Bad Accounts

Bad Accounts

Kate McVaugh

2014

1

There could have been any number of reasons why Pia had found a gun lying in her front yard. It didn't necessarily mean that it had been dropped there by a careless hitman. Admittedly, she had stolen files from her employers implicating them in illegal activities. But would they really have put a contract out on her? According to her friends, they would. Whether or not she really was a marked woman, Pia had decided that it was probably a good idea to get out of town for a few days. At least that had been her reasoning earlier in the day before boarding a Greyhound bus headed south. Now she wondered if this crazy plan to flee Monterey, travel to San Diego, and then on into Mexico, had really been her only option.

Miserable did not come close to describing how she felt. Her knees ached, her backside was numb, and no amount of squirming and repositioning helped. Fifty-two was entirely too old to be squished into a small seat on a long bus journey. And why had she decided to wear skinny jeans, vintage clogs, and a wispy tank top? Her lower half felt like it was in a vice grip, and her arms kept sticking to the nasty vinyl seat back. It was at rare times like these that Pia wished she could ditch her well-honed fashion sense for a velour track suit.

If only she'd taken a plane, she'd already be in San Diego. Then, if necessary, it was a quick trip to San Ysidro where she could walk right through the US-Mexican border to Tijuana. But, as her friend Brad had pointed out, plane trips require ID checks. Pia couldn't chance airline personnel noticing that her passport possessed someone else's name and picture.

It was too late now. She'd already committed to the plan so there was no use getting upset. Pia leaned her head against the dirty window and thought about that conversation she wished she'd never had two weeks ago in Saul's Bar, back Monterey, California.

2

"Girl-Dude, you really took another accountant's job? Pia, my friend, when are you gonna learn to enjoy life?" Brad grabbed his beer bottle off of the bar and took another swig.

"I always enjoy life, Brad," Pia replied. "And why would I possibly choose to stay unemployed?" She glanced down at her new, fire-engine-red manicure looking for a distraction. She did not want to get sucked back into the old conversation the two had been having for years; Brad's lifestyle choices versus hers. Maybe she shouldn't have agreed to meet up for a drink. It had been a long day and she was not up for hearing about Brad's objections to her *conventional* life, as he put it.

Anyone looking at the two friends seated at the bar in Saul's would probably think they were strangers. Pia, the long and lean, well-groomed business woman, with chin length raven hair always perfectly colored and styled. She wouldn't be caught dead in a business suit, but you'd also never catch her in the office in yoga pants. She had dubbed her unique style as *professional funk.* Today she wore a Malaysian sarong, topped with a fitted silk top. Brad, on the other hand, was still living the surfer lifestyle even in his early fifties. His six-foot-two frame was invariably dressed in tattered board shorts and a faded t-shirt, exposing a good part of the surf-toned body of sun-damaged skin. He accessorized with shell necklaces on leather twines around his neck and wrists.

"Come on," Brad insisted, "you could've taken some more time off and found something better to do." He shook his head. A loose strand of long, salt-water bleached hair fell across his face.

"Like what? Granted, three months off was certainly lovely. I got back to my painting, took afternoon naps, drank a few too many cocktails—but I do have a lifestyle to maintain." She knew the two would never see eye-to-eye on the matter, and it had never interfered with their friendship. But right now she simply wasn't up to defending herself.

Pia picked up her martini, swirled the toothpick pierced olive around and popped it into her mouth. "Anyway, how is your life as a senior citizen surfer any better than mine?" On second thought, she might as well get in a few playful digs.

"See?" Brad said, reaching over to grab a handful of peanuts from the bowl in front of him. "That's your problem Pia, you think like an old person. Senior citizen? Get real!" He'd never been able to understand how his buddy had gone from high school party girl to corporate drone. "Tell me, my friend, do you ever have any fun? '

"I have plenty of fun," Pia answered, "it's just a little more grown up than your brand of entertainment."

"I'd disagree there. Anyway, your work's so boring. Accounting?"

"It's not at all boring, Brad. I like taking charge of other people's money. Not only that, but I'm good at it and get paid quite well, thank you very much."

Actually, if Pia were being one hundred percent honest with herself, she would have to agree with Brad. Her job had become mind-numbing and soul sucking. She'd reached that stage where you pretty much hate everything that has to do with your profession. However, Brad would not hear those words coming from her lips. It would be like admitting that she might have chosen the wrong career. And that might mean her life had been a waste. It wasn't something she cared to consider.

"Really? Good at your work?" Brad countered. "If that's true, why did you lose your job?"

Pia looked closely into Brad's eyes and once again wondered about the long term effects of his weed and beer consumption. She was never quite sure if he had actually forgotten what she had told him, or if he was just winding her up to get a reaction. It was no use trying to get a read—her buddy was a world-class fibber.

"Brad, you know very well that the new owners relocated the office up to San José and gave me the option of moving up there. You also know that when I declined the offer I was given a very nice severance package." She did not need to tell him of the two months she had spent applying for new jobs and getting turned down.

"*Exactly!* You could have taken all that dough and lived off the money a lot longer than three months."

"But then I wouldn't have been able to pay off my mortgage or purchase a few more stocks." Pia took another sip of her martini. "Brad, you've never considered the long term gains that come with financial planning. I respect that, but it's not how I can live. I like making money and having security."

How many times over the years had they had this very same conversation? Brad trying to convince her to go all bohemian, and Pia subtly suggesting he might want to look for a full-time job. In the end, their separate paths had worked out for both of them. It was only lately that Pia had begun to question her choices and wonder what life would have been like if she'd been a little less conventional. She doubted Brad had ever had any reservations about his choices.

"My man Bob," Brad called out to the old guy stacking glasses at the other end of the bar.

Bob, head bartender at Saul's for as far back as anyone could remember, looked up. Never a really big man, the years had shrunk Bob down and thinned him out, yet he had a presence that demanded respect. All those years of dealing with drunks and crowds meant nothing much addled the man. He no longer moved too quickly, but his hearing was just fine. He ambled down to where Pia and Brad sat.

Saul's-Bar-on-the-Wharf was one of those old style cozy places; lots of worn wood and aging faux red leather seating. Several cocktail hour customers lined the long bar, and a few more sat at booths running along the front windows. Tinted glass filtered out light and nosy eyes, along with the 70's style stained glass swinging doors that opened onto the wharf. They'd finally removed the hanging ferns a few years back but the place still felt stuck in another era. Saul's had plenty of tourists in the right season, but also more than the usual amount of locals who found the dark, dank atmosphere comforting.

"What can I get you Brad?" Bob asked when he got to where the two sat, wiping down the bar that didn't need wiping. Except when ringing up a sale, Bob refused to wear his glasses. He compensated by repeating the bar moves that were hard-wired into his brain, constantly moving up and down the bar—whether or not there were customers, running a bar towel over the surfaces, and emptying the ashtrays he insisted on putting out even though they couldn't be used.

"Set us up with another round," said Brad. "And I got a question for you Bob. I say Pia here's led a boring life. What do you think?"

Bob set down a bottle of beer, wiped the counter, and grabbed the martini shaker. "It's her life, Brad."

"Thank you, Bob," said Pia, while he shook her fresh cocktail. "See Brad? Bob doesn't have a problem with my choice of profession."

"But dude, she had the perfect opportunity to change it up when she got laid off from that establishment job she's had forever. But what does she do? Goes to work in another office." Brad shook his head in disbelief.

"So you found another job?" Bob asked Pia, setting down the fresh martini. He'd been the only one Pia had confessed her fears to about not finding work. "Good to hear. Who you working for now?"

"I doubt you've heard of them," said Pia, "It's a small firm over on Lighthouse Avenue. Houston and Melrose Accounting."

Bob immediately stopped wiping out a clean ashtray, rested his hands on the bar and leaned forward.

"You're working for Jack Houston and Bernie Melrose?" he asked in a hushed voice. "Why didn't you say something about this before now?"

"I just started about a month ago, Bob," Pia answered, rather surprised at Bob's reaction. "I didn't really think you were interested in accounting firms."

Bob threw the bar towel over his shoulder. "All I can say is to watch your step, young lady." Bob thought anyone under the age of seventy was young.

"Watch myself? What do you mean?" Pia rarely wondered if Bob's age was starting catch up with him, but maybe she should. "I've been in the work force long enough to know how to behave." She turned to look at Brad. "Our friend here, on the other hand, might have a little difficulty with a nine to five routine."

"Jeez, Pia, get with the program!" Brad interjected. "Bob's not talking about getting to work on time." He reached across the bar to pat the bartender on the shoulder. "I get ya, dude. You think the bosses might want a little something extra from Pia here." Brad laughed. "But Bob— get real, my man! She's still good looking, but she ain't no twenty year old."

"Honestly Brad, what decade do you live in?" said Pia, thinking that Brad really might have brain damage. "And I'll overlook the reference to my age. Don't forget, we were born in the same year."

"Yeah, but the young babes still think I'm hot. Isn't that right, Bob?"

Bob ignored Brad's comment, the concern on his face clearly visible. "Listen Pia, Jack Houston is one bad animal. You need to keep clear of him."

"Come on Bob," Pia scoffed, "he runs a small accounting firm with Bernie. Both of them are close to retirement age. They're your average dull accountants. How bad can aging money-crunchers be?"

"How bad? How bad, you ask?" Bob said, his hushed voice rising in pitch. He glanced around to make sure no one was in earshot. "You ever hear rumors of the Fishing Run?"

"Whoa, Bob, hold up a sec," Brad cut in before Pia could say anything. "This Jack dude works for the Fishing Runners?"

"He and his partner *are* the Fishing Runners," Bob answered. "Or at least a big part of them."

Pia looked at Brad. She looked at Bob. They seemed to know what each other was talking about, but their conversation had come to a halt.

"You two want to let me in on this?" she asked.

The men exchanged glances. "You tell her Brad," Bob said.

"My pleasure," he said, and turned to face Pia. "Maybe if you got out more often you'd know that the

Fishing Run is code for a mondo drug operation that's been going down in these parts on and off for years."

Pia turned to Bob, the more even-keeled of the two even if he might be getting a little senile. "You're telling me that I'm working for drug traffickers?" She tried not to laugh. "I don't think so."

"Well, you are," Bob said. "Houston and Melrose run the money end of it." Bob began to polish a spotless glass.

"Sorry Bob, but you're wrong," she said shaking her head. "Accounting's been my life for more years than I care to think about and I'd know if I were working for drug dealers." Pia picked up her glass, took a sip, and ignored the knot that was beginning to grow in her stomach.

"Maybe," replied Bob, "but then maybe you haven't been at Houston and Melrose long enough to see anything."

Pia chuckled, avoiding any comment.

"I wouldn't laugh about this if I were you, Pia," said Brad. "You might want to listen to Bob. He's been around a long time and knows the score." Pia reached for the peanut bowl.

"He's right about that, Pia," said Bob. "I know what I'm talking about. Do the smart thing. Get out of that office before they take you down with them."

"Dude, you really think Pia's in danger?" asked Brad, clearly worried. "The Fishing Run's been going on for years. Except for a couple of minor busts, nothing much has ever happened."

Bob glanced around again to see if anyone might be listening. Then he leaned in closer to Pia and Brad. "What I hear is that something big is going down soon. My advice to you Pia…don't wait around to see what happens. I doubt you want to spend the next several years in the pen…or worse." A customer called out to Bob. He straightened up and headed off down the bar.

"You believe us now?" Brad asked.

"No I don't," Pia said with all sincerity, hoping that her well practiced, stoic business face wasn't giving away her rising blood pressure. She picked up her cocktail and finished it one large gulp.

~~~

That night, sleep did not come easily to Pia. She couldn't get the thought of working for drug dealers out of her head. As crazy as it all sounded, it might just be a real possibility. Regrettably, she'd had her own suspicions about Houston and Melrose right from the start, but had consciously ignored them. Of course, she had only assumed that her bosses were cooking the books for a few clients— nothing she hadn't run into in the past. And as long as she kept her books on the up and up, she wasn't in danger of breaking any laws. But drug barons? That was an entirely different matter.

Pia had no desire to ever again be involved in anything that might entail dealing with law enforcement. She'd had her fill of the boys in blue when she was in her teens.

Back in high school, Pia was generally the dutiful student during the week, while Brad could often be found surfing and partying rather than in class. Weekends, however, were another matter. That's when Pia would let her hair down and hung out with Brad and their surfer friends. More often than not, there was plenty of booze and weed. They never really did anything bad. Just your run-of-the-mill teenage antics. And since they kept their partying to the beach area, which they always cleaned up, there had never been any run-ins with the law. That is until that night in May during their senior year.

Pia, Brad, and six of their friends had been down at the beach, minding their own business, drinking cheap wine and smoking cigarettes. Suddenly, they saw a flash of headlights and heard a screech of tires. For a minute, they thought they were going to be plowed over right there in the sand.

Jumping into action, they all ran to where a fancy sports car had jumped the small barrier and proceeded along a low dune before coming to a stop. It sat stranded in the sand. The car had torn up an entire natural plant area.

When the driver, apparently not injured, jumped out of the car and tried to make a run for it, several of the guys tackled him and held him down. Pia went out to the road to flag down a cop while the others quickly disposed of the wine bottles. When the police arrived, the friends gave their statements and went home.

A few days later they found out that the offender, some rich young businessman from Pebble Beach, had been released the same night of the accident and that no charges had been filed. Pia, Brad and their pals were outraged, but it was Pia who took the next step. She contacted the police and questioned why the man hadn't been charged with property damage. When that didn't go anywhere, she wrote an article in the school newspaper which included the name of the man, the arresting officer, and the police chief. After the local news picked it up, and even a radio station in San Francisco, things started to change—although not how Pia had hoped. She got pulled over and hassled more times than she could count until she went off to college in Santa Cruz. And then even when she returned home for visits. The cops didn't like her and she didn't like them.

And even though it was years ago and all the hassling parties were now retired, the bad memories remained locked in a corner of Pia's brain. They only surfaced at the mention of law enforcement. Times like now, with this whole crazy situation.

She looked at the clock. It was nearly two a.m. If she didn't get some sleep, she'd be useless at work in the morning. Drug dealers or not, for now she intended to keep her job.

As she reminded herself, it had been a minor miracle she'd even been hired at Houston and Melrose. She'd only ever confided in Bob about the near panic she'd gone into a month after she'd left her previous job. At the time, Pia hadn't considered that finding a new position might be difficult. After all, she was extremely qualified with years of experience…and those years of experience turned out to be the problem. Apparently, she was too old.

It seemed that anyone over the age of thirty-five had little chance of landing a good job. When Bernie Melrose had only asked for a resume, her CPA license, and given her a brief interview, she'd seen no reason to question why they, and no one else, would take her on. Certainly, it was not because they were looking for a shady accountant. *That* she would have known before taking the job. Nonetheless, if they *were* into illicit practices, she wanted to find out before her reputation could be jeopardized and she was out of a job for good and headed for the bread line.

Pia flipped off the bedside lamp and flopped onto her pillow. Just forget about it, she told herself. Brad and Bob's fantasies about narco-traffickers were not going to keep her awake any longer. She closed her eyes and nodded off.

3

It wasn't until a few weeks later, when Pia had all but forgotten about the talk of drug dealer accountants, that the tide began to change. She had arrived at the office early as usual, her thoughts focused on the beautiful August morning of bright sunshine and warm air.

Huston and Melrose Accounting occupied a small, non-descript, one story building on Lighthouse Avenue, with a cramped parking area in the rear. Clients entered through the front into a bland reception area. A framed print of the coastal waters off of Lover's Point hung behind the secretary's desk. Two fake, potted ficus trees framed the front window. A utilitarian, uncomfortable loveseat with two matching chairs filled in the rest of the space. A hallway on the right led to three offices, a small kitchenette, and the back door. Jack Houston's office, the largest, faced the street. Across the hall was the kitchenette and Bernie Melrose's office. In the back corner facing the parking lot, in what might have been designed as a storeroom, is where Pia worked.

At eight in the morning, only Bernie Melrose and Pia were in the building. Jack Houston never arrived before ten o'clock, and the new secretary, the daughter of Jack's sister, only came in after her university classes at The Monterey Institute. This was the time when Pia could work without noise from the other offices.

Pia rolled her chair up to the desk and turned on her computer. Waiting for it to start up, she glanced around the cramped office space and its bland, barren walls. Brad was right...what was she doing in this place? Once again, as she had been doing with increasing frequency, she questioned her life as an accountant. She came to work, did her job, went home. And not much more. Up until her mid-forties, she really had enjoyed the challenges and calculations. But somewhere after that it had become a monotonous routine of doing figures and dealing with people she would rather not associate with. But what were her options? Start a new career? At her age? No; once you hit fifty it was either win the lottery or bite the bullet and stick with what you'd been doing your whole life. She sighed, pushed her hair out of her face, and bent down to take a file from her desk drawer.

She was trying to focus on Mr. Wilson's business statements when she heard a car pull into the parking lot and glanced out the window to see who might be arriving. You could tell a lot about a person by the car they drove. In Monterey, a beat-up truck might be a surfer or maybe a fisherman. A Lincoln Town Car most likely had driven over from Carmel. This car, however, caught her eye. Pia scooted her chair closer to the window and stared at the shiny black, late model Mercedes with darker-than-legal tinted windows. It was the type of car movie gangsters drove.

And that's when she remembered that conversation she'd had with Bob and Brad a few weeks back. Was this a drug dealer's car? She still couldn't believe Houston and Melrose were in the drug trade. Certainly she would have gotten at least a slight whiff of this type of illegal activity. She craned her neck a little closer to the window hoping to get a better look at the driver. Even without a clear view of the man, Pia knew it was no one she'd seen before at the office. The car door slammed shut, she shook her head of ridiculous thoughts, and attempted to get back to Mr. Wilson's papers.

But then the back door opened and a man's voice called out to Bernie. She dropped the file on the desk and tuned in to the goings-on outside her door. She heard her boss walk out to greet the man in a hushed voice. *"Not in the hall!"* The other man warned in a loud whisper, followed by the sounds of padded footsteps on the carpet, Bernie's office door clicking shut, and the lock turning.

Now that was odd. Why would Bernie lock the door? Pia tapped her fingers on the desk trying to decide what to do. Continue on with Mr. Wilson's file, or find out who was in Bernie's office? *You never take any risks,* Brad had lectured her on countless occasions. Although that was not entirely true, spying on a private conversation at her place of work was not something she had ever done. So why not now? If nothing else it would prove that Brad and Bob's assumptions about this Fishing Run organization were way off the mark. Or at least with this client they were.

How to go about eavesdropping was another question. She couldn't exactly listen in at Bernie's door. There was, however, the door that connected the kitchenette to his office. It was worth a try, especially considering that her mind was as far away from balancing spreadsheets as it could be. Pia waited a few more minutes and then set out for the kitchenette.

The cover of making a fresh pot of coffee would work if she got caught snooping, but it was much preferable if Bernie and his guest didn't know she was there. She quietly entered the kitchenette and tip-toed over to the door that led to Bernie's office. She carefully placed her ear against it but all that penetrated was a muffled conversation. She looked around the room and spotted a water glass in the drying rack. If it had worked to spy on the camp counselor and her secret boyfriend when she was a kid, it would still work now.

Carefully placing the glass against the door, Pia leaned her ear against the bottom of it.

"...right, it's all been transferred, Joe." It was Bernie speaking.

"You sure you got it to the right accounts?" the other man asked, in a low, raspy voice.

"Joe, I've been working for you and your father for too many years to start messing things up now."

"Got to cut you off for a second Bernie. Remember to call him *The Captain*, even if it's just you and me talking."

"Sorry Joe. I forgot." Bernie didn't usually slip up. Not calling The Captain, *The Captain,* could prove fatal. "But getting back to your question, yes, everything's in order. Half in the Cayman's, the rest in your other off-shore accounts. Here, look at the screen. See? All taken care of."

"Yeah, it looks fine, but The Captain wanted me to make a personal call today," Joe said.

"I was wondering about that. Usually he likes to take care of business out of the office. Why the visit?"

"He's worried about security. Seems the feds are beefing up surveillance in the area and we heard some undercover agents may've infiltrated parts of our operation."

"That doesn't sound good, Joe. Any real details?" Bernie asked.

"Nothing other than to keep a sharp eye out." Joe stopped talking, making Pia think the conversation was over. Just as she started to remove her ear from the glass, Joe continued. "The Captain wanted me to ask about that new broad you got working here. Who is she?"

Pia's hand gripped the glass tighter and her eyes widened, but she remained frozen in place.

"Pia? Just an accountant. No need to worry about her. She's good at what she does. And it goes without saying that she has no idea about our arrangement."

"You sure she won't start digging around, Bernie?"

"Nah, not her. She got downsized out of her last job. The gal was desperate for work, and Joe, she's no spring chicken. That makes her the perfect candidate to keep her nose to the grindstone, counting the days until retirement. It's the young hot-shot's you have to worry about—always looking for a way to better themselves at the expense of their employer."

Pia had heard more than enough to be convinced that something suspicious was definitely going on. It was time to get out of there before she was discovered. Taking carefully placed steps, she moved back to the sink, silently set down the glass and picked up a coffee mug which immediately slipped out of her hand and banged on the counter. She did not need the glass-on-the-door to hear the expletive from Bernie's office. The door flew open.

"Pia, what are you doing here!" Bernie boomed, watching Pia's back while she poured coffee into a cup.

"Hum?" she said turning to face him. "Oh hi Bernie. How's it going?" The Joe guy stood directly behind him. He might have been good-looking in that Mediterranean way about twenty years ago, but clearly Joe had taken to fatty foods and nicotine. His pudgy, soft body could not be disguised by the expensive threads, nor could the stench of a three-pack-a-day habit. In his mid-forties, Joe was not looking forward to a long life.

Pia set the coffee pot back on the warmer and smiled across to her boss and Joe. "Sorry if I interrupted the meeting with your client," she apologized, shaking out her right hand. "It's the darn arthritis. I seem to drop things right and left these days." She took a step towards the door. "Back to work," she called out while retreating from the kitchen before Bernie could respond.

Once back inside Bernie's office, Joe began to pace.

"She doesn't look too stupid to me, Bernie," Joe said, making sure he spoke in a whisper.

"I never said she was. She's an accountant Joe, they don't make them stupid. I said she hasn't, and won't, put her nose in our business," Bernie assured him.

"I sure hope you're right."

~~~

For the next several hours Pia, being the professional that she was, shut her mind off to anything but the accounts in front of her. But at 11:30 on the dot, she grabbed her bag and headed for the door.

"I'm off for my lunch," she called out, quickly passing by Bernie and Jack's office, not waiting for a response.

Her normal lunch-time routine took her down to a bench overlooking the Monterey Bay. Today a brilliant sun shown down through cloudless skies on what Pia considered to be one of the most spectacular vistas on earth. The Pacific Ocean crashed along a coast of breathtaking rock formations, tide pools, and sand. Pelicans, seagulls, otters, and seals, made up for some of the wildlife that inhabited this rich landscape. In the right season, whales could be spotted travelling through the waters. As magnificent a day as it was, Pia's mind was not on the scenery in front of her.

Sitting down on the first empty bench she found along the walking path that faced the bay, she pulled out her phone and called Brad.

"Brad, it's Pia," she said, glancing around to make sure she was alone.

"Hey girl-dude, what's up?"

"I was hoping we could get together later. I need to talk to you. Do you think you could drop by my place this evening?"

"Let me check my schedule," Brad said. There was a slight pause. "Nope. No plans. What's this about? Why can't we meet up at Saul's?"

"Not at Saul's. I need you to come by the house." It suddenly occurred to her that she might be acting a little paranoid. What, exactly, was she supposed to tell Brad? Her mind temporarily froze.

"Pia? You still there?"

"Yeah, I'm here. OK, this might sound a little crazy, but do you remember that conversation with Bob we had a few weeks back?"

"Which conversation would that be?" Brad asked.

"The one about the people I'm working for and what they might be into?" Pia watched two joggers pass by on the trail, waiting for Brad to recall their talk about drug dealers. And then it clicked.

"Whoa, hang on...you talking about the narcotics dudes?"

A middle-aged man in a business suit sat down next to Pia, talking loudly on his phone. She got up and walked closer to the tall outcropping of coastal rock.

"Look Brad, we can't discuss this on the phone. Just come by my house later, OK?"

"No problemo. I'll be there. Just make sure you have a cold one ready."

4

Pia had just poured water through the coffee filter when the doorbell rang. She looked up at the clock glad to see that Brad had arrived at six, and not at a late hour. You never knew with Brad. Trustworthy; yes. Punctual; not often.

Their friendship dated back to high school when they were both part of the surfing crowd. Pia loved the ocean but didn't have the passion for riding the waves like Brad and some of the others. She'd often spend her time on shore sketching scenes of her pals flying across the water. At some point, Brad had asked her to draw out a design to put on the custom board he was making. It turned out to be such a hit that soon most of their friend's boards were decked out in Pia's work. She'd even gotten a few jobs with a pro shop up in Santa Cruz.

Never seeing any real profit in taking up surfboard painting as a career, Pia had gone off to college after high school graduation, while Brad had gone off to surf competitions, beer, and hot young beach bunnies. He'd never made the big time, but that had never bothered Brad. He was happy to pick up whatever work came his way as long as it didn't interfere with his wave time. Something about his low-key personality, semi bad-boy air, and those California surfer good looks, had ensured Brad a long list of girlfriends who would happily put him up in their homes for years at a time.

And then one day they would see the light and realize that even though he was a nice enough guy, he didn't want a family and didn't help much with the bills. The latest had kicked him out two months before and he'd been forced to take up residence in his mother's garage.

"Hey Brad," Pia said, opening the door, "Come on in, I'm just making coffee."

Brad walked in and followed Pia through to the tiny kitchen on the left where she took down two mugs and set them on the counter. Brad wrinkled his nose.

"My friend, it's after five, where's the beer?" he asked. Pia continued pouring coffee into the cups.

"We need clear heads, Brad. Caffeine is what you're getting." She passed him his filled cup.

"I think better on alcohol," he reasoned.

"Maybe, but for now we're sticking to this," she said, starting to walk back to the living room. "We might be able to get to the beer later."

"Girl-dude," was all Brad could say, shaking his head.

Coffee in hand, the two went into the living room of Pia's cottage in Pacific Grove, the small town that bordered Monterey. The community had all the charm of its more well-known neighbor, but with much cheaper property prices, and minus the tourists. The cottage fit her perfectly; big enough to move around in but tiny enough to never get overwhelmed with the upkeep. She was halfway up a hill that led straight down to one of the entrances to The 17 Mile

Drive and Pebble Beach, and just as close to the Monarch Butterfly Reserve.

Pacific Grove had seen its share of religious colonies and artists over the years, and prided itself, up until 1969, on being the last dry town in California. Although it had evolved like everywhere else in the state, it still retained a small town, artsy feel. Pia felt very much at home in this community.

Brad took a seat in the worn recliner, and Pia settled in across from him on the sofa. Sun streamed through the open living room windows. The fog was starting to roll in and soon she would have to close them. Pia looked out at the changing weather. There were quite a few other things she would rather be doing than embarking on the conversation she was about to have with Brad.

She turned back to face her friend. "I suppose there's not really a good way to tell you this, but I may not have been one hundred percent honest when I told you and Bob that I didn't have any suspicions about Houston and Melrose." Pia waited for Brad to respond.

"Cool," said Brad. He took a sip of his coffee and grimaced. "Think maybe I could get a shot of Jameson in this?"

"No, I don't."

"Worth a try." He took another swallow. "So what's up with the boss-men?"

"Well... it's just that even before Bob mentioned that Houston and Melrose might be involved in drugs, I already had a pretty good idea that they might have questionable

25

accounting practices..." Pia noticed Brad's increased attention to the story, "...but it had nothing to do with my accounts and I didn't think it was anything major. Like drugs."

"So why didn't you tell that to me and Bob? You know you can trust us. What was it you said? Oh yeah, something about them being old guys about to retire."

"Some things are better left unsaid, Brad. Anyway, I'd thought it was only a little creative bookkeeping. Nothing I couldn't ignore."

"And now you think there's something more to their practice than just a few fudged accounts?" Brad asked.

"Yes, I do. I think they could be financing something illegal. Maybe it's drugs, maybe something else. Or maybe they're laundering more than just a little cash. Whatever's going on, it's more than I bargained for with a new job."

"Bummer," said Brad. "Maybe you should follow Bob's advice and get a new job."

"Easier said than done, Brad. And right now I can't afford to quit."

"Maybe you should have held off on buying those new stocks. Or I guess you could sell them."

"Look Brad, I'm not ready to leave a job I just got simply because I think there might be something questionable going on. On the other hand, I have no desire to work for drug lords. Anyway, if they really are these Fish Run guys, maybe I should do something about it." Pia looked back out through the window before turning back to Brad. "Do you think I should go to the cops with my suspicions?"

Brad nearly dropped his cup. "You been smoking loco weed, girl? Go to the fuzz? Don't you remember what happened last time you did that?"

"How could I forget? But that was years ago and this is a lot different from a bunch of teenagers trying to get justice for a damaged beach front." Pia set her cup down on the coffee table. "But maybe you're right. Maybe I should get some hard evidence first. I'm just not sure how to proceed."

"How *to proceed?*" Brad blurted, almost jumping out of his chair. "Pia, if these dudes are working with the Fishing Run, you do *not* want to proceed with anything. Didn't you hear what Bob and I said? They're crazy-dangerous dudes." He was beginning to think his friend might be on medication he didn't know about. Thinking of calling the cops? "Anyway, you still haven't told me why you even suspect them. Give me the low-down."

"It's not much. So far, it's just a conversation I overheard in the office today," she told him. What if she were wrong? After all, it could have been a completely innocent exchange between a client and his accountant.

Neither of them said anything for a minute. Pia, not sure if she was starting to pick up on Brad's paranoia; Brad, hoping she would offer him that beer.

"Go on," Brad finally said, "tell me what you think."

"OK. This is what happened. I was in the kitchen at work today and Bernie was meeting with some guy I've never seen before named Joe. I heard them talking about off-shore accounts and as far as I know, Houston and Melrose don't have that sort of set-up." Brad waited for her to continue. "Thinking about what you and Bob told me it makes sense that something more than a few bookkeeping manipulations are going on in that office. Now I just have to figure out what to do."

Brad remained silent, sloshing his coffee around in the cup. It looked like he might be thinking. Finally, he took a large gulp and set the mug down on the rug.

"My advice homie?" he told his friend, "turn in your notice and find another job."

"There *are* no other jobs, Brad, but that's not even the point. You and Bob said these guys were big-time dealers, right?" Brad nodded. "How are we supposed to ignore that? Brad, these aren't you're local pot grower friends."

"So now you're getting all socially conscious Pia? You want to save the world from the criminal element? I don't think these are the kind of dudes you want to mess with."

"And I certainly don't want to stir up any trouble, but how can I ignore that I might be working for dealers? And by the way, what exactly is it they deal in?"

"I hear it's along the lines of black tar heroin."

"So it really is the bad stuff." Brad nodded, but said nothing. "How can you back off from that? You're OK with having heroin dealer's right here in town? Brad, you've seen how bad the drug situation has gotten over the years. And don't you remember what happened to our high school friends who went the way of a nightly fix? Maybe I'm wrong about Houston and Melrose, but I have to at least check it out." Pia tried to look Brad in the eye, but he was now staring down at the floor. "Come on Brad, you know we can't ignore this."

He raised his eyes to her. "Hell, Pia, of course I'm not down with the hard drug scene. But what can we do about it? Like we told you, this shit's been going on for years and no one's stopped it." Brad picked up his cup and swirled around the dregs. "Can I get some more coffee? I kinda like the buzz I'm getting."

Pia got up, grabbed both cups and went into the kitchen, returning with refills and a bag of cookies.

"All right," Pia said, handing him his cup, "So you agree that we can't just overlook this, right?" She didn't wait for him to respond. "What we need now is a plan."

"What do you mean by a plan?" asked Brad, reaching into the bag and grabbing several cookies. "What do you intend to do? Hell, all you heard was part of a conversation. You don't have any hard evidence on your bosses."

"Not yet I don't," Pia admitted, grabbing a cookie but not eating it. "But there has to be proof in Bernie's office. I'm sure I could find something. It's at least worth a quick look."

"How you gonna do that?" Brad asked, cookie crumbs sticking to his face. "Ask this Bernie guy if you can search his office?"

"Actually, I thought I'd go in tonight and see what I can come up with. And that's where you come in." Pia took another sip of coffee. "You want in on this, right?"

"Are you talking breaking and entering?" he asked. "Damn Pia, you're starting to get all rad on me!"

"It's not technically breaking and entering if I have a key."

"Not sure the cops would agree with you on that," he said. He waited for Pia to withdraw the plan, but she said nothing. "What the hell. It might be worth checking to see if I still have the chops."

"You've done this before?" Pia asked, just a little bit concerned. She'd never known her friend to engage in anything illegal other than a few pharmaceuticals.

"B and E-ing? Just to get into a few rock concerts."

"That's not quite the same thing, Brad."

"No, but it still might be fun." He looked to make sure Pia wasn't just joking around. "You're sure about this?" he asked. She nodded. "Cool. So when's this going down?"

"How about ten o'clock tonight?"

A large grin spread across Brad's face. "There's hope for you yet, girl-dude!"

~~~

A little after ten, they parked Brad's beat-up '64 Chevy truck three blocks from the office. Just in case any security cameras caught them driving around, it would be a much more logical explanation that an aging surfer was out at a local watering hole.

"I'll try to get in and out as quickly as possible," Pia told Brad. They stood partially hidden from view in the group of trees next to the office. "If you see anyone coming towards the office, send me a text message." Pia took a final glance up and down the street making sure the coast was clear. "Are you ready?"

"Go for it. I'll man the post." Brad slipped farther into the trees and disappeared from sight.

Pia walked up the driveway and entered through the back door, half expecting an alarm to go off when she unlocked it. Again she wondered if she had made a mistake in assuming Houston and Melrose were in the drug business. If they were as big as Bob said, wouldn't they have a state of the art alarm system? Or were they intentionally trying to keep a low profile? Too late now, she was already inside and heading to Bernie's office.

Even though it was nighttime, enough of the corner streetlamp shone through the blinds enabling her to see the around the premises without bumping into anything. She walked by Jack's office hoping she wouldn't need to come back and search it. Fortunately, with Bernie's office facing the back, light from her small flashlight wouldn't be easily noticeable unless someone was in the parking lot at night.

Pia walked over to Bernie's desk and took a double-take at the papers lying scattered all over it. The man had always been a neat freak, but this looked like he'd been in the middle of work and had gone out to get a cup of coffee. Pia froze. What if he were still in the office? That was crazy. No one was there. But it did prompt her to move with more urgency.

She carefully leafed through the papers by the thin beam of her flashlight. Peering closely at one, she saw it was a printout of deposits to an off-shore account. On a separate piece was a list of names with account numbers. Quickly, she gathered all the papers, walked out to the copy machine in the hall, and ran them through the feed tray.

Returning to the office, she was rearranging the originals as she had found them, when her elbow accidentally knocked the mouse. Suddenly the computer came to life. She stared at the screen and then sat down in Bernie's chair.

Pia scrolled through what looked to be more spreadsheets of business transactions she didn't recognize. Considering the papers that lay on the desk, it was easy to assume that the two were related. About to print it out, she noticed there were several other files in the same folder. She jumped up, ran to her office, and grabbed a flash drive from the desk drawer. Once back in Bernie's office she plugged in the drive. Drawing her hand back, her bracelets caught on the edge of the screen nearly knocking it over. She tore the bangles off and began to download files, trying to remain calm.

A sound from the parking lot made her jump and Pia immediately switched off the flashlight. About to text Brad to find out what was going on, her files finished downloading. She pulled out the flash drive, leaned back in Bernie's chair and exhaled. Suddenly, her eye caught sight of the tiny red flash from the security camera on the ceiling in the corner.

"*Darn!*" she blurted, shoving the drive into her pocket and grabbing the stack of photocopies. She scrambled out of the room and out the back door. She locked it and walked quickly over to where Brad was hiding.

Brad stepped out from the trees, dropped his joint and ground it out.

"Couldn't you wait until this was over?" she asked.

"That coffee had me too wired. I needed to calm down."

"Come on. We need to get out of here," Pia said, walking back towards his truck. Brad shrugged his shoulders and followed, feeling a little too mellow to make any comment.

"You get the goods?" Brad asked when they'd reached his truck.

"I got something," Pia answered. "Let's wait until we get back to my place to talk."

Neither of them said anything more on the short drive back.

Pia walked into the house, threw the papers on the coffee table, and went straight to the kitchen. She grabbed two glasses and pulled out a bottle of single malt. After pouring generous shots into each, she returned to the living room where Brad was glancing through the photocopies.

"Drink up," she said taking a large gulp before Brad had a chance to take his own glass.

"Breaking out the good stuff, I see," he said.

Pia walked over to the couch and sat down. Brad took his spot in the recliner.

"Mind if I light up another doobie?" he asked, pulling a baggie out of his short's pocket.

"Yes Brad, I do. Just drink your scotch and be quiet for a minute so I can think."

"You're looking a little stressed, Pia. Seems to me we pulled it off. Chill out."

Pia pushed her hair out of her face and exhaled loudly. "Brad, this isn't good. I think they'll know I was there."

"What are you talking about? No one even came by walking a dog. Although I do think I saw a raccoon mosey around the back."

"Are you sure about that?" Pia asked. "It seemed to me you were too busy getting high to notice much."

"Come on girl, I was just heightening my senses. Honest Pia, no one was there. Why do you think anyone saw you?"

Pia explained about the security camera in Bernie's office. There was probably even one at the back door.

"Bummer. You're sure the camera was on?" Pia nodded. "Why didn't you erase the tape?" he asked.

"How would I know how to do that?" She picked up her glass and finished off the scotch. "Anyway, it's too late to think about what I should have done. What am I going to do now?"

"Let's slow down here. First off, did you get any evidence of illegal activities?"

"I can't be sure until I check it out, but yes, I think I did."

Brad paused a second to think this over. "Girl-dude, don't tell anyone I ever said this, but you might just have to go to the police before your bosses find out what you did."

"And admit I stole files from them? No, going to the cops isn't a good idea." Pia squeezed her eyes shut forcing herself to concentrate. "Maybe no one will look at the security tape. After all there's no reason to suspect a break-in."

"You sure about that?" Brad asked.

Pia thought about it, at the same time absentmindedly rubbing her right wrist. "*Oh no!*" she blurted out, pounding her fist into the sofa. "Where are my bracelets?" She quickly patted down her pockets, jumped up and ran out to Brad's truck and then retraced her movements back into the house. "I don't believe it! I think I left them on Bernie's desk."

"Not cool," Brad offered, wondering how Pia could have been so stupid, but not voicing his opinion. "Maybe your boss won't notice."

"Three, shiny gold bracelets sitting on his desk?" asked Pia. "He'll notice."

She got up, left the room, and came back with the bottle of scotch, poured her friend another shot and then one for herself.

"Ya know Pia," Brad started, "I wouldn't be so sure that the bosses will think you were there." Pia raised her eyebrows at him. "Well, OK, they might." He shot back his drink and placed the glass on the table. "If that's the case, that they do know you were in there, then I don't think you should go into work tomorrow."

Brad grabbed the bag of cookies that were still out and waited for a response from Pia. None came.

"Girl-dude. We'll figure it out. Meanwhile, do you mind if I crash out on your couch? I don't think I should be driving."

"Only if you stay up long enough to help me go through at least some of the papers and files I got from the office. If there really is anything of substance, I think you're right, I better not chance going into the office tomorrow." Pia reached for the purloined photocopies.

"Homie, what would you do without me?"

5

The following morning, Jack Houston was not in a good mood. *"What do you mean you don't know where the bitch is?"* he yelled at Bernie. Although Jack and his partner were friends and had worked together for years, sometimes the man really got on Jack's nerves. "It's already ten-thirty."

"I told you Jack, Pia didn't show up for work today and I had no reason to worry about it. I'm sure she'll be in touch." After what he'd seen on the security tape, Bernie was pretty sure he'd never hear from Pia again, but kept the thought to himself.

"And you're sure she saw the files?" Jack questioned, trying to pace around in the small confines of Bernie's office. "How could you let that happen?"

"Like I told you Jack, I was working on the books last night when I got the call that my uncle was in the hospital. It was seven-thirty at night, for Christ's sake. Pia gets to work at eight in the morning and leaves at four. Like clockwork, every single day."

"So you just left everything out for anyone to see?" Jack's face was getting redder and if he didn't calm down soon he might end up in a bed next to Bernie's uncle.

"What could I do? Uncle Walt's eighty-nine with a bad ticker. My cousin said it was the big one and I needed to get there quick."

"He's eighty-nine, Bernie. Couldn't you just let the old guy croak?"

"You're all heart, Jack," replied Bernie. "Remind me not to visit you in the hospital next time your heart acts up."

"Well at least I'm not stupid!" Jack lowered his substantial girth down into the big green leather chair across from Bernie's desk and lit up the cigar stub he'd been carrying.

"Do you have to smoke that in here?" asked Bernie. "I thought your wife made you give up smoking."

"The wife don't tell me what to do and you know that." Bernie knew the exact opposite was true, but said nothing. "Besides, I told her I'd give up cigarettes but not my Cuban's."

"That cigar stinks too much to be Cuban," Bernie noted. "Who sold you that line?"

"OK, so maybe it's Honduran, but who's gonna know if I say it's Cuban?"

"Anyone with a nose." Bernie got up to open the window and turn on the fan.

"Maybe we're wrong Bernie—jumping to conclusions. You're sure it was her?"

Bernie flipped the computer screen around so it faced Jack, then hit the play key.

"That's her, Jack," he said pointing to the surveillance tape of Pia entering the office. He nodded at the scene before them. "See? She's going through my papers and then goes out and comes back with two stacks. I presume those are copies. Then she goes through the files that were up on the screen and it looks like she downloaded all of them. If she hadn't left these bracelets, I never would have checked the security camera." Bernie shook his head. "Still can't figure out why she snuck in at night in the first place and then went right to my office."

"You must have said something," Jack accused Bernie.

"Of course I didn't!" Suddenly, Bernie remembered the incident in the kitchen. "Oh hell! She might have heard me and Joe talking yesterday."

Seeing Jack start to hyperventilate, Bernie quickly explained the prior day's episode when he and Joe had found Pia in the kitchenette.

"Great, Bernie! Just great! Now she not only has our files, she knows about Joe. You also mention his father? You know what he'll do if he finds out we blabbed his name." Bernie decided not to mention that Joe had reminded him to only refer to his father as The Captain.

"Forget about that Jack…what do you think she'll do with the information?" Bernie asked.

"We're not going to wait to find out. You tried calling her, right?" Jack sucked on his cigar that had gone out.

"Well….not really," Bernie admitted. "I mean I called her cell thinking she might be on the way in, but she didn't answer and I didn't leave a message. I hadn't thought to call her home phone."

"*What?* You see the security tape and you don't make any real effort to track her down?" Jack began to chew the end of his cigar.

"I thought I'd wait for you."

"Damn, Bernie, you're really starting to lose it." Jack reached over and picked up the desk phone. "Dial her number for me." Bernie punched in Pia's number.

Jack listened to Pia's home phone ring and then waited for the answering machine message to finish.

"Listen Pia," Jack said to the recorder, "you need to get your ass into the office pronto. Don't think we don't know what you did. You can deal with us, or you can deal with the police when we turn over the evidence of your actions. I wouldn't put this off if I was you." Jack slammed the phone down.

"Jack, you think threatening her is the right move?" Bernie asked.

"You got a better idea?"

"What if she just goes straight to the police? We're screwed," reasoned Bernie.

Jack thought for a moment. "You're right. Even though we can prove she broke in and stole that information, it could still be bad for us." Jack leaned back in his chair, re-lit his cigar, took a few puffs, and tapped the ashes on the carpet. Bernie cringed.

"OK," Jack continued, "here's the plan, we get my nephew Junior in here to do a little creative bookkeeping. He can attach Pia's name to files that will incriminate her. Or put in a few phony pay-outs. If we do go down, the broad's going with us!"

Jack leaned forward, picked up the phone again, hit re-dial, and waited for the beep on Pia's answering machine.

"Listen doll-face, it's me again. You might want to think twice about taking that information to the authorities. I just re-checked our books and it seems your name is mentioned in more than a few places, including a Swiss bank account. I'll give you one hour to get your ass to the office."

"What if she doesn't show up?" Bernie asked. "Then what do we do?"

"I'm not going to wait to find out," Jack answered, pulling out his phone. "I'm calling in a clean-up team."

"Since when do we have a clean-up team?" asked Bernie.

"Since my ass and yours could land in the slammer, which has been for years now." Jack looked back at his phone and punched in a number.

"Larry," he said to the party on the other end, "I need you to do a job. Meet me at our regular place in one hour."

"Who's Larry?" Bernie asked as soon as Jack had put the phone back in his pocket. He wasn't sure how he felt about Jack having contacts he'd never heard of.

"He's the guy who's gonna take care of the Pia situation."

"Just to be clear, Jack, what exactly is this guy going to do?"

"What do you think he's gonna do Bernie? Bake her a cake?" Bernie didn't respond. "Larry's gonna get rid of the broad for us."

"He's your enforcer? How come I've never heard of him? And what kind of name is *Larry* for a hitman?"

"Shut up Bernie," Jack warned, glancing up at the security camera. "Did you disable that security equipment yet?"

"I turned it off as soon as I found the evidence that Pia was here. It's just you and me. So how exactly does this Larry take care of things?"

"The less people that know, the better. I'll get Junior in here to work on the books and you're going to work on finding Pia. We'll need all the information you have on her. Address, any contact numbers, any friends and family."

Bernie looked sheepishly at Jack. He'd really screwed up this time. "All I have is her address, Jack. The gal's only been working for us for a month. I don't know anything else."

"What?! You hired someone without references?" Jack boomed.

"She had a resume and is a registered CPA. What more did I need? Hell Jack, the broad's over fifty and was in a rough way. Got laid off a few months back. What would you do if you lost your job now? You're how old—sixty-three? Who'd hire either of us? And by the way, who ever heard of someone Pia's age causing problems?"

"Bernie, you still got a lot to learn about the human character. I don't care how old she is, she's already a problem. And I'm not about to let her mess up the business."

~~~

"You're righteously fucked, girl-dude," Brad unnecessarily stated.

Sitting in Pia's living room, sorting through the photo-copies and computer files, the two had just listened to the second of Jack Houston's threatening messages.

"You're assuming that Jack and Bernie can actually do something other than fire me," replied Pia, "or maybe get me arrested for stealing files."

"You ever been arrested Pia?" Brad asked.

"You know I haven't."

"Believe me, you don't want that experience."

"I think they're bluffing," said Pia, picking up a few documents. "Attach my names to fake accounts? Who does that?"

"I'd say Houston and Melrose do," Brad answered. "So what are you going to do? Ignore them?"

"I don't know what I'm going to do, but I'm not making any rushed decisions." She rifled through a few documents. "I have to say, though, that it does look like there's money laundering going on here. But I'll need more than a few hours to come up with hard proof." Pia dropped the papers on the coffee table. "And maybe there isn't any. Maybe they covered their tracks well enough, or maybe I'm just reading too much into a bunch of off-shore accounts." She leaned back on the couch. "And honestly, none of this means they're working with drug dealers."

"Pia, you got a better reason why they'd have off-shore accounts with beaucoup bucks? Especially after what Bob told us? If you were anyone else, I might agree that we don't have any real proof. But money's your gig. Give me a professional opinion. Is there a whole lot of funny money running through Houston and Melrose or not?"

Pia paused for a second and then nodded her head. "Yeah, there's definitely something illegal going on."

"Then what we need is a plan that won't get you offed or arrested."

"I'm not planning on getting arrested and why would they want to kill me? Come on Brad, this isn't Las Vegas and the mob's not going to bury me in the desert. Jack just wants me in the office to hand back the papers. Then he'll fire me."

"Again, for someone with brains you're acting stupid," Brad said. "You think some big-time narco-dudes are just gonna let you walk when you have the goods on them?"

Pia thought about it. Her bosses would really kill her? She seriously doubted either of them even knew how to rough someone up, let alone handle a gun. Brad needed to lay off the weed and quit watching crime shows.

"We'll debate someone wanting to kill me later. But one thing I do know is that I'm not going to hand these documents back to Jack. I know I took them illegally, but I still think the best idea is to contact some government agency."

"Whoa, hang on there, partner. No authorities just yet. Didn't you hear what your boss said about linking your name to a Swiss bank account?" Brad grabbed his cup of coffee and took a swallow. "Tell you what, let me go home and get on some clean clothes then I'll head down to Saul's Bar and check in with Bob. He knows more about these guys than either of us."

Brad stood up and looked out the window at the beautiful day. "Or I could catch a few waves first...." He glanced over at his friend and saw the unease in her eyes. "All right. Saul's first and then the beach."

6

It was nearly noon when Brad sat down at the bar in Saul's. He watched Bob serve up martinis to a group of businessmen, then called out to him. Bob waited until the group had taken their glasses back to a table along the side wall before walking over to Brad.

"Brad," said Bob anxiously, looking around, "where's Pia? Did she go into work today?"

"Why so jumpy, my man?" Brad asked, noting Bob's uncharacteristic anxiety. "Pia's back at her pad. Why do you ask?"

"She needs to keep a low profile. Maybe get out of town," Bob whispered.

"Yeah, we were just talking about that. Give me a—" About to order a beer so that he could think more clearly, Brad stopped. "Hey, how do you know about the break-in?"

"What break-in?"

"Last night me and Pia went to the Huston and Melrose office after hours to dig up some dirt on her bosses."

"Why would she do that?" Bob asked, glancing down the bar and then back to Brad.

"After you told her they had drug connections the other week, she finally started to pay attention. And then yesterday she overhears Bernie and some guy named Joe talking about off-shore accounts. Last night I went with her to the office and stood guard while she went in to look for drug-dealer evidence," Brad explained.

"I told her to find another job, not start nosing around," said Bob.

"You know Pia," Brad replied.

He then told Bob about the threatening phone messages Jack Houston had left that morning. "Is that why you say she needs to hide?" Brad shook his head. "But that doesn't make sense. You didn't even know about our undercover operation until just now."

Bob straightened up and looked out to check on the customers in the bar. Seeing that they were all taken care of, he returned his attention to Brad. "If you'd gotten here fifteen minutes ago you would've seen Jack Houston. And he wasn't alone."

"So? What good would that do me? Hey, I don't even know who this Jack guy is."

"But I do, and I didn't like who was with him." Bob bent over the bar and whispered in Brad's ear. "He was meeting with Larry the Lawnmower."

"Who?" Just when Brad thought he knew anyone of importance in town, Bob would come up with a new name.

"Larry the Lawnmower. He's only the most notorious hitman in the Monterey area."

"There are hitmen in town?" Brad asked in disbelief.

"Brad, a lot of things go on in this town besides surfing and cold beer."

"Clue me in, Bob," said Brad, giving Bob his undivided attention. "You never know when I might need a professional."

"The story goes that Larry started out doing lawn maintenance for a big outfit that takes care of the yards on The 17 Mile Drive. From what I hear, some homeowner pulled him aside one day to see if he wanted to do a little off-the-records job. So Larry goes back to the house that evening and meets the homeowner in the back shed... that's where he sees a body that needs disposal. A stack of bills convinced Larry to do the job and he's never looked back, graduating all the way to hitman in no time. He started his own lawn company to keep his cover and pay the bills between hits."

"That's some heavy stuff, Bob. But what makes you think this Larry dude is after Pia?"

"About an hour ago Jack came in with Larry. They ordered a couple of drinks and then walked over to the booth in the corner. When I saw the exchange of a large pile of green-backs, I got curious. I walked over to see if they wanted a refill and that's when I saw Larry holding a photo of Pia and telling Jack that he would take care of the situation." Bob wiped the bar in front of Brad and continued. "It's a good thing they assumed I'm a little senile or I might not have gotten the information. I was just about to call her when you arrived. I'm pretty sure Jack was paying Larry to take care of Pia."

"You're for real, man?" Brad asked. "They got a contract out on Pia?"

"I wouldn't joke about this sort of thing."

"Damn! This is worse than we thought! I better get back over to Pia's and fill her in."

"That's a good idea. And just make sure she gets out of town." Bob looked at the clock behind the bar. "You should have until nightfall, and after that, she's a goner."

"You heard Jack tell the hitman what time to take her out?"

"Didn't need to. Larry only works at night—not before nine p.m. During the day he runs the landscape business."

"I'm on it Bob," Brad said, getting up from the bar stool. "Think you could give me a beer to go?"

"No booze 'till after you help Pia. Then the drinks are on me."

"My man!" Brad raised a hand to high-five Bob, who ignored the gesture and headed off towards a customer. "I'll be in touch."

~~~

"Time to pack," Brad announced when Pia opened her door.

"What are you talking about?"

"Let's go inside and I'll fill you in." Brad turned around to check if anyone was watching. "Looks like no one tailed me here."

Pia sighed, ushered Brad in and closed the door. "Again, what are you talking about?" she asked, waiting for an answer before moving into the living room.

"It's worse than we thought, my friend. Seems there's a hit out on you."

Pia leaned close to Brad and took a sniff. "Are you already smoking? I thought you agreed to stay sharp for now."

"No weed involved, Pia, honest." His friend didn't move. "This comes straight from Bob. Larry the Lawnmower is gunning for you."

"Larry the Lawnmower?" Pia asked, turning to walk into the living room, Brad trailing behind. "What kind of name is that?"

"It's the name of the top hitman in the county, according to Bob." Brad sat in the recliner facing Pia on the couch. "I hear he chops up his bodies into little blade-like pieces, then drops them off the coast by Point Lobos and the sharks take care of the rest." Brad liked to embellish stories.

"Brad, I'm beginning to think you really have done permanent damage to your brain. Anyway, what makes Bob think someone's out to get me?"

"Only that he saw your boss Jack handing Larry the hitman a picture of you and a pile of cash. And then he heard Larry say he was going to take care of you. But don't worry—we still have a few hours to get a plan together. Bob says Larry doesn't take people out until after dark."

Pia sank back into the couch. "Come on Brad, you can't possibly believe that Jack hired someone to kill me. Who puts a contract out on an accountant?"

"Seems like your boss does."

"Right," said Pia, "that makes sense. One day I'm an accountant and the next day I'm on a hit list."

"Girl-dude, would I make something like this up?" She raised her eyebrows, knowing well the jokes Brad liked to play on his friends. "Well maybe I'd try it on one of the guys, but not you."

Pia had to admit that Brad really did sound quite serious. She ran her fingers through her hair, jumped up from the couch and went to her desk to grab a pen and pad of paper. She returned and started taking notes. It's what she did when faced with a problem, either in life or in accounting. Her very orderly mind had a need to see the situation laid out in front of her. She scribbled for a few more moments while Brad looked on.

"Writing your last will and testament?" Brad asked. "Could you leave me your house?" Pia ignored the comment and continued to jot down notes.

"I'd be happy with just this chair," he told her.

Pia finally looked up from her notepad. "I can't say that I believe the whole hitman theory but even if I didn't, I think maybe I should get on the road until I can come up with some hard proof against Houston and Melrose. Then I have to figure out how to get the information to the authorities without implicating myself."

"Great. You can do that while you pack," Brad said starting to get up. "Where do you keep your suitcase?"

"Hold on Brad. I said you might be right that I need to leave for a few days, but I'm not going now. I can't possibly leave town until tomorrow morning."

52

Brad sat back down in the recliner. "Spontaneity's never been your thing Pia, but it might be a good idea right now."

"No, Brad, it wouldn't be. I have too much to do first."

"Like what? And what about Larry the Lawnmower? He's probably dropping by later tonight."

"Like organizing a travel plan, figuring a way to safeguard the files I stole, getting some cash from the bank. Lots of things."

"Girl-dude, I sure hope you're right."

7

Later that evening, just as Bob had predicted, Larry was sitting in his wife's bright red Fiat 500, parked at the corner closest to Pia's cottage. He tried to stretch out his legs but only managed to bang his knee on the steering wheel for the fifth time. The damn car was not built to accommodate his six-foot-four, two-hundred and thirty pound frame. His wife, at barely five feet, had no problem. It had been his tenth anniversary present to the little lady and he had never planned on driving it. He hated the Italian piece of shit that no real man would be seen driving, but his Mustang was still in the shop. Car headlights headed his way and Larry tried to duck down in the seat. It didn't work. Fortunately, the driver was too busy chatting on his phone to notice Larry. Maybe he should have just come in his van, but it had large lettering proclaiming *Larry the Lawnmower.* At thirty-eight, he was getting too old for this type of work. But the money was just something he couldn't pass up and he liked his reputation of being the premier clean-up man in the area. He checked his watch—just turned eleven-fifteen. The lights inside Pia's house had gone off thirty minutes before and he figured she should be asleep by now.

Larry unfolded his legs out of the miniature car, tried to extract himself, and promptly smashed his head on the doorframe. Being the tough dude that he was, he didn't even let out a curse word. He reached back in to grab his Berretta, silencer attached, from under the passenger seat. Suddenly he found himself trapped between the steering wheel and the dashboard, in danger of dislocating a shoulder. He really should have taken up yoga classes with his wife. He might have been more limber. If anybody was to drive by now, it might look like he was trying to hot wire the car. Finally, with a few contortionist moves, he freed himself from the metal trap, stretched to his full height, and tucked the gun into the back waistband of his jeans.

After one more check of the quiet neighborhood, Larry set out towards Pia's house. The fog was in, making for good cover but also making it harder to see without using a flashlight. Why was it always at times like these that Larry remembered the things he should have done, like investing in night vision goggles? Screw it. It was only a middle-aged broad, nothing like the philandering black-belt karate instructor he'd taken down last year. This would be an easy paycheck.

A four-foot front gate with a metal latch led onto Pia's property. Latches could be tricky; they tended to make a lot of noise. Judging the height, Larry figured he could easily climb over it. What he hadn't counted on was the two foot drop below street level on the other side. Once over the gate, he lost his footing and tumbled in the dirt narrowly missing the garbage can. Sitting on his butt, he pulled out the Berretta that was digging into his back, thankful the safety was on. He should have used the holster. Yet another thing he'd forgotten. What was up? He never used to be this off the mark when it came to jobs.

Larry placed the gun in front of him, crouched down and checked out the darkened front door. A window on the right looked like it might be an easy entry point. Larry was always grateful for targets that lived in 1930's dwellings that had not been upgraded. About to stand up, he heard the front door click and then open, and watched as someone walked out onto the porch. He pushed himself back into the shadows of the garbage can and the large Monterey Pine.

It was too dark to tell, but the person by the front door looked a lot taller than the description he'd had of Pia. Had he gotten the wrong house? And then the person fired up a lighter and held it close to his face. It was a man. Jack hadn't mentioned a husband or even a boyfriend. In fact he'd been adamant about how easy the job would be on the aging spinster. Larry stayed dead still and soon got a whiff of cannabis. This was not part of the contract. No mention had been made of some pot-head on the premises. Now what was he supposed to do? Still crouching, his knees began to complain. Attempting to reposition his body, he lost his balance and fell backwards into the garbage can.

"Whoa, what's going on?" called out the man with the lighted joint. "Better the fuck not be a skunk. I told you guys to leave me alone."

This was worse than Larry had thought. The guy might be on hallucinogenics.

"I'm just going back in to get a flashlight and then we'll see who's the boss," the stoner called out, opening the front door and going inside.

Larry grabbed his chance to escape. Any noise he made would be attributed to a skunk, so he didn't bother to hop over the fence but undid the latch. Hell, it hadn't even made a sound.

Sticking to as much coverage as possible, Larry got back to the Fiat and squeezed himself inside just as he saw the beam of a flashlight from Pia's front porch. He waited a full ten minutes before starting the car up and backing out into the intersection. He was going to jump all over Jack's ass for this set up.

8

The next morning, Pia was up early as usual, putting on the kettle anticipating a cup of coffee. Maybe yesterday had all been a dream. Was she really working for drug dealers who'd hired a hitman to silence her? Did she really need to spend the day running around getting cash, storing files, and possibly getting out of town? For now, all she wanted was some hot coffee.

Six in the morning was her favorite time of the day. Only Brad, snoring on the couch, broke the silence of the early morning. She gazed out through the kitchen window to her front yard. The fog had already lifted, meaning it was going to be a warm day. About to grab the coffee bag from the freezer, Pia did a double-take. Why was her front gate open? Brad must have gone out sometime in the night. If the deer had gotten in and eaten her roses, she was going to be very unhappy with that surfer crashed out of her couch.

She slipped into a pair flip-flops and set out to close the gate. After latching it, she turned back and stopped. Something *had* gotten in; the garbage can had been moved. She did a quick spin to see that the roses still had all their blooms and turned back to straighten the can. That's when she noticed that gun lying next to it. She bent down and stared at the shiny object. One thing she did know; deer did not carry weapons. Instinctively grabbing an old tissue from the pocket of her bathrobe, she picked up the gun, checked to make sure no neighbors were watching, and went back into the house.

She put the gun on the counter and returned to making coffee. It wasn't until after the first few sips that her head started to clear and Pia found herself mesmerized by the weapon. She was no expert, but had seen her fair share of firearms on the nightly news. She knew that the silencer attached to the gun was not something one bought at the local sporting goods store.

"Smells good," Brad said, walking into the kitchen. Reaching for a mug, he stopped short and pointed to the firearm. "What's that?"

"What does it look like, Brad? It's a gun with a silencer."

Brad walked over and bent closer. "Girl-dude, what are you doing with a Berretta?"

"You know guns that well?" Pia asked. "I thought you were all peace and love."

"Doesn't mean I don't know my weapons. Remember Jim Benson from high school? He's a survivalist—lives up in Big Sur now. I ran into him a few years back and went for a visit. The dude is armed to the teeth." Brad grabbed a cup of coffee and the two continued to stare at the gun.

"So where did you get it?" Brad asked.

"I found it out by the garbage can. I was out there because the gate was open." Pia straightened up and looked at Brad. "Did you go out there last night?"

"I might have had a little night-cap......."

"Brad, I told you, no weed at my house."

"Looks like if I hadn't done that, you might not be here," he reasoned.

"What do you mean?"

"Girl-dude, I warned you about Larry and the contract out on you and you ignored me." Brad pointed to the Berretta. "Appears he showed up. I must have scared him off."

"Are you serious?" Pia looked back at the gun. "You really think someone came to kill me last night? There has to be some other explanation, right?" She looked hopefully at Brad.

"Not that I can think of." Brad reached down to pick up the gun and then thought better of it. "You didn't get any fingerprints on this, did you?" Pia shook her head. "Gotta say, this Larry must not be too smart if he dropped his weapon. Maybe you'll be OK."

"Maybe, or maybe not. But there's nothing right about a gun in my front yard." She took another sip of her coffee and set it on the counter. "That's it," she said, walking over to the kitchen phone, "I'm going to have to call the police."

"What?" Brad said, blocking her way to the phone. "Don't you remember what happened last time we decided to report a problem to the cops? You got hassled for years, and that was just about some dickhead who messed up the beach. What do you think they're going to do when you call in a gun like this? And then it's just a matter of time before your bosses tell the cops about the break-in. Girl, you'll be locked up in a New York minute." Brad wasn't sure he had convinced his friend. "And just so you know, you can forget about ever getting a real job again."

Pia had to admit that Brad had some good points. Possession of a gun that may belong to a hitman would not look good on a resume.

"So what do I do now, Brad?"

"You gotta get out of town, girl. Larry for sure will be back tonight."

Pia topped off her coffee and stared out the window. "Assuming you're right, how do you know he'll keep to this supposed schedule? Maybe he'll be back sooner."

"Well," reasoned Brad, "he's at least going to have to get another gun." This did not make her feel any better.

Pia took in a deep breath and exhaled. "This certainly is not what I'd planned when I took those files." Not that she had actually given any forethought to her little foray into espionage. She took several more sips of coffee and looked at Brad. "Do you really think I need to get out of town?"

"Girl-dude, we're staring at a Berretta with a silencer and you really need to ask?"

Pia couldn't very well argue with that. When she'd talked about leaving town the day before, she wasn't really thinking that it would be necessary. Certainly by now this whole situation would have resolved itself, right? It would likely turn out to be a giant misunderstanding. Apparently, it hadn't. She remained silent a moment longer, running through her options.

"How about if I head down to San Diego?" she said. "I haven't been there in years. If I have to really get out of town, it might as well be someplace hot."

Brad thought about it. "San Diego's nice. I got some surf buddies down in Ocean Beach. Then again, it might not be enough. This is an international organization, you know, and they probably have contacts everywhere in the state."

"Oh come on, Brad. You can't really believe that I need to get out of the country. What, go to Mexico? I'm sure you'll now tell me I can't do that because Houston and Melrose are connected with the Mexican drug cartels, right?"

"Damn Pia, didn't you listen to what Bob and I told you the other day?"

"That's the problem. I listened to you two and look where it got me. Now I'm thinking about hitmen and drug cartels."

"Pia, the Fish Runners don't have anything to do with Mexico. It's a Turkish cartel behind it all."

"Not that you ever mentioned that, but what difference does it make where they're from?"

"It makes a whole lot of difference. Actually, Mexico might be a good place to go until we can figure this out." Brad's mind wondered off for a moment. "Think maybe you could head down to Oaxaca? I been looking for a reason to get down that way. I hear they got the really good blow, and Puerto Escondido's known for its primo waves."

"And here I thought this was about wanting to save me from a drug dealer's contract," said Pia. Brad looked a little chagrined. But not too much.

"Well, you know…since you have to go there anyway…"

"If I go Brad, I go alone." She already felt bad enough for having involved her friend in what was turning out to be much more than what she'd expected. "Anyway, I'd need you here to watch the house and keep me updated on what's happening."

"Girl-dude, you asking me to housesit?"

"Unless you prefer staying in your mother's garage."

"Sweet."

"OK, so here's what I can do. I'll head down to San Diego and then we'll see what happens. I bet in a few days all this will have turned out to be nothing." She looked at the Beretta. "Or maybe not. Anyway, I'll need you to drive me up to up to San José so I can catch a flight down south."

"Uh uh," Brad said shaking his head. "No way José can you fly out of that airport."

Pia was really trying to follow Brad's train of thought, but it was becoming rather difficult. "Why not?" she asked. "I thought you just told me I had to get out of town."

"But not on a plane. These drug barons have connections with airport security."

"Now you're just being paranoid, Brad." She reached for the coffee pot and refilled his cup. "Or maybe you're still half asleep."

"I'm plenty awake and not being paranoid—just taking precautions. What if I'm right? Do you really want to risk that?"

Pia shook her head at the craziness of it all, and walked back to the living room. Brad followed her and sat in the recliner. She paced around for a while longer before taking a seat on the couch.

Her employers were into some sort of illegal activities, apparently there had been a hit put out on her, and there was a Beretta sitting on her kitchen counter. Pia didn't really believe that there could be a connection to airport security, but considering everything that had happened in less than a day, why take the chance? She could easily enough get down to San Diego on a bus or the train. If she were going along with this entire insane scenario, what difference did it make how she got out of town?

She grabbed her laptop off the coffee table and started searching for the easiest alternative to plane travel.

"What are you doing?" Brad asked.

"Figuring out if bus travel or train is the best way to get to San Diego."

"For someone so smart," Brad said, "you'd think you'd know not to use a computer."

Pia stopped typing in searches and lifted her head to look at him. "Now you really *are* getting paranoid, Brad. No one's put a tap on my laptop."

"Yeah, but if Jack Houston gives your name to the cops, I can think of a few agencies who might be interested in looking into what you've been searching for on that laptop of yours. You'd be leaving a trail right to you."

"Fine. Before I leave I'll destroy the hard drive." Pia had no intention of doing this, but it might help to keep Brad quiet for a few minutes while she mapped out an escape plan. It worked for a whole forty seconds.

"So how you gonna get down south? You could always hitch-hike." Pia didn't even bother to look up from her work. "Just a thought," he added.

"It's either train or Greyhound," she finally said, "but it looks like the bus will be easier." She typed in a few more words. "Looks like I'll have to take a local bus from Monterey to the station in Salinas."

"I could drive you over to Salinas," Brad offered.

"No, you've already done enough. If you could just get me to the bus stop in town, that would be great." She returned to her laptop screen and perused the bus schedule. "There's a Greyhound leaving Salinas for San Diego at two this afternoon."

"Sounds good to me."

"OK, I'll make a reservation." Pia began to fill in the online form.

"Whoa, Pia, hang on there a minute! You can't use your real name and no way can you use a credit card. From here on out, you need to fly under the radar."

"So how do I get a ticket?"

"You go to the Salinas Greyhound station and pay cash. I'm pretty sure you'll get a seat."

"They're going to ask for ID, won't they? One way or another I'll eventually have to show some form of identification."

"Nah...you look too old and respectable. You'll be fine."

"Is that supposed to be a compliment?" she asked. "Don't bother answering that. I already have enough to worry about without thinking that I've gotten to an age synonymous with little-old-lady safe. Still, I'll need some form of ID just in case."

"I'll go and see Bob in a while. He can get you something, I'm sure."

Pia gave a questioning glance at Brad. "How come, after all these years, I'm just learning about Bob's connection with the underworld?"

"Like I been telling you, girl, you need to get out from behind that desk you work at."

9

Mrs. Arlington put down her binoculars and checked the clock on the mantle; not quite six a.m. Then she looked back across the street to Pia's house. It seemed the surfer staying at Pia's hadn't left during the night. His beat-up truck was still parked across the street. Ever since he had arrived the night before, Mrs. Arlington had kept a sharp eye out on Pia's cottage, going to bed late and waking up early. She'd seen the bum drop by now and then, but he'd never stayed the night. Just when Mrs. A had decided that Pia must be one of those new-fangled lesbians, not that any women had ever spent the night, she had a man for a sleep-over. This troubled Mrs. A. She was miffed that she'd been thrown off her theory on Pia's love life. It had been the only thing that made sense. Why else would an attractive, successful woman be single?

She and Mr. A had been married for forty-eight years and had planned on at least another ten. But deciding to bungee-jump for his seventy-fifth birthday had proven too hard on his heart. She'd never be able to wipe the picture from her mind of Mr. A's lifeless body bouncing up and down on that cord over a gorge in Costa Rica. Worse, their medical insurance wouldn't pay to bring the body back so she had had to agree to a cheap cremation or bury him in that god-forsaken jungle. Mrs. A glanced over at the old paint can that held her husband's remains, inscribed only with the company's name: *Los Colores de America*. She hadn't yet had the strength to have the ashes transferred to a proper urn.

Sitting in the living room window, she stroked the binoculars Mr. A had given her as a gift for bird watching. She'd never cared too much for the birds, but fortunately had found spying on the neighbors and the passing cars to be quite satisfying. This early in the morning not much was going on, and Mrs. A had just decided to fix herself another cup of coffee when she saw Pia walk out her front door and then over to the garbage can. She raised the binoculars to her eyes and spun the focus wheel, giving Mrs. A a clear view of Pia retrieving the gun from the ground.

Mrs. A, a devotee of all TV police dramas, recognized a lethal weapon when she saw one. She also knew that to report the sighting would cause all sorts of complications, which she didn't need. For now, she would continue her surveillance and try to stay out of the way of any stray bullets.

Meanwhile, across town, Larry searched his wife's Fiat yet again. It wasn't there. He'd lost his Berretta. He'd have to chance a drive past the hit's house on the way to a lawn maintenance job on The 17 Mile Drive. At least Jack had given him two days to do the job so he wouldn't have to make a report just yet and explain misplacing his weapon.

10

"Get over to Pia's and see if the job's done," Jack instructed Bernie. He looked up at the office clock from behind his desk. It was nearly two-thirty in the afternoon and he still hadn't heard from Larry. The guy swore he would have the job done by now. He should have taken out Pia the night before, although Jack had given him longer in the event of some unforeseen obstacle.

"*What?* You want me to check for a dead body?" Bernie answered. His partner was getting way out of hand. "Screw you Jack."

"How else we gonna know if she's still a problem?"

"*You* go over there, Jack. I don't want to know anything about this."

"Look Bernie, just knock on the door...maybe look through a window. I don't know...just find out if Larry took her out."

"Why can't you go?" Bernie asked.

"I got a meeting with Joe and his father. So far, they don't know about Pia stealing the files and I intend to keep it that way. Seeing as this is all your fault in the first place, I'm not about to let you come along and the accidently let the cat out of the bag." Jack used the leverage of his desk to hoist himself out of his chair.

Bernie could only look on, not being quick enough to come up with a response before watching Jack's large backside lumber out of his office. Why should he have to do this? Hell, he hadn't even known about Larry and his association with Jack. All right, he might have suspected that Jack used a hired hand now and then, but he'd made sure he was no part of it. Bernie shrugged in defeat, put on his sports coat, and grabbed his keys. Maybe he'd be lucky and Pia's body would be hidden from view. Then Jack could make the trip himself.

Fifteen minutes later, Bernie stood on Pia's front porch not knowing exactly what to do. He leaned his head closer to the door and was sure he heard voices coming from inside. Dead girls don't talk. He listened a second longer and realized it was the TV.

Bernie hadn't really known Pia that well, but he didn't have anything against her. Certainly nothing that would result in a hit. He tried not to think about her getting a bullet between the eyes while watching a nature show. Or did Larry go in for strangulation? With a sigh, he knocked on the door. At least he could tell Jack that he tried to get in.

Bernie counted to ten, banged the door one more time, then took a step back and suddenly stopped. Something had fallen onto the floor inside. God, what if Pia were still alive and soaked in blood, struggling to reach the phone? What if she managed to call the cops? How would he explain what he was doing there? Or possibly worse, what if Larry were still in there? So far, he still had plausible deniability. Deciding that the best plan of action was to high-tail it out of there, the front door abruptly opened.

"Dude, what the fuck you doing?" Brad asked, pulling open the door and staring at Bernie. "Can't anyone take a nap around here?"

Bernie, trying to not look startled, gave the man the once over. *Surfer*, he thought with disdain. At least it wasn't a hitman.

"Where's Pia?" Bernie asked, trying to peer behind Brad.

"Back to the question of what're you doing here, my man?" replied Brad.

"I'm looking for Pia. I know she lives here."

"Hold your horses dude, I don't know who you are. Why should I answer your questions?" A thought crossed Brad's groggy mind. "You're not a cop, are you?"

"No. I'm Pia's boss, Bernie Melrose. Now where is she?"

"I'm the only one here now, boss-man. Anyway, Pia never mentioned you to me." All those years of weed made it hard to tell when Brad was lying.

"Well then, where is she?" Bernie asked.

"Bern, my man, chill! I don't know where she is." Brad stretched and yawned. "What time is it anyway?"

Bernie, slightly distracted, looked at his watch. "It's three o'clock."

"Whoa, beer time!" said Brad. "Wanna brewski?" He turned and headed towards the kitchen.

Not knowing what else to do, Bernie followed him into the kitchen where Brad grabbed a can from the fridge and popped it open.

"That's disgusting!" Bernie commented. "You wake up at three and then start drinking?"

"Wrong, my man. I got up at six, did me some waves, came back and took a snooze. Now it's cocktail hour. Sure you don't want one? Looks like you need to mellow out some." Brad figured this guy would believe just about any excuse he came up with for drinking a beer in the afternoon. Bernie didn't need to know what he'd really been doing, which had been driving Pia to the bus stop.

"Look, I need to know where Pia is." Suddenly it occurred to Bernie that he'd never bothered to find out if Pia were married. He couldn't picture the sharp, attractive accountant with this low-life, but one never knew. "She never told me she was married."

"Whoa, dude, just 'cause I'm in her house doesn't mean we're hooked up." Bernie looked confused. "We're just friends, Bern. No hanky-panky between us."

"Then what are you doing here? And where is she?" Apparent that Bernie was starting to get upset, Brad offered him his beer. Bernie swatted away his hand.

"Lighten up Bern, don't go all apoplectic on me. I don't keep tabs on Pia and she doesn't keep them on me. She's a big girl. I'm sure she'll be in touch."

Just when Bernie decided he'd had enough of the surfer, his eyes caught sight of a fancy-looking gun resting next to the toaster on the counter behind Brad. Holy Moses! Maybe this *was* Larry. Maybe he'd already done the hit. Then why hadn't he introduced himself as such? It was too much to figure out at the moment. He'd take it up with Jack at the office. For now, he just needed to get out of there.

Bernie strode back to the front door. "When you hear from her, you tell her to get in touch with me." He started to leave and stopped. "By the way, I didn't catch your name."

"Thought you'd never ask. The name's Brad." He stuck out his hand but Bernie had already turned, headed back to his car.

Brad waited at the kitchen window until Bernie had driven off. He looked at the oven clock. It was nearly three-thirty which meant Pia was already on the Greyhound out of Salinas and headed for San Diego. He really should go and check in with Bob to give him an update, but that could wait for later. Right now he was craving a sandwich made from Pia's assortment of quality foodstuffs.

~~~

Larry, still breathing hard from the walk up the hill to Pia's house, leaned against the phone pole and tried to catch his breath. He used to be able to jog the hills that ran up from the Pacific Ocean. When had he lost that ability? Maybe he just should have driven his van up the hill and to hell if the neighbors spotted it. He was here now, breathing easier, and hoped he looked like someone out taking a walk. He began the short stroll towards Pia's. That's when he saw a little old man leaving the house. What was this girl into? Derelict surfers *and* retirees? He waited until the man had driven off before continuing to the cottage.

A car was parked by the front gate. It could be Pia's. In front of it had to be the surfer's truck, judging by the marijuana decals and surf shop bumper stickers. Ordinarily, Larry would have simply kept walking and come back at night. Ordinarily, he wouldn't have left a Beretta in the front yard of a hit. He walked up to the house and bent down as if to tie his shoe. It seemed the little old man hadn't bothered to latch the gate and Larry duck-walked into the yard and over to the garbage can where he had set the gun down the night before.

Searching through the pine needles and a pile of dried cat shit he came up empty and then nearly fell into the can again when someone inside cranked up the stereo. Some sort of hideous music assaulted his ears, but it meant Pia was probably inside and it offered good cover. Even if he didn't find his gun, he could take her out easily enough, seeing as she was a girl and kinda old. The stoner shouldn't prove to be a problem except that Larry wouldn't be getting any extra cash for that one.

Larry crept up to below the kitchen window on the left of the front door and slowly straightened his legs until he could see inside. It looked like no one was in the kitchen so he stood up further. Now all he had to do was gain entry and do the job. His hand felt down to the Bowie knife case on his hip, only to grip an empty piece of leather. It was then that he remembered he'd taken the knife in to be sharpened. Without taking the time to feel like an ass for the second time in two days, he quickly scanned the kitchen counters for an alternative weapon. That's when he saw his Berretta nestled next to the toaster. And that's when Brad walked into the kitchen heading for the refrigerator.

Larry sank back quickly to the ground. He stayed there for several minutes until he thought he heard the surfer leave the kitchen. It had given him just enough time to come up with a plan that would take care of the gun situation. He'd deal with the hit problem later on.

By the time he made it down the hill and into his truck, Larry had it all worked out. He drove two blocks to one of the few remaining pay phones that stood outside the laundromat in a small strip mall. He'd used it on occasion and remembered the tip-line stickers plastered on the phone booth wall. He stepped in, noted the first number listed, and punched it in.

A woman's voice got as far as *hello,* before Larry cut in. "There's a gun on the kitchen counter at the house on 601 Blue Jay Drive. It was used in the murder of that karate instructor last year." Then he hung up.

Sally, the receptionist in the office of 16 Mile Drive Security, pulled the receiver away from her ear and stared at it. In this line of work you got used to all sorts of nuts calling, and more than a few prank calls from bored kids. Working for a company that profited off a name bearing a close resemblance to The 17 Mile Drive, those brain-dead, computer-addicted punks, thought they were cool calling in false reports to millionaire's row. Not many of the clients serviced by 16 Mile Drive Security had the money to buy a park bench in the Pebble Beach area, let alone a home. But there was something about this call that struck Sally as odd. It was not a kid calling and it did not sound like a prank.

"Hey Ray," she called out to the security officer who'd just clocked out, "you ever hear anything about a karate instructor that got killed?"

Ray stopped at the door and walked back over to the desk. Medium height, and in his early thirties, Ray had an overall, bland, pudgy appearance. He tried to compensate by adopting a military style crew-cut, thinking it gave him a look of authority.

"Sure, Sally," he replied, "don't you remember? That was last year. Not too far from here. Why you asking?"

"That call that just came in? The guy said where to find the murder weapon."

Ray's interest increased. "Did he give you a location?"

Sally, who had been working so long at the job she rarely needed to write things down, repeated the information.

What a break! Ray saw his chance to finally crack a case that the police hadn't been able to. This could bode well for him. Get him a position on the force. Get him away from running security for this tacky operation. What he would give to escape the boring street patrols and start chasing down real criminals.

Nearly salivating at the thought of it all, his little fantasy was interrupted by Sally's voice. "Ray? You all right?"

"Yeah. Yeah. Just fine. Hey Sally, what time does Alvin finish today?" If he was going to apprehend a killer, it might be best to have a co-worker along.

"He finished about half an hour ago. Said something about heading over to McDonald's, if that's a help."

"It is Sally," he said, walking towards the door.

"What do you think I should do about that call?"

"Forget about it, Sally. Probably just one of those rich spoiled kids trying to get someone to do a raid on a friend's house."

"That's what I thought," said Sally, returning to her bookwork. "You'd think they'd have something better to do."

11

An hour after her Greyhound bus had left Salinas, Pia finally pulled out the passport that Bob had secured for her getaway. Brad had given it to her when he'd dropped her off at the bus stop in downtown Monterey, and Pia had quickly shoved it to the bottom of her purse. At the time, she'd been more concerned with handing off the stolen files to Brad who'd arranged to take them to Bob for safekeeping. By the time she got to the Greyhound station in Salinas, she'd all but forgotten about the fake ID and hoped that no one would ask to see it. Brad had been right. The ticket agent didn't care who she was.

Without reading glasses, all Pia could make out was a woman with long blond hair. That wouldn't be hard to pull off. Women's hair styles and color often didn't match their ID photo. She squinted at the tiny print and thought her new name might be Carol, but it was too difficult to read anything else, especially on a moving bus. Hating to rely on the glasses she generally refused to acknowledge were needed, she finally broke down and dug them out of her bag. Five seconds after putting them on Pia wished she hadn't bothered.

The name was not Carol. It was Carl Jones. He was ten years younger than Pia and although he may have had a somewhat delicate face, he was definitely a man. *You'll have to get creative with the new identity,* had been Brad's advice when he'd given it to her. Several scenarios ran through her head: she'd recently gone through a sex-change operation; it had been a joke; the government had misspelled her name.

The guy was three inches taller than Pia's five foot seven, and weighed sixty pounds more. OK, she could cover that. All women lie about their height and she could say she'd recently lost weight, which might account for why her face looked so different. Her best bet was that no one asked to see her ID. She didn't waste any time thinking about the real Carl Jones, or wondering if he might be some dead guy. That would be really bad karma.

The only thing to do now was to close her eyes and try to fall asleep. Maybe with a rested brain she would be able to better deal with her new identity as a man.

~~~

Back at Pia's cottage, Brad had just about nodded off again after his awesome snack of baguette, Swiss cheese, and roast beef, when there was pounding on the front door, accompanied by, *"Open up, police!"*

Brad flew off the couch, checked his pockets for any illegal pharmaceuticals and then waited a few breaths more before going to the door. He opened it and stared at the two men standing before him, 16 Mile Drive Security emblazoned on their shirts.

"You're not the police," Brad said, about to close the door.

"I told you this wouldn't work, Ray," the shorter of the two said. "I told you we should wait for the real police before we knocked on the door."

"We *are* real police, Alvin. We carry guns, don't we?"

"No, you're not," Brad answered him. "And this isn't the 16 Mile Drive, so beat it." Brad yawned and focused his attention on the company logo. "Where the hell's the 16 Mile Drive, anyway?"

"Come on Alvin," Ray said to his partner, ignoring Brad's question, "we can't wait for the police to get here. We need to secure the premises." At this point he placed his hand on Brad's chest and gave him a shove.

Brad may have been fifty-two, and may have looked like a dead-beat, but anyone who has surfed the freezing cold waters and rough waves off the Monterey Coast for most of his life, was no wuss. Not only did Brad not budge from the shove, but he grabbed Ray by the wrist and proceeded to hurl him off the porch and onto the dirt path.

Ray jumped up and was about to go for his gun when a real cop car came screeching to a halt in front of the house. A woman in uniform flew out of the car and ran to where Ray was getting up.

"Just in time, officer," said Brad. "These clowns were trying to break into my house."

"Ray, I thought I told you to wait until I got here. What were you thinking?" said the officer. She was shorter than Ray, but her muscled body could have thrown him into a head-lock in one easy move—something she had often considered doing.

"Hey, it was me who got the info and passed it on to you," Ray reasoned. "Anyway, you were late showing up, Jackie."

"I swear Ray, if you weren't my second cousin, I'd haul your ass in right now." Officer Jackie gave Ray the stink-eye and he sheepishly stepped aside.

"See Ray?" Alvin whispered. "I *told* you we should've waited!"

"Shut up Alvin," Ray answered under his breath.

"Now that that's settled," said Brad, who'd been enjoying the cop altercation, "I'll just get back to cleaning the house."

"Not so fast, buster," Officer Jackie said, placing her hand on the door and preventing Brad from closing it. "This your house?"

Damn, I'm screwed! thought Brad. This lady was the real-deal. Her platinum blonde ponytail didn't fool him into thinking she was soft. No way could he play with her like he did with the rent-a-cops. Then again, he had nothing to hide. He'd flushed his pills down the toilet after Bernie had left, and thrown his weed in the compost bin.

"Actually, it's my friend's house. She's not here at the moment. How can I help you?" Brad had learned that being polite to the law usually helped.

"We got a report about a gun being in the house. Know anything about it?"

"Gun? Lady-cop, I don't do guns."

"Lady-cop?" scowled Officer Jackie, furrowing her eyebrows.

Just about to give Brad a talking-to on how to address women in uniform, Ray, who'd snuck off to the left to peer in the kitchen window, yelled out,

"Jackie! I can see the gun! It's on the kitchen counter!"

In quick succession, Ray ran towards the front door, Brad turned to dash for the kitchen, and Officer Jackie whipped out her gun and aimed it at Brad.

"On the ground, dickhead!" she ordered. Brad, having heard those words before, carefully raised his hands and kneeled down.

"I said on the ground!" Officer Jackie yelled. At that exact moment, Ray ran over and tried to slip past the two, knocking Officer Jackie straight into Brad who then fell to the floor.

"God damn it, Ray!" screeched his cousin. "Get out of the way!"

"It was my tip and I'm gonna get the credit!" Ray attempted to get by her but Officer Jackie was quite the agile cop. With one foot pinning the now supine Brad, she quickly moved her other foot and tripped Ray, who proceeded to land partially on top of Brad.

"This is police brutality!" Brad yelled out from down on the carpet. "Get that stooge off of me!"

Officer Jackie rested the nose of her gun on the back of Brad's head. "Shut up," she said, then grabbed his wrists and clamped on the handcuffs. Ray scooted on his butt towards the kitchen.

"*Ray*," barked his cousin. "Be of some help and keep this man on the ground." Ray complied, stood up, and placed his foot in the middle of Brad's back.

Brad turned his head towards the kitchen but he couldn't get a clear view. He heard the lady-cop call in for backups and a forensic team. Fifteen minutes later and five more cops, the cuffed Brad sat on the couch, trying to remember the meditation chants his mother had taught him.

Officer Jackie and three other male cops inspected the Berretta that now rested inside a plastic zip-lock bag.

"Sure looks like the type of gun that was used on the karate champ," one of them said.

"You don't run across this kind of thing in Pacific Grove too often," commented another.

"You sure the surfer knocked off the karate guy?" asked a third cop, looking warily at Brad. "Doesn't look the type to carry a lethal weapon."

Brad, tempted to shout his innocence and yell at the authorities, kept his mouth shut. He glanced over at Ray who had been allowed to stay as long as he kept quiet and didn't move from the recliner. Ray's co-worker Alvin, on the other hand, had slipped out the front gate as soon as he had seen Ray sneaking off to check through the kitchen window.

"You want us to book him?" one of the cops asked Jackie. "We called this in, and it isn't even his house. Maybe he was trying to rip it off."

This time, Brad couldn't keep quiet. "It's my friend's house but I have her permission to be here." He nodded to the pile of mail on the coffee table. "See? All my mail is being forwarded to this address. And right next to it is my wallet. Check my ID."

One of the cops picked up the pile and Brad's driver's license. "He's right Jackie. It looks OK to me."

"See?" said Brad, feeling triumphant, "I told you so. And by the way, you can't book me. I haven't been arrested. I haven't been read my rights." He'd spoken too soon.

"Well, I guess we'll just have to arrest you then," said Officer Jackie. She really didn't want to deal with the surfer, but she didn't like his attitude. "Rick," she, ordered one of the men, "read him his rights and get him down to the station."

"Ahh…." Rick began, not sure he should question his boss. "What are we arresting him for? It looks like he's here legitimately….and there's no law against owning a Beretta. Although I'm not sure about the silencer part."

"Yeah," said Brad, "you can't just arrest me because there's a gun in the house."

Finally, an hour after Brad had answered the door to Ray the security guy, the house was free of the cops, although he was given a warning not to leave town. The first thing he did after they were well gone was to call Bob.

"I may need a lawyer Bob," he said. "And I think Pia's totally fucked for sure this time. I can't talk on the phone, but I'll be down later tonight."

For now, Brad just needed to calm down. He went outside and dug into the compost bin until he found his stash that he'd carefully wrapped in an airtight bag just in case he might have to retrieve it.

From across the street, Mrs. A kept her eyes glued to the house. There had never been this much action in all the years she had lived there.

12

The Greyhound pulled into the downtown San Diego terminal at eight-thirty, twilight just setting in. Pia stretched as best she could before attempting to get out of her seat. She was seriously concerned that both her hips and elbows might be permanently locked in a sitting position.

The neighborhood had undergone a radical upgrade since last she'd been there, when it was still the scummiest downtown west of the Mason-Dickson line. In those days, the neighborhood had been filled with winos and hookers and junkies and bums, decrepit buildings and filthy streets. Even in sunny San Diego, the area had always seemed to have a grayish pallor hanging over it. Too bad. Old school downtown would have been a perfect place to remain anonymous. In the new upscale edition it might not be so easy. Honestly, Pia thought, she was starting to sound as paranoid as Brad. Even if her employers were connected to drug dealers, she really didn't think they were criminal masterminds tracking her every move.

After easing her way off the bus and retrieving her bag, she sat on a bench and pulled out the hand-drawn map with directions to the cheap hotel she'd found online. Following Brad's advice, she hadn't called ahead to book a room. Considering the establishment offered both hourly and weekly rates, she figured there wouldn't be a problem with room availability.

OK, let's go, she prodded herself, and headed for the hotel a block down and around the corner. Walking past a few shady characters, it was apparent that the urban renewal hadn't quite reached all the blocks of downtown.

Pia walked in through the dirty glass front entrance of The Downtown Central Hotel, past a couple of drunks snoozing in dilapidated chairs around the cramped lobby, and on up to the receptionist's desk. She peered in through the barred window that fronted the small, alcove office.

"Hello," she called out to the back of a man busy watching a tiny, grainy television. He didn't turn. "Excuse me?" she said, this time in a louder voice.

The man spun around and glared. "What?" he snapped, running a hand through greasy, thinning dark hair.

The clothes he wore were clean, but had seen better days. The name on the patch of his worn work shirt read *Sam*. Pia briefly wondered if that was really his name.

"Hey Sam, I need a room for the night," she said, reaching into her bag for her wallet.

"Name," said Sam, not looking up while he flipped open the log book.

This was one more thing Pia had not thought through. She wasn't supposed to be using her real name and she couldn't really use the new identity of Carl.

"Jane Doe," was the best she could come up with. Inventing stories on the spur of the moment was something Brad was good at, but not Pia.

"Do you have a reservation?" Sam asked, still not looking up.

"Do I need one?"

"Some people have them, some don't," he answered, now meeting Pia's eyes.

"No reservation," she confirmed. "Do you have a room?"

He rolled his chair over to the other side of the tiny cubicle and grabbed a key off the rack.

"That'll be thirty dollars. Cash or debit card only." Pia pulled out the money, slipped it under the barred window, and took the key.

"Up the stairs, third floor, down the hall on your left," Sam said, pushing the key through to her. He swung his chair around, deposited the money through a slot, and returned to watching his show.

Pia dragged her small bag up the stairs. She swore it hadn't been that heavy when she'd packed it. Twice she'd banged it into the back of her ankle and wished she'd taken a small back-pack instead. She considered taking off the uncomfortable clogs, but opted for pain rather than dirt-encrusted carpet. At least she was finally off the bus and looked forward to getting some rest. She stopped in front of room 306, unlocked the door, and kicked her bag inside.

The stuffy third floor room reeked. There were obviously no laws against smoking in this hotel. Pia walked across the small space and pulled back the thin, shabby drapes. Not more than twenty feet separated the hotel and the next building. No lights were on in the window across the way making it impossible to tell if it were an office or an abandoned building. In this area, it could be either. With a bit of effort, she managed to get the window open a mere four inches. She briefly considered opening the door to get some cross ventilation but thought better of it. After all, it would only be for the night. She flopped down onto the lumpy mattress and stretched her mangled body.

All she really felt like doing was closing her eyes and dozing off, but she'd promised to check in with Brad. She forced herself to sit up, grabbed her purse off the end of the bed, and dug around until she'd found her phone.

On Brad's insistence, she'd turned it off before leaving Pacific Grove. She doubted Jack, Bernie, or even this Larry guy could trace her using the phone's GPS, but they *could* call her. The last thing she wanted was to be distracted by a ringing phone and demands to get into the office. Tossing the phone around in her hand, Pia was now faced with a dilemma. If she turned it on, there was the possibility of more threatening messages from Jack, which she just did not want to hear. If she kept it off and used the phone booth in the lobby, anyone down there could overhear her conversation. In the end, the cell phone won out and she called Brad's number.

"Hello," said Brad. With all the noise in the background, Pia knew she'd reached him at the bar.

"It's me. I just got here."

"Girl-dude, why are you calling me on my phone?" Brad shouted over the noise. "It could be tapped!"

"Brad, no one has tapped your phone." Pia hoped her soft voice, brought on by exhaustion, would calm Brad down.

"You calling from a phone booth?" If anything, Brad sounded even more agitated.

"No, I'm using my cell."

"Are you *tripping?*"

"Brad, take a deep breath and settle down. Remember, you told me to check in with you once I got here. I'm just calling to let you know I arrived in one piece, if a bit sore, and that I'm staying at—"

"Don't say another word!" Brad cut in. "We've got trouble."

Pia yawned. "What could possibly have happened since I left town this morning?"

"Look," said Brad, "we shouldn't talk about this on the phone." Pia leaned back on the mattress and felt her eyes start to close. "Pia? You there?"

"Yes, Brad, but just barely. All I want to do is go to sleep, so please just tell me what's going on."

"Bad news, girl-dude. The cops came by the house today and they found the gun."

Pia shot straight up and leaned her back against the headboard, now fully awake. "What were they doing at my house? And how did they find the gun?"

"Can't say why they decided to drop in, but a little weasel rent-a-cop spotted the Beretta on the kitchen counter. The real fuzz said something about the Beretta being used in the murder of that karate instructor last year. Long story short, I got cuffed but they released me...at least for now. They were asking about you but I said I didn't know where you were." Brad listened to the silence at the other end of the line. "Pia? You still with me?"

"Yeah," Pia answered, brushing her hair out of her eyes, "I'm just not sure what to say."

"Look, your name hasn't hit the news yet, but I'm kinda thinking it might." Brad thought for a moment. "Listen, we have to get off the phone. Let me talk to Bob and then I'll call you back from the pay phone here. And then you *have* to ditch your cell."

"Fine, Brad." Pia was simply too beat to try and make sense of this latest news. "The only thing I'm planning on doing is taking a long shower and then going to sleep. Call me whenever. Bye."

Brad disconnected, looked down the bar and called Bob over.

"She's in San Diego, Bob. Now what do we do?"

"We discussed this Brad. You already told me you have friends down there and you know the area. Like I said before, you have to go down to San Diego and then help Pia get across into Mexico."

"You really think she's got to split the country?" Brad hadn't been to San Diego in years and was always up for a road trip, but he'd never smuggled anyone into Mexico.

"It's the only way. Go back to her house, call your friends in San Diego, then book a flight out of San José."

"Aren't you forgetting that I'm supposed to be watching Pia's house?" Brad asked.

"We'll figure that out later." Bob turned when a customer called out to him from down the bar. "I can at least get someone to check on her place daily. I've got to get back to work now. Call me when you get to San Diego."

Brad slapped down a tip on the bar and headed back to Pia's to make arrangements.

13

Pia woke up early feeling far from rested. The combination of a stinky room, lumpy mattress, and thoughts of life as a fugitive had kept her tossing and turning most of the night. She dragged herself out of bed, took a long shower, and made a cup of instant coffee provided by the meager room amenities.

It had been close to midnight when Brad had called her at the hotel, insisting that she needed to get to Mexico. To help her get across the border he'd be flying down to San Diego in the morning. At the time, she'd simply been too tired to argue with him so agreed to the plan. Now, with the light of a new day, she wasn't so sure. Brad was probably right that she should get south of the border. However, she didn't want him drawn in any further into this problem with her bosses.

Pia checked her watch. Brad would be arriving in a few hours and they were to meet on the Ocean Beach pier. There was nothing to say that she *had* to make that appointment. Why not just head down to Tijuana by herself and figure it out from there? If the coast were clear, she could easily cross back over to California.

Pia slipped into a pair of sky blue cotton palazzo pants, an off-white tank top, and a pair of flip-flops. She pinned her hair up off her neck and put on a bit of makeup, then made one final check of the room. Not spotting any incriminating evidence, she headed down to the lobby.

Sam was still on duty in the reception room and looked like he might have just woken up.

"Morning Sam," Pia said, passing her room key through the slot below the barred window. "Could you tell me where can I get a bus to the border?"

Sam yawned, displaying teeth in need of a dentist, and then reached down to scratch his balls. "You trying to get to Mexico?" he asked.

"Yeah, that's the plan."

Sam pointed to the TV. "Don't think that's a good idea today."

Pia leaned forward trying to make out the picture on the small screen. The volume was too low to be heard clearly. "Why not? What's going on?"

"Big-ass dope bust at the border crossing. Some sort of joint US-Mexico deal. The border's been all but shut since around four this morning."

"Oh dear," Pia said. Now what was she going to do? She hadn't planned on border delays, or on the heightened security issue which pretty much assured that her passport would be scrutinized. "They're really not letting anyone through?"

"You might be able to get into Mexico—at least it'd be easier than trying it the other way." He stopped to look at Pia noticing, as he had the night before, that she was not like his usual clientele. "And if there's some reason you're trying to get across the border undetected, today wouldn't be the day to do it."

"Well, that certainly puts a damper on my plans," she said mostly to herself.

"So you *do* want to get out of the country?" Sam asked.

Pia looked him straight in the eye. Quickly sizing up a person was a skill she'd become quite adept at after years of working with clients and their tax returns. He may have been a little rough around the edges, but this guy dealt with a non-stop supply of folks who were on the lower end of the money scales and often with shady motives. She couldn't imagine that he'd even care why she was in a hurry to get south of the border.

"Let's just say I *did* want to cross the border without any possible hassles. What would you suggest?"

"You're best bet is Arizona. Unless you want to hang out here for a day or two." He gave her the once over. "I know a lot of good hangouts I could show you where no one will ask your name."

"Thanks for the offer, Sam." Pia nodded her head towards the lobby. "You run a nice place but I've got to be on my way. Tell me about the Arizona route."

"Catch the bus to Tucson and head on down to Nogales. Never heard of any big problems there." Sam reached under the counter, pulled out a sawed-off shotgun and placed in his lap. He reached down again and retrieved a tattered bus schedule.

He glanced through it then turned it for Pia to read. "Looks like the next bus out leaves in thirty minutes."

"Thanks for your help. I guess I'll be off, then." She grabbed a twenty out of her pocket and slid it under the barred window. "Buy yourself a few beers."

"Good luck, Jane Doe."

A few minutes later, Pia found herself in front of the Greyhound station. She stood there looking in through the glass doors. She simply could not go inside. The thought of another bus ride, to a city she didn't know, in a completely different state, made absolutely no sense. There was no guarantee that she wouldn't get stopped at the Arizona-Mexico border, which would make the trip totally pointless. She turned around and walked off down the street.

A block and a half later, she found a city bus stop and sat down on the bench. People were just starting to come out of hotels down the street and the traffic had begun to pick up. She glanced up to the route information sign on the bus stop pole. There was a direct bus going to Ocean Beach. It seemed the fates had decided she was going to meet Brad after all. Twenty minutes later she was seated on the bus headed for the beach.

Once Pia got off the bus in Ocean Beach, it wasn't hard to find the pier. She checked her watch and saw that it would be a while before Brad arrived. She walked over to a café on Newport Avenue and ordered a grilled cheese sandwich and coffee.

14

Back in the offices of Houston and Melrose, Bernie heard the back door open followed by Jack calling his name. He looked up at the clock on his office wall. It was only 8:45 in the morning; something serious had to be up for Jack to be there so early. Bernie took a deep breath in anticipation of the tirade from his partner that was sure to come. He'd managed to avoid Jack after the episode at Pia's and hadn't picked up on his phone calls. Now, he would have to tell him what had happened.

"Bernie," Jack said, coming into his office, "I been trying to call you since yesterday. Where were you?" Jack dropped into the chair across from Bernie's desk with a loud thump.

"Sorry Jack, but I had to go back to the hospital to check on my Uncle Walt. The doctors say he's still got a fifty-fifty chance." Jack was not impressed.

"Great, Bernie. The old guy lives to see another day." He looked heavenward and shook his head. "What's wrong with you?" he snapped. "We got more important things than your uncle Walt! What the hell happened when you went to Pia's yesterday?"

"Wouldn't Larry know the answer to that?" asked Bernie, trying to shift the conversation in another direction.

"No news from Larry yet. But he doesn't always check in right away. That's why I had you go over to her house."

"I didn't see her, Jack. The only one there was the guy who answered the door." Bernie felt it was better not to mention that he hadn't searched for a body.

Jack leaned forward in his chair and probably would have jumped out of it had he been a smaller man. "What?" he yelled. "You saw Larry? Damn, he's really starting to lose it."

"Is Larry a surfer? Scraggily hair, shorts, and a lot of necklaces?"

"No, Bernie, Larry's not a fucking surfer! Necklaces? What kind of pussy do you think I'd hire to take care of business?"

"Calm down, Jack. I was just asking. Pia wasn't there, only the beach bum. What was I supposed to do, ask him if there was a dead body in the house? Maybe he was Pia's boyfriend, although he said he wasn't."

"And how are we supposed to know who he was or what he was up to? How do we know he didn't see Larry? Christ, Bernie, maybe if you'd done a better job when you hired the broad we'd know who she was shacking up with."

"Jack, you know it's against the law to ask if she's got a husband. How was I supposed to know her marital status?"

"There are ways to get around that, and you know it. Never mind that for now, just tell me if you noticed anything else. For all we know Larry already disposed of the body."

"I wasn't there long enough to check for signs that Larry had been there, but I did see something rather odd."

"Yeah? What?" Jack asked, leaning forward in his chair.

"You're not going to believe this, but Pia had a Beretta sitting on the kitchen counter."

"Pia has a gun? Huh. Didn't strike me as the type."

"That's what I thought. Or it could have been the surfer's, not that I was about to ask him. The man appeared to be high on something so I thought it was better to leave."

"But you didn't think it was important enough to call me?" Jack, again, looked toward the ceiling. "What am I doing working with a bunch of morons? How hard can it be to take out one, over-the-hill gal?"

"How do you know Larry didn't come through? Maybe he was too busy getting rid of the body to get in touch," Bernie suggested. "Jack, you're getting all worked up about nothing. I know you said you'd wait for Larry to call, but maybe you should try to reach him."

"You're right, Bernie, this can't wait. I'm calling Larry." Jack hoisted himself out of the chair, walked out of Bernie's office and headed for his own.

Just as Jack was about to call Larry's number his niece, and current secretary, Heather, popped through the door.

"Uncle Jack, I'm so glad you're here," she said excitedly. "Did you hear the news?"

"What news? And why are you here so early? Don't you have classes?"

"Yeah, I do, but this is important." Heather closed the door and walked over to her uncle's desk. "Uncle Jack, you're not going to believe this but there's an APB out on Pia! It's crazy! She seemed like such a boring person. I can't imagine what she's done. Do you have any idea?"

Jack tried to remain as calm and emotionless as possible. His niece had no idea about his clandestine business dealings and he planned to keep it that way. "An APB on Pia? Where'd you hear that?"

"My roommate has a police scanner. She's hoping to get in with the CIA after graduation and she thinks it will help sharpen her skills. Anyway, we were having coffee in the apartment before classes and the bulletin came through about Pia." Heather glanced at her watch. "I need to go. I've already missed the first hour of my Mandarin class but I thought you'd want to know."

"Thanks, Heather. And maybe don't mention this to your mother." That's all he needed, his sister butting into his affairs.

"Bernie!" Jack yelled out through the open door after Heather had left. "Get in here now!"

Bernie walked into Jack's office. The man was starting to turn red. "What's wrong? Was that Heather? Why was she in so early?"

"Only to tell me that the cops have an APB out on Pia!"

"What! Pia's alive? What the hell's going on?"

"That's what I'd like to know. Hell, we don't know for sure if the broad's dead or alive. Maybe Larry got rid of the body. But why the hell are they looking for her?"

Jack pulled out his small address book and started looking through names. "There's got to be someone I can call." He flipped through a few more pages and stopped. "This should do." He looked up at Bernie. "Remember Constance? Used to work at the Chevrolet dealership in Seaside?"

"The one who got you all the deals on the cars?"

"That's the one. Her son Ray works for some security outfit—always trying to get on the local police force. See if you can locate him. He might be able to help us find out why there's an APB out on Pia."

"Jack, I don't even know the lady. How am I going to find her son?"

"You got a point. OK, I'll call her and try to find Ray. Meanwhile, get back over to Pia's and find out what the surfer knows. Better yet, let's put a tail on him."

"He wouldn't tell me anything yesterday, so what makes you think he'll talk today?"

"I don't know Bernie," Jack responded, "maybe you could put the squeeze on him and do your job."

"I'm an accountant Jack, not an enforcer. Isn't that why you have people like Larry?"

"OK, OK….morons…," he said under his breath. "I'll get in touch with Larry, seeing as it seems he might of fucked up the hit, the least he can do is pump the surfer for info."

15

Pia had been in the café for well over an hour when she finally swallowed her last bit of coffee, paid the bill, and wandered outside. There was still time before she was to meet Brad on the pier, but with her suitcase loading her down she couldn't very well take a walk around town. She headed back across the street, up the steps to the pier, and plopped down on a bench.

The day was clear and warm, with just a few scattered clouds in the sky. Joggers ran along the beach, surfers rode the small waves. Pia leaned back and must have dozed off. Next thing she knew, Brad was shaking her awake.

"Huh?" she muttered, confused for a second, wondering what she was doing sleeping in the sun. "Brad...hi," she yawned. "I wasn't sure if you'd make it."

"Gotta have the faith, girl-dude. Said I'd be here and I am." Brad took a seat next to her and looked out at the surfers. Only the small-sized waves kept him from running down to the beach and jumping in.

"OK, we're in Ocean Beach, now what do we do?" Pia said, getting up to stretch.

Brad turned back to her. "No worries, I got it all under control. I already called Skip and he said to drop by whenever we got in."

"Skip?" Pia asked. "Who's that?"

"He's an old buddy of mine from the surfing circuit."

"And he doesn't mind a stranger dropping by? Are you sure he has enough room?"

"No problem there. Skip earned a little bit more money on the pro circuit than I ever did—actually a *lot* more money—and invested in a line of cruise wear. All the old ladies on those Mediterranean cruises pay top dollar to be dressed in *Skipper of the Seas* outfits. I tried giving a few to my mom, but she told me they were the ugliest clothes she'd ever seen. Course, she's still pretty much a beatnik and constantly reminds me of her time with Kerouac. She wrote a note to Skip thanking him, then donated the clothes to the Salvation Army."

Pia briefly wondered what Skip my live in. Recalling the homes she'd passed coming in on the bus, Ocean Beach seemed to be comprised mostly of adorable little cottages, low commercial buildings, and ugly 60's apartment complexes. Very cute, indeed. She assumed that even though Brad said his friend was doing well, he was probably like all of his other friends and lived hand to mouth. Not that it mattered in the slightest. He was offering to hide her and Pia was certainly grateful.

"So where does Skip live?" Pia asked.

"He's up on Sunset Cliffs. It's not too far," Brad said, looking at his somewhat bedraggled friend. "But we're gonna have to walk. Taking a taxi in OB ain't cool. Don't want to be pegged as tourists."

Pia looked at Brad who blended in with everyone she had seen so far and then looked at herself. She'd do well enough, especially in her ragged state. She stood up and extended the handle on her suitcase.

"Then let's get a move on. I certainly don't want to be mistaken for a tourist." For the first time Pia noticed that Brad only carried a medium-sized messenger bag slung across his chest. "That's all you brought?"

"I wasn't planning on moving down here. Bob just wanted to make sure you got to Mexico. Anyhow, I don't need much and I can always borrow from Skip."

"Right," said Pia. "Lead the way."

The two walked off the pier, up Newport Avenue a few blocks, and then turned right onto Sunset Cliffs Boulevard. It had been a fairly level walk, but soon the street began a slow incline and Pia now understood why it was called Sunset Cliffs. Normally, she'd enjoy the walk but after the last couple of days, and then dragging her suitcase which kept bumping and turning on the uneven sidewalk, it was getting more than a little tiresome. She'd tuned out Brad's non-stop commentary on the places he'd been in OB, the parties he'd attended, and the ladies he'd encountered.

"Are we getting close, Brad?" Pia asked, stopping to lean against a bench and take in the scenery looking out over the Pacific Ocean. She turned around to look at the houses that ran along the other side of the street. The farther along they had walked, the bigger and newer the houses had become. "Your friend must be doing pretty well. These are mansions."

"Much better than I even imagined," Brad said, taking in the rambling homes across the way. "Last time I was down here, Skip still lived down on Cape May Avenue, not far from the beach. It was a nice enough house. I'd trade it for any of the places I've ever lived. Funny, he always swore he'd be one of the *people* and not sell out to buy one of these new houses up on the Cliffs. Seems Skip's gone all capitalistic on me." Brad pulled out the address he'd written down. "Hey look. It's just two houses up."

Skip's house was a large, modern, Mediterranean style home, set a ways back from the street. Pia was too spent to admire the carefully manicured garden entrance, or notice the expensive sports car in the driveway. She just wanted to sit down, kick off the flip-flops, and drink about a gallon of cold water.

A barefooted man walked out dressed in off-white linen, drawstring trousers and a thin, aqua-toned cotton t-shirt. He was a little shorter than Brad, and the beer-gut more substantial, but generally he looked to be in great shape for a man close to sixty. The big difference between the two men was Skip's shaved head.

"Dude!" Brad yelled, embracing his friend in a bear hug. "You hit the mother lode with this place!"

"Good to see you, brother!" He grabbed a handful of Brad's long locks. "Damn, you still have this much hair? I gave up years ago and now just go shiny-topped." He then turned to Pia and wrapped her in an embrace before she had a chance to resist.

"So you're the gal on the run. Welcome to OB! Come on in."

~~~

From behind a car parked across the street from Skip's, Larry crouched in an uncomfortable position. Sweating profusely, and already feeling his sun-burnt face beginning to blister, he watched the three go into the house. Fuck it! He should never have agreed to tail the surfer.

When he'd finally gotten in touch with Jack, he'd been pleased to find out his gun tip had lead to an APB on Pia. Apparently, some cop named Ray had been at Pia's when they'd found the gun. Larry didn't want to think about how it was that Jack was on a first name basis with a cop. All that mattered is that Jack was none the wiser that the weapon really belonged to Larry. Better yet, Jack had believed his story about Pia not being home when he'd gone to do the job. But then Jack had asked him to maybe rough up the surfer a little and find out where Pia had gone. Larry had tried to argue that that wasn't something he did, but Jack had him by the balls, telling him he'd smear his name. He didn't really have a choice and Jack knew it.

So Larry had hopped back into his van and driven over to Pacific Grove. Just as he was pulling in front of Pia's house he saw the surfer jump into his truck and drive off. Larry started to tail him, thinking it would be just out to the beach, or maybe over to Carmel. When he'd called it into Jack, he was instructed to keep on the surfer's trail.

It wasn't until he was driving into the San José airport that Larry had a feeling his goose was cooked. He parked his van a row away from Brad's truck and called Jack again, all the while following the surfer into the airport and up to the ticket counter.

"Now what do I do, Jack?" Larry asked. "Looks like he just bought a ticket to San Diego."

"Hah! We got her! So our little Pia decided to do a runner. Bet she's already down there." Larry doubted that. What reason would she have to go to San Diego?

"OK. So now can I go home?"

"No, Larry, you can't go home. Get on the fucking plane and keep up the tail!" Jack demanded.

"What? Fly down to San Diego? How do you know that Pia's even there? And what am I supposed to tell my old lady?"

"You should have thought about that before you didn't do the job I paid you to do and the target got away. Anyway, didn't you tell me your wife's away on a girl's weekend in Vegas?"

"So what? I don't even have a toothbrush with me!"

"Just get on the damn flight and call me when you get in. I have friends down there who can help you out with brushing your teeth!"

So Larry begrudgingly bought a ticket and got on the same flight as Brad. He was pretty sure the surfer didn't know who he was, but all the same made sure he kept a low profile. Once in San Diego, Larry hopped into a cab and followed Brad until they arrived in Ocean Beach.

No one had been more surprised than Larry when he saw Brad meet up with Pia on the pier. Holly crap! Jack had been right. But what was she doing here? Jack said there was an APB out on her, right? Maybe he should just call in a tip again. But then he called Jack who made it very clear that Larry was to do no such thing. It was too risky. What he needed was for Larry to finish what he'd been hired to do. Off the bitch.

Swearing under his breath, Larry continued to follow the two until they arrived at the house up on the cliffs. Now that he'd found out where the surfer and Pia were holed up, he wandered back down the street until he found some shade.

He pulled out his phone to call Jack and soon realized that his battery was dead. This was beyond fucked! He checked his wallet and found fifty-five dollars in cash. That wasn't going to last long which meant he'd need to find an ATM. It wasn't the way he liked to do things, leaving a money trail, but it was that or credit cards. Meanwhile, he was not about to sit on the street waiting for Pia to leave the house.

Walking back into OB, he stopped at the first phone booth he found, dug out all his change, and called Jack.

"This is crazy, Jack! I don't have any clothes, no phone, and my van is parked in short-term parking at the airport. What the hell am I supposed to do?"

"Calm down, for one. Look Larry, you're a professional, right? Find a motel in town, drop by Radio Shack and get a charger, and then call me."

~~~

Once Pia and Brad had been shown their rooms and dropped off their bags, they joined Skip out on the back terrace which resembled a mini-tropical oasis. Glass doors from the living room opened onto a terra cotta tiled patio, shaded by a wooden awning. Lush grass filled in the back yard which was bordered by brightly colored bougainvillea, various palm trees, and tropical plants not known to Pia.

"You've got quite a beautiful place, Skip," Pia said, admiring the peaceful setting and enjoying the luxury of expensive garden furniture. "How lovely it would be to live in such great weather. I'm sure you know that it rarely gets this warm up in the Monterey area."

"I've been telling Brad for years he needs to move down to a better climate," said Skip.

"And put up with all the spoiled surfer's here who know nothing about battling the elements? No way, dude." Brad took another sip of his beer. "So how's the family, Skip. Got another wife yet?"

"Damn Brad, you know that I only ever had one... and that was enough. But the kids are doing great. My son graduated from San Diego State a few years ago and now is running a lot of the daily operations of the business. My daughter, on the other hand, won't have anything to do with *Skipper of the Seas*. She can't see making cruise wear for people who go on *"those damn ships that pollute the ocean"*. She's majoring in marine biology out at Scripps." Skip reached over to get another beer out of the cooler. "What's up with your life? Still no wife or kids?"

"Too old for either of those," Brad replied. "Isn't that right, Pia?"

The men turned to see Pia, stretched out on the sofa, slumbering peacefully.

"Guess it's been pretty tiring for her," said Brad.

"Then now's a good time to fill me in on the details, brother."

16

When Pia next opened her eyes, long shadows covered the patio. She sat up, disturbing the multi-colored sarong that had been placed over her. For a brief moment she forgot that she was hiding out from some drug dealer's accountants. Maybe she should just doze off again and it would all go away.

"You're awake," Brad called out, walking out of the house and over to Pia. "Skip's just about to fire up the grill. We're having fresh fish. Hungry?"

"Sure," Pia answered, yawing. "How long have I been asleep? More importantly, is there any news from Bob?"

"You've been snoozing for several hours now," Brad said, taking a seat in a rattan chair next to the lounge. "I talked to Bob a while ago. Sorry, but it's not good news."

Pia reached for the bottle of water on the ground and took a few sips. "What could have happened now? Does someone know where I am?"

"No…which is the good news."

Pia leaned back and rubbed her eyes. "Maybe I don't even want to know anything else." She'd never been one to run away from adversity, but this might be a good time to start.

Brad saw the exhaustion on his friend's face and debated if he should give her a little longer to wake up before launching into the latest news. But that wasn't going to help anyone.

"Look Pia, I'll give it to you straight," he said. "The fuzz have issued a warrant and there's an APB out on you. Something having to do with that gun you found in the front yard."

"*What?* A warrant out for my arrest?" Brad nodded confirmation. "How can they do that? I didn't own that gun. Someone left it on my property." This further confirmed why Pia had avoided any association with cops for all these years.

"Seems there's pretty good evidence that it was the Beretta used to kill that karate instructor last year."

Pia thought for a moment and vaguely recalled the incident that had happened the year before. "What would that have to do with me? I certainly didn't kill him."

"No, but someone did. Probably Larry the Lawnmower. And then he lost the murder weapon at your pad. And then the cops found it."

Pia stood up, stretched, and paced around the patio. First her bosses were out to get her and now the police. This just didn't happen to law-abiding citizens in their fifties. And an APB meant that she probably wasn't safe anywhere in California. She couldn't decide which was worse; gangsters looking to take her out or the police searching for her.

She finally stopped walking and turned to Brad. "I guess maybe I do need to get to Mexico." She gazed around the tranquil back garden. "Too bad. I was starting to like it in Ocean Beach."

"Then come back when you get this all straightened out," said Skip, who had just walked outside. "Brad and I've been talking and figure you're safe enough here for a few days until I can set up something with my clothing distributor down in Puerto Vallarta and we can get you down there."

"You don't mind aiding and abetting a fugitive for a few days?" Pia asked.

"Nothing I haven't done before," he replied.   Pia decided not to ask for clarification.

Remembering her conversation with Sam at the hotel that morning, she said, "Do you think the border will be open by then?"

Before Skip could answer, Brad cut in. "The border's shut? They don't close the border." He looked to Skip. "Do they?"

"It was never shut completely," Skip answered, "but there were a few hassles there this morning, which is not that unusual. It should be OK by now." He turned to Pia. "But how did you know about it?"

"I almost crossed into Tijuana before deciding to meet Brad here in Ocean Beach. The only reason I didn't go was because the hotel manager warned against it."

"You would have gone alone?" asked Brad. "Into Mexico?"

"Oh course I would have, Brad. What's wrong with that? I'm completely capable of taking care of myself. Plus which I took enough Spanish in high school to get by. Anyway, living in Monterey County is sort of like being in Mexico. Navigating the real thing wouldn't be a problem."

"Pia," said Skip, "Tijuana is not Monterey."

"Agreed," Pia answered, standing up, "but I'm sure I could manage. Now, if you'll excuse me, I want to run some water on my face and then get down to planning." She walked back into the house.

"Seems your friend might need to mellow out a bit, Brad," Skip commented after Pia had left.

"Try telling her that." Brad leaned back in the chair. Since there really wasn't anything to do for now, a few tokes might just hit the spot.

"Hey Skip, my man, got any of that San Diego Stardust you used to grow?"

"Brother, has it been that long since you've been here? I haven't heard that name in years. Anyway, I've come up with a much better crop. OB Oblivion."

"Skip, my man, you should have gone into horticulture!"

"I prefer to grow my own and share it with friends. Cruise wear is a much safer line of work." Skip stood up. "Let me get the fish on the grill and then I'll fire us up a reefer or two."

~~~

Larry, not wanting to call attention to himself, had secured a room at the local youth hostel. He now wondered what had made him think it'd be a good idea. It wasn't even that cheap a deal. He had his own room, but had to share the john and shower with three other rooms. From the look of the other residents he'd seen in the lobby, he wasn't planning to sit on any toilet seats any time soon.

He'd bought a charger for his phone, a toothbrush, some t-shirts, boxers, and a few other things at the local drug store. He'd called Jack and was now waiting for a return call. If Jack wanted him to take out Pia in her surfer haven, he needed a gun and a safe plan of exit. And fuck if he'd dispose of a body like Jack had suggested. He checked his watch; it was nearly seven o'clock and still no word from Jack. He wanted to get out and get a better lay of the area before nightfall. He also wanted something to eat. Screw Jack. He wasn't going to waste any more time sitting in a cramped, musty room.

Larry checked out his image in the mirror. His jeans fit in with the local scene, and the new flip-flops, as fucking uncomfortable as they were, beat out his sweaty work boots. The navy blue t-shirt, screen-printed with *Han Ten in San Diego*, looked too new but the one he'd been wearing stunk to high heaven and was now at the bottom of the trash can. Larry pulled off the pristine shirt and went about tearing off the sleeves. Then he dusted the room with it, hoping a little dirt would give it a worn veneer. At least he still had the body to go with exposed arms. In jeans, no one could tell he had laborer-white legs, and it was getting too dark to notice his ghost-white feet. His face was pretty sun-burnt, but a hat at this time of the evening wouldn't do any good. It amazed him how just a few hours in the sun down here could do such damage; something that he didn't have to worry about back home.

Stopping for a whiz before leaving the hostel, Larry bumped into two smoking hot babes walking out of the room next door. The brunette was nearly as tall as he was with an outstanding set of ta-ta's. Her slightly shorter friend had blonde hair so light it nearly looked white. Larry wondered if it was natural. Neither was wearing a whole lot of clothing.

"How're you ladies doing?" he asked, stretching an arm over his head, then leaning it against the wall to better show off his buffed biceps.

"You just arrived?" asked the tall brunette, her bra-less titties in danger of popping out of that skimpy sundress. "You don't look like the other guys here." Larry picked up on a slight accent.

"Is that good or bad?" he asked, starting to see the advantages of being in a place where no one knew you, and of not having the old lady along. Larry had never worn a wedding ring; too dangerous for someone who worked with machinery, as he'd told his wife. Gazing into the eyes of the leggy gal in front of him, he wondered if she'd even care if he was married.

The brunette reached up to run a hand over Larry's bicep. "That's a very good thing. The guys we've met here are too young and too skinny." She turned to her friend, also bra-less in a tiny tank-top and miniature shorts. "Isn't that right, Karen."

"Yah, it is. We like strong men." Yeah. Definitely an accent.

Larry was in serious jeopardy of getting a full-blown woody. He crossed his legs and squeezed. *Fuck.* He hadn't been this turned on in years.

"The name's Larry," he said, taking his time to give the gals a thorough up-and-down. "What do you lovely ladies go by?"

"I'm Karla, and this is Karen."

"Karla and Karen. The two K's. I like it. Where're you girls from?"

"We're from Sweden," Karla answered.

Larry had hit the lottery! Not one, but two young babes from Sweden, and they seemed interested. Fortunately for Larry, who may not have had much recent experience in the flirting game, he'd always been a quick thinker.

"I was just going out to get a bite to eat. Could I interest you ladies in a little dinner? My treat?" He offered his arms to the girls and they immediately latched on.

"That would be wonderful," said Karen.

"What kinda food you gals up for?"

"Mexican," said Karla.

"We love the margaritas," added Karen.

"Then Mexican it is," said Larry, already anticipating the effects of tequila on these desirable young Swedes. "Let's go find us a restaurant." He led the girls to the stairs and then down to the lobby, through a few other tourists with backpacks checking in, and out onto the street.

Next, Larry, who had grown up in a tourist town and knew about finding a good eatery, walked the girls to the corner gas station and into the mechanics bay.

"Hey there, friend," he said to the mechanic, "can you steer us to a good Mexican restaurant?"

"You're best bet is Marco's," answered the man. "It's a little rough looking but the best food this side of the border."

"And the margaritas are good?" asked Karen.

"The best."

"Gracias, amigo," Larry said. He turned to the girls. "That's Spanish for *thank you, my friend*."

"Ohhh," cooed Karla, "he even speaks the language!"

"You gals stick with me, and you'll be all right." The three locked arms and sauntered off to Marco's restaurant.

~~~

Jack sat in his office up in Monterey, staring at the phone on the desk and his cell next to it. What a crazy day it'd been. He mentally checked off the positives, like getting the dirt on the cops' involvement with Pia, thanks to Constance's son Ray-the-security-man. And then the minor miracle that Larry had been able to track the surfer to Pia, and on to where she was holed up. Now if only his buddy Alan down in La Jolla would get back to him. Maybe he shouldn't have relied on him, but how was Larry supposed to take out the broad with no weapon? Maybe he'd just send the hitman to the sporting goods store to pick up a new gun, even if it was a risky venture.

"Hey Alan," Jack had said when he'd called that morning, "it's Jack Houston. How ya doing?"

"Jack? Where the hell are you calling from?"

"Up in Monterey, same as always. I thought maybe you kicked off, seeing how I haven't heard from you in what....three years?"

"That's about right. You know Jack, you also could've called me."

"True Alan, but you know how it is."

"So why the call? Maybe you need something?"

"Sharp as ever, Alan. Yeah, I need a favor."

"Is it one of *those* kind of favors? 'Cause I got to tell you Jack, I'm retired now."

"What? Retired? What do you do? Play golf all day?"

"You should try it. It suites me. Don't have to keep looking over my shoulder any more. What we do Jack, it's a young man's game."

"Maybe you're getting old Alan, but I still got a lot left in me. So can you help a friend out?"

"Depends on what you need."

"I got an associate down your way right now who needs a little extra power, if you know what I mean."

"Flew down from up there, did he? Jack, I tell you, it's not like the old days where you could bring anything onboard an aircraft, though I preferred to ship through with my luggage."

"Sure was an easier time, pal. So you think you can give me a hand?"

"Let me get back to you. Might take me a while to get something untraceable, but I should be able to help out an old friend."

And now it was nearly eight in the evening and still no word from Alan. Jack played with the contact list on his cell phone. It was generally bad etiquette to call a second time, but maybe Alan was suffering from a bit of short term memory loss. Maybe he'd forgotten about the earlier call. He'd certainly forgotten about calling Jack in the past few years. Screw it. He was calling.

"Alan," Jack said when his friend picked up, "it's Jack."

"We must still have the old connection. I was just about to dial your number." Jack could hear voices in the background, then the sound of a door closing.

"Got you at a bad time?" Jack asked.

"Actually, you got me at a perfect time. I needed an excuse to get out of the living room. The missus has her girlfriends over for a game of mahjong, and they're trying to rope me into playing."

Jack didn't give a hoot about what was going on in Alan's house, he just needed that gun. "So were you able to come up with something?" he asked.

"It took a while, but I got what you need. Most of my boys are retired from the game so I had to go through other channels."

Jack did not like the sound of that. "You contacted someone you don't know?" he asked. He might be right about Alan's mental state.

"Don't get your panties in a twist, Jack. It's a reliable source. Now do you want the merchandise or not?"

"Yeah, yeah…sorry Alan. It's been a rough day. Where can my man pick it up?"

"My contact wants as few people involved as possible. The only way he'll do this is by texting the pick-up spot to your man. You got his number?"

This wasn't getting any better. Jack did not like handing control over to a third party. "You sure that's the only way he'll do this?"

"It is. You still interested?"

Jack thought about it for another moment. What choice did he have? He'd give Larry's number to Alan, then call Larry with specific instructions to keep him posted about every single move. He gave Alan the information, hung up, and immediately called Larry.

Larry didn't answer and Jack hung up. He thought about sending a text message but had never been able to figure out how your thumbs were supposed to tap out a message on those tiny little letters. He dialed again.

"Larry," he said after the message tone, "a friend will be sending you a text about where to pick up the gear. Before you do anything, you have to call me and give me the details. Don't fuck this up."

17

Pia, Brad, and Skip, after finishing their meal of grilled fish and fresh salad, remained in the back patio enjoying the warm evening.

"If you really think the best thing is to fly down to Puerto Vallarta out of Tijuana, then I guess that's what I'll do," Pia said, picking up her bottle of Dos Equis. She had to agree that she'd never get out of the US using a fake passport at an airport. "I guess I'll just have to try walking across the border tomorrow and hope they aren't as diligent about checking passports."

"Sure you don't want a hit?" Brad asked, offering her the joint of Skip's homegrown. Pia shook her head.

"I'm still worried," she continued, "about getting across the border and then on to a plane, even if I do that on the Mexican side. I don't think I want to trust that Carl Jones ID. And by the way Brad, who is the guy?"

"Didn't ask Bob. It's better that way." He took another deep drag of the reefer. "Anyway, what choice do you have?"

"Hold up," said Skip, before Pia could come up with a response. "I've got this part all under control."

"Oh, thank goodness. You've found me a better ID?" She asked hopefully.

"Nope. We're going with Carl," Skip said.

"And just how is that going to work?" Pia wondered if both the guys were now so stoned they didn't know right from left.

"I've got it all planned out. I've booked you on a package tour with a travel agent I know. You get on the bus here with the group, cross the border and pick up a flight in TJ bound for Puerto Vallarta. Once there, the rest of your group will board a cruise ship, but you'll stay in town."

"Skip, I really appreciate all that you're doing for me, but that still doesn't explain how the passport I'm holding will get me across the border. It says my name is Carl. It says I'm a guy. Won't they check?"

"It's different when you're on a tour that makes regular trips across the border. All they do is collect the information from the group leader," Skip explained.

"You still can't be sure custom agents on either side won't come aboard the bus or worse, grab me trying to board a plane. Someone's bound to notice that I am not Mr. Jones," Pia reasoned.

"Not gonna happen," said Skip pausing to exhale some smoke. "You'll be on a bus full of transgender gals and their dates."

Pia furrowed her eyebrows. "And how's that going to help me?"

"You'll be dressed transgender, of course," Skip replied.

This did not clarify much for Pia, but she was too relaxed to care about much other than drinking her beer and enjoying the ambiance of Skip's abode. She yawned, stretched her arms over her head, and stood up. "Skip, can I offer to do the dishes tomorrow?" she asked. "I think I'd keel over at the sink if I tried to do them now."

"Don't worry about that," said Skip. "I have the cleaning crew coming in the morning and they'll take care of it."

"Dude, you have housekeepers?" said Brad, glancing around his surroundings. "No wonder this place is spotless. Maybe I should get into the clothing business."

"You know Brad, I've been thinking of opening a shop in Carmel. I could use someone I trust up there."

"Brad selling resort wear?" Pia smiled at the thought. "Then again, he always has been a charmer. It just might work."

"Retail?" Brad said. "Closest I ever did to that was working in a coffee shop right after high school." He mulled it over in his mind. "Skip, would I have to wear a polyester leisure suit?"

"Brother, you could dress like me. Casual, but classy. Although you'd need to do something with your hair."

Before the men could get further into their discussion of how an employee of Skip's should dress, Pia excused herself.

"Talk to you guys tomorrow."

~~~

Larry emptied the last drops from the pitcher of margaritas into Karen and Karla's glasses. He'd thought of ordering another, but he wanted to make sure the gals didn't do something stupid like puke or pass out and ruin his chance for a night of Swedish lovemaking. He had to admit that these ladies certainly appeared to be able to hold their liquor, unlike his tiny wife who generally passed out after two glasses of wine. Now the problem was where to take them. In a new town, Larry had no idea and going back to the hostel wasn't quite the atmosphere he needed. He might as well check the messages he'd felt buzzing in his pants pocket.

The voicemail from Jack told him to be on alert for a text message about the merchandise, and to keep him informed. Larry then checked his text messages. One from the wife saying she'd won one hundred dollars on the slots. The second came from a blocked number: *Meet me. 10 tonight. The Wild Side. I'll be wearing a red rose in my lapel. Code phrase: "nice place they got here."* Shit! Just when he was getting into one of the best nights of his life, he had to go to work. And how was he supposed to know where this Wild Side was?

Just then their waiter appeared with the check. "Hey buddy," Larry said, "you know of a place called The Wild Side?"

The waiter stopped, looked at Larry and the ladies, hesitated a moment, and then bent over to whisper in his ear. "Yeah...it's a third-rate titty bar over past the Sports Arena."

"Ladies who get naked?" asked Karen, who apparently had very good hearing. "See Karla, we were right! Larry is very special."

Larry and the waiter exchanged grins, but stopped short of a fist-bump.

"You gals interested in going?" Larry asked with a sly grin. This was just getting better and better.

"Oh yes!" they answered in unison.

Larry glanced up at the waiter's name tag. "Maybe Shawn here can tell us how to get there."

"It's not far at all. Want me to call you a cab?"

Larry pulled out his wallet, took out a hundred dollar bill and handed it to Shawn. "I like a man who knows how to work," he said, "keep the change."

"I'll get right to it," Shawn responded, heading off to order the cab.

While the ladies excused themselves to go freshen up, Larry pulled out his phone and debated calling Jack. Why should he? He had the instructions and he knew where Pia was camped out. The last thing he needed was for Jack to find out he was taking a couple of hot babes along to the pick-up. He'd call him when the transaction was completed.

He was standing by the front door of the restaurant when the ladies came back, big smiles on their faces. Now with a Swedish beauty on each arm, Larry strolled out of the restaurant feeling like the king of the world.

Fifteen minutes later, the threesome stepped out of the cab in the parking lot of The Wild Side. Cars, trucks, and motorcycles filled a good amount of the spaces. The club itself, in a low building set quite a ways back from the street, had that look of a place that was either on its way up or down. Noticing the neon sign surrounded by white bulbs, many of which had burned out, Larry figured it had seen better days.

A burly doorman sat on a stool just inside the doorway, his body and a curtain blocking the view into the club, but doing nothing to soften the pulsating music. Typical bouncer: husky, shaved head, large waxed handle-bar mustache, and lots of tattoos. He looked at the three, asked to see ID's, stamped their hands, then pulled back the raggedy black velvet fabric to let them inside.

Larry hadn't been to a stripper joint since his bachelor party, which was all a haze thanks to multiple shots of Jack Daniel's. Staring in at the sight he suddenly felt like he'd been missing out on a whole lot. Why the hell hadn't he ever been back?

A small stage encircled by a bar filled the center of the club. Tiered semi-circle booths ran along both walls. Red and purple lighting gave the place an otherworldly glow. A few black lights and a disco ball hanging over the stage added to the exotic ambiance. It was hard to make out details of the patrons, although it was clear that a group of about five sailors sat on the stools surrounding the stage, directly across from a couple of bikers. So mesmerized was Larry, that he'd momentarily forgotten about his dates. Karen squeezed his arm.

"This is just like in the movies!" she said with excitement. "Let's get a table."

They walked over to an empty booth, up two steps, and scooted around until they faced the stage. A young woman dressed in a baby-doll nighty sauntered up to their table.

"What can I get you folks?" she asked.

"You girls want to get more margaritas?" Larry asked.

"We want one of those tropical drinks," Karla said. "The ones with rum."

Larry, being a beer and straight shot man, was lost on that one.

"What do you suggest?" he asked their waitress.

"My bartender makes a killer Mai Tai."

"Yes! That's what we want!"

"Three Mai Tais?" asked the waitress.

"Two for the ladies and bring me a Coors." If he hadn't been there to pick up a gun, Larry would have gone for a double shot of Jack on the rocks, but right now he needed his wits about him.

After their drinks had been served and the girls had taken a few sips, Larry excused himself to go to the men's room. Once out of the booth, he began to case the club and look for his contact, even though he was still early for the meet time. On deals like this, it was always good to know the location of the fire exit.

The Wild Side extended much farther back than Larry had initially thought. The back side of the stage connected to the service bar, where a guy worked at lightning speed pouring drinks and ringing up sales. Three waitresses stood in line to give orders, while another stowed her tray and money behind the bar and headed onto the stage. Two pool tables filled in the space past the serving area. Along the left wall were two more booths in all but darkness. Larry noted the emergency exit sign at the very back corner next to a door marked *Office – Employees Only.* Across from the exit were the restrooms. Larry circled the rest of the way around the club and arrived back at his booth, pleased to see the girls looking mighty happy.

"You have to taste this!" Karla said, offering her umbrella topped cocktail to Larry. "It is simply delicious!"

"Thanks, but I'll stick to my beer for now."

On his stroll around the bar Larry had seen an array of men: military, bikers, blue collar workers, and businessmen, but no one with a rose in their lapel. He checked his watch. It was just after ten.

From the vantage point of the booth, he had a clear shot of the entrance and kept it in the corner of his eye. Fortunately, with the music so loud, he didn't have to worry about keeping up a conversation with the girls. Anyway, both of them seemed too taken with the gyrations on the stage to worry about talking.

Larry watched a few customers enter the club, lit up by the door light when the curtain was pulled back. Then an immaculately dressed, slightly built Hispanic man, in a three-piece suit walked in. It was only a brief glimpse, but Larry was sure this was his man, even without certainty that it was a rose in his lapel. There's a lot to appreciate when one professional observes another. The man moved through the club with an air of strength, yet no one turned to look twice at him. Larry's eyes followed him as he walked the entire premises before taking a seat in the shadows of a booth on the opposite side. Once the man had been served a drink, Larry decided it was time to make his move.

"Ladies, please excuse me for a minute while I stretch my legs," he told his companions. "I'm not used to sitting in one place for long, and after the time in the restaurant, my muscles are getting a little tight."

Suddenly, Larry felt a warm hand grad a hold of his cock. He flinched slightly and looked over at Karen.

"Your muscles hurt?" asked Karen. She looked over at Karla. "I think Larry is maybe getting a little....what do you say? Horney?" Karen giggled.

Karla leaned over, ran her hand through his hair, and then stuck her tongue in his ear. "Maybe it's just me and Karen who feel the heat, yah?"

Holy Moses! Larry felt the blood rush to his privates and used all his strength to keep from grinding into Karen's grip. He had to get the weapon first, then he could get back to the girls. Carefully, he reached down and removed Karen's hand, placing it in own, and bringing up to the table. Then he tired to focus on the job at hand. It didn't do any good, he was getting harder by the second. Next, he thought of his wife and what she would do if she knew what he was up to. Worked like a charm. He felt the momentary excitement drain out of his body.

"You girls sure now how to get a man turned on. But let me move around for a few minutes and then we'll get back to this."

"We'll be waiting," said Karen. "Don't be too long or I might have to let Karla take care of me." Larry just kept visualizing his wife.

Walking first towards the back of the club, Larry went into the men's to splash water on his face. He checked himself in the mirror, practiced his tough-guy look, and went out to meet the arms dealer.

A quick glance over at the girls proved they hadn't been following his moves. Their eyes were glued to the dancer on the stage who, at the moment, was lying on her back, hips in the air, pumping away at an invisible body.

Larry stopped at the side of the booth and slowly turned his head to make sure the man wore a rose in his lapel. Their eyes met and Larry nodded once.

"Nice place they got here," he said, repeating the code words and stepping up to the booth.

"Not bad," replied the man.

"Mind if I have a seat?" Momentarily, Larry worried that maybe this wasn't the right person and he might be mistaken for a fag making a move. Remembering the man's small build, Larry figured the guy wouldn't try to punch him out, should that be the case.

"So where's it at?" Larry asked, dispensing with any small talk.

"I got it out in my car," the man answered, keeping his eyes on the stage. "I'll walk out, you wait a minute, then

follow. I'm parked way over on the left. Black '69 VW bus."
Then he got up and left.

A gun dealer in a hippie van? This was worse than
Monterey. Hell, what did Larry care? He counted out the
minute, took another glance over at the girls—still enthralled
by the stage action, and headed for the door.

Once in the parking lot, he had no trouble spotting the
decrepit VW bus. It didn't fit with the fine threads the man
had been wearing, but it certainly was good camouflage. He
walked over.

Opening the side door to the van, the man shown a
flashlight over the floorboards, then pulled back an old beach
towel. Christ! What the fuck was Larry supposed to do with
an AK-47? Couldn't exactly put it down the back of his
pants.

"Amigo," Larry said, "think you got your orders
mixed. I need a hand gun."

"No one said anything about that to me. The call was
for a weapon. I assumed you'd want top-of-the-line."

"I need something I can carry concealed. How am I
gonna do that with this? You must have something else."

The man covered the weapon, shut the door, and then
opened the front passenger side. He reached into the glove
compartment and pulled out a small, pink, zippered bag.

"You can take this, if you want," he said handing it to
Larry.

Unzipping the bag, Larry stared at a tiny little
Derringer revolver; like the ones ladies carried in the old
west.

"And what's this? A toy?"

"Used to be my grannies, but she died a few months ago and I wasn't sure what to do with her gun. Couldn't very well leave it around for the grandkids to discover."

"No, you couldn't. Guns and kids don't belong in the same house. But I can't see how this will do me any good. What kind of range does it have?"

"About two feet, if you're looking for serious injury."

"You got nothing else, amigo?"

"That's it. And it's clean so no trace problem. Look, I've got to go, so make up your mind."

What was he supposed to do? He knew taking out the broad with this tiny weapon would be almost impossible. But if he called Jack and told him the situation, he wouldn't understand. Hell, he'd take the miniature gun and figure out what to do later. Right now, he had two ready-to-rumble hot chicks inside a topless bar.

"OK. I'll take it." Larry stuck out his hand. "Muchas gracias, amigo."

They shook hands and went their separate ways.

Larry re-entered the club, glancing quickly to see how his ladies were doing. Shit! Where were they? That's when he noticed the increased whooping all around. His eyes shot to the stage. Karen and Karla were up there in nothing but their tiny thong panties, driving the crowd wild.

He walked up to the edge of the stage and took a seat, right as Karla squatted down, legs apart, mere inches from his face.

"Larry, where did you go?" she shouted over the noise. "We got bored and the nice manager said we could dance." The guy next to Larry reached over and stuck a twenty in the waistband of her knickers. Larry grinned. Yeah, the private show was going to be his alone.

18

The smell of freshly brewed coffee greeted Pia when she stepped out of the shower the next morning. The day was off to a good start. There was nothing like a good night's sleep and a cup of strong coffee to vanquish the prior day's troubles.

"Morning," said Skip, pouring her a cup of the steamy brew. "You sleep OK?"

"Best night's sleep I've had in days." She took a sip from her cup. "Skip, I don't think I ever thanked you properly yesterday. I'm not sure I'd do the same for a total stranger who also happens to have a warrant out for her arrest."

"Sister, you're not a stranger, you're Brad's friend. And the man's helped me out more than a few times over the years. No problem at all. "

"By the way, where is the guy?" Pia asked, looking around. "Still asleep?"

"Brad? In bed when there are waves like we have this morning? No, he took off an hour or so ago."

"Wasn't he saying that the surf wasn't cold enough for him here?"

"Just his crazy talk. He loves the weather in San Diego but his ties to Monterey are just too strong to make a permanent move."

Pia looked out at the morning sun through the open kitchen window. A warm breeze blew over her body. "I don't know…I might just be able to give up life in the north for this kind of weather." She turned back to Skip. "Who knows? It could be that I'll have to go underground for the rest of my life and will never be able to return home."

"I'm sure it will all work out. Once Brad gets back, we'll all go over to my friend's office. She's the one running the tour that will get you to Puerto Vallarta."

~~~

A few hours later the three piled into Skip's aging surfer van and made their way over to Pacific Beach, the next community just north of OB. Immediately, Pia became aware of the different vibe from the tie-died atmosphere of Ocean Beach. For one thing, it was a much larger and more commercially built-up, with wider main streets and much more traffic. Although it lacked the quaintness of OB, it retained a beach town atmosphere.

Skip parked his van in front of Tranquility Vacations. A rainbow flag hung over the doorway of the small store, and hand lettered promotions covered one window. Skip opened the front door, setting off soft wind chimes, and the three walked in.

"Skip, darling," said a woman, getting up from behind her desk, and walking over to hug him. "These must be your friends."

"Brad and Pia, this is Anastasia, proprietress of the company that's going to get the young lady to Puerto Vallarta."

Anastasia had quite a regal air. She stood a good six feet tall in her flat, gold, sandals. The healthy tan was not overdone, and it set off the blond hair arranged in a loose, carefully styled coif. Her flowing sundress of purple-orchid-printed fabric accentuated her thin, but fit frame. Pia was fairly sure she'd had some work done, but it was understated.

"Anastasia and I went to high school together," Skip explained. "She's made a name for herself in two fields—travel and fashion makeovers."

Anastasia pulled Pia away from the others and spun her around. "This is *Carl*?" she asked, squinting her eyes. "We'll have to do some work to make sure she passes."

"So the plan is to make me look like a guy?" Pia asked, not having given anymore thought to what Skip had told her the night before. It certainly would be a new experience.

"Oh darling, of course not!" laughed Anastasia. "I'm going to make you look like a drag queen. My hair stylist Arturo is setting up in the back."

"You're going to do what?" asked Pia. This was a possibility she hadn't considered. "And you're going to do this right now? I thought the bus didn't leave until tomorrow."

"One always needs a dress rehearsal, my dear," she said, playing with Pia's hair, leaning back and moving her head side to side. "Basically all we need to do is a lot of makeup and big hair. Of course we'll have to ditch the clothing and go for a more convincing look."

"She looks enough like a girl to me," Brad said.

"That's the problem," said Anastasia. "We want a more flamboyant appearance."

Pia wondered how on earth flamboyance could make her incognito. Brad just looked confused. Skip smiled.

"Not to worry," said Anastasia, noting Brad and Pia's look of puzzlement, "I've got it all under control."

"So what do you need us to do?" asked Skip. "Help you pick out some new duds?"

"Oh Skip, you're very funny," said Anastasia. "I'll give it to you that you know how to dress for that moneyed-casual look, but theater is not in your repertoire." Anastasia turned and called out to the back room, "Arturo, can you come out?"

Wearing black skinny jeans and a body-hugging white t-shirt, Arturo appeared from the back. Shorter than Pia by several inches, his brown, flawless skin, nearly glowed beneath jet black hair loaded with a lot of product. One heavy gold chain hung around his neck.

"This is Arturo, my genius of a hair stylist-slash-makeup artist," said Anastasia.

"What is it you want me do to?" he asked his boss, already running fingers through Pia's hair, picking up clumps and randomly arranging them.

"Big hair, Arturo. One of your nightclub specials."

"It's a little on the short side to do really big hair. Maybe add some extensions? What about a new color?"

Pia was up for going incognito, but the idea of hair extensions and new color seemed a little unnecessary. However, she did not want to appear ungrateful. Fortunately, Anastasia spoke up.

"Just the up-do, Arturo. I'm sure it will be sufficient without any extras." She turned back to Skip. "You two boys can take off for now. Give us a couple of hours. That should be enough."

"Cool," said Brad. "That means me and Skip can head on over to our buddy's surf shop. Been a long time since I've seen the guys."

"You'll be fine here, Pia," Skip said. "While we're out I'll also check with my sources to see if your name's come up on any police alerts."

"Skip, my man, you have police sources?" asked Brad.

"Brother, I have all sorts of sources. Now let's get out of here and let these folks do their thing."

"Can't wait to see what Pia looks like in drag," Brad said.

"Maybe Anastasia can do you next, Brad," Pia laughed. "Your hair's certainly long enough."

Arturo stepped over and took a hold of a lock of Brad's hair. "Now this, I could work with."

"Time to go, Brother," Skip said, steering Brad towards the door. "Catch you in a few."

Once the men were out the door, Anastasia turned to Pia. "Are you ready?"

"I'm not exactly sure what I'm getting into, but ready I am."

"Great. Just follow me and I'll show you were all the magic takes place," Anastasia said, leading Pia to the back of the store where Arturo had already gone.

The room off the back was twice as big as the front section. And this was no travel agency back store room. It looked more like the dressing room of a theater, complete with a hair salon station and a three sided, department store mirror. Racks of clothing, neatly arranged, ran along the side walls. Tidy, stacked bins, labeled with various items of clothing and accessories, filled in any empty spaces.

"I think I'll let Arturo do your hair and make-up while I search for just the right outfit." Anastasia ushered Pia to the salon chair, then walked over to the racks of clothing.

The stylist immediately began to brush out Pia's hair, grabbing sections and pinning them up.

"Are you sure you don't want to go blond?" he asked.

"Not today, thank you. Maybe when I get back from Mexico. If I ever do get back, that is."

"Why shouldn't you?" Arturo asked, all the while shoving clips here and there.

"I'm guessing you don't know the whole story," Pia said. She hoped she wouldn't sound rude by not explaining her situation to Arturo. "It's probably better if I don't give you the details."

"All I know, and all I need to know, is that you have to get across the border undetected." Arturo stopped and looked at Pia in the mirror. "You don't look like a terrorist or drug lord, so I'd say this will only be a short excursion."

"And how would you know I'm not either of those?"

"Baby," said Arturo, "I know how to spot them. I used to do it for a living."

Pia stared at Arturo's reflection in the mirror. That's when she noticed the medallion hanging from the gold chain around his neck. She pointed to it. "That looks like some sort of military insignia."

"Marines."

"You were in the Marines?" she asked.

"Sure was. Four good years. It's how I got my citizenship."

"Really? Where are you from?"

"I was born in Guatemala but came here twenty-five years ago when I was eighteen. A cousin sponsored me and I decided I wanted to become a citizen. The fastest way was to join the military."

"Funny, you don't look like a Marine."

Arturo grabbed Pia's hand and placed it on his thigh. "Feel that baby? Solid muscle. I may be little but I'm tough." Pia couldn't think of how to respond to the statement. He let go of her hand and continued toying with her hair.

"All right. I think I know what I'll do. You're going to look gorgeous!"

~~~

Back at the hostel in OB, Larry lay in bed not wanting to open his eyes. This had to have been the best night in his entire life, and he wanted to keep re-visualizing all that had taken place. After he'd picked up the gun and gone back into the club, the night had really gotten going. The girls had stayed on stage for two more numbers before putting their clothes back on and joining Larry in the booth for an after-dance liqueur. This time, he couldn't help but to slip a hand up Karen's leg, surprised to find nothing between his fingers and her warm pussy. Once he'd gotten her off, with Karla on the other side whispering sweet nothings to him in Swedish, the three had decided it was time to head back to the hostel. They'd been at it the rest of the night and Larry had nearly forgotten why he was in San Diego in the first place.

Before he got any more aroused, Larry disentangled himself from the sleeping beauties and reached for his phone on the nightstand. Crap. It was already almost noon. He quickly checked his messages; two angry voicemails from Jack wanting to know why he hadn't checked in, and a text from his wife saying she'd decided to stay a few more days in Vegas. One more quick glance at the girls, and he headed into the shower. He needed a cold one and then a lot of hot coffee before calling Jack.

Thirty minutes later, cleaned up and caffeinated, Larry placed the call to Jack from out in the hostel's back patio.

"Where the fuck have you been?" Jack yelled into the phone.

"Sorry Jack, I couldn't call you last night. I was in a public place and then it got too late."

"Too late? What kind of bullshit excuse is that? Don't answer. Just tell me if you got it done."

"I got the package and I'm just on my way to take care of things."

"I'm gonna tell you one more time Larry—don't fuck this up!"

"Gotta go, Jack, I'll call you when I've taken care of business."

After he'd hung up, Larry wondered just exactly how he was going to do what he'd promised. He'd have to wait until the evening and try to get into the house up on the cliffs. Maybe he'd get lucky and no one would see him. But in his experience, places like the one where Pia was staying always had security cameras and alarms. Screw it. He had a whole long afternoon before he'd have to go to work. The girls had mentioned going to the zoo and he thought that might be fun.

~~~

"And how about that tournament out in Hawaii during the big storm?" Skip asked. "We sure showed those candy-asses what California surfers are made of!"

Brad and Skip and Topper and Beamer sat around on the couch and bean bag chairs at the back of Boogie Down Surf Shop in Pacific Beach, reminiscing about their time on the pro surfing circuit thirty years earlier.

"Dude," Brad exclaimed, hoisting his beer, "those were some really gnarly waves! But we smoked 'um!"

"Ah, come on Brad, we remember you wiped out on the third ride," said Beamer.

"But up until then, no one could touch me." He took another swig. "Then after I ate sand, I had all the ladies *wanting* to touch me. Worked out just fine." The crew clinked bottles.

"Must admit, Brad," said Topper, "you may not have had the goods to make the big time, but you always had all the babes lining up for some of that West Coast dick."

Brad briefly lost himself in memories of the non-stop selection of hot bods he'd had the pleasure to service over the years. "Those were the days, boys."

"Don't tell us they're over," said Skip. "You're the only one of us that managed to stay single for all these years. Me and the guys have all been married and divorced at least once and have a whole slew of offspring."

"Yeah," piped in Beamer, "the ex-old lady's been with some rich banker up in La Jolla for years but won't get married so she can get the alimony and profits from the store. She don't even need the cash. Just likes to stick it to me."

"That's the problem we all had with hooking up with hard-bodied surfer groupies," Skip said. "We were the catch of the day until we retired. When the glamour's gone, the babes are gone. Although I don't think there's quite the selection these days, what with all the pro women surfers. Now that they can make money on the waves, they don't need us. Brothers, it's a whole different ball game out there now."

"No shit, it is," said Beamer. "Hey Skip, remember when you were just getting started in your business and had to get those bikinis down to that surf shop in Mazatlan? How was it you snuck them in?"

"Loaded them in the door panels of the truck." Skip said. He shook his head. "We won't see days like that again."

A silence descended over the group, each man remembering some of the highlights of their youth. Only Brad didn't seem bummed out by all the nostalgia.

"Dudes, what's with the down faces? Look at us! We're still in great shape, we still surf, and I, for one, still get laid on a regular basis. Or at least I did until the last girlfriend kicked me out...living at my mom's is kinda cramping my style, but that won't last forever."

"You got a point, Brad," said Topper. "My last girlfriend was twenty-two years old. Didn't last more than a month, but I was sort of tired of her by then anyway."

"See?" said Brad. "We've got it good now! Hey, why don't we go out and see if we still got the goods as a group? We could head on down to the beach."

"Waves suck right now," said Beamer.

"Who said anything about surfing?" said Brad. "Let's say we hit a beach café and start the surf talk. That always brings the ladies by."

"Brother," said Skip, "you always did have the best ideas. Beamer, can you lock up the shop?"

Beamer was already headed for the counter to get the keys. "Hell yes I can! Let's go get us some babes!"

19

"Bernie, I got to tell you, this is totally screwed." Jack sat behind his desk, puffing on his rancid cigar. His partner tried to keep from coughing. "I don't like relying on those numbskulls down in San Diego when we got real problems right here in Monterey."

"Didn't you tell me that Larry had things under control? That your friend down there had delivered?" Bernie asked.

"That's what I thought. But Larry was acting a little cagey." Jack re-lit the cigar that had gone cold. "And it's not like I can meet with him to straighten his ass out."

"We're just going to have to wait it out, Jack. I mean what else can we do?" Bernie batted away the noxious fumes. "Who knows? Maybe Pia will give up and hand over the documents she stole."

Jack exhaled another large plume of smoke and stared out the window. Suddenly, his face lit up, he whipped around in his swivel chair, and stubbed the cigar out in his coffee cup.

"Bernie!" he exclaimed. "That's it! Why should we wait on Pia? I bet she's got all the information stashed at her house. We need to get over there and find it." Bernie knew where this conversation was going and he didn't like it. "How about you run over there and see what you can find?"

"Now you want me to break into her house? I don't know, Jack, that seems kind of risky. What if she has an alarm system?"

"Quit being a pussy, Bernie. Larry said there wasn't one." This wasn't exactly true, but since Larry hadn't mentioned one, it was the logical conclusion. "Broads like that always have a key stashed under a planter box."

"Broads like that?" asked Bernie.

"You know what I mean."

Bernie didn't, but it was best not to question Jack when he was on to a hot new idea. He didn't like the idea of breaking in, but he liked the idea of landing in a federal pen even less.

"OK Jack, I'll give it a try."

On the drive over to Pia's, Bernie mentally ran over what his cover would be should any neighbors happen by. He could be a relative checking up on her house when she was out of town. Or he could just tell the truth and say he was her boss and add the little lie that he said he had been asked to check on the mail. At least that way he wouldn't have to try and sneak in through the front gate. The bold approach seemed his best bet.

Upon arriving at her house, he first checked her mailbox, which was empty. What if someone were staying at the house? Well, he'd just go knock on the door and find out.

When no one answered, Bernie did a quick look around the property and across the street to see if anyone was about. Assuring himself that he hadn't been observed, he went about checking all the obvious places where someone would hide a key. There was nothing. Then he looked at the front door lock. Nothing he couldn't handle.

From his inside, sports coat pocket, he pulled out the locksmith's tools he hadn't used illegally in ages. Souvenirs from a misspent youth, Bernie had never lost his natural ability to pick a lock and kept his skills honed whenever he went to visit a relative. They always got a kick out of timing just how long it would take him to break in. He was inside Pia's house in under thirty seconds.

He was glad she lived in such a tiny place. It would take no time to search it. He already knew that Pia was as orderly as he was and hoped that would help him to zero in on where she might keep her records.

The filing cabinet contained neatly arranged files all clearly labeled and color coded, not that he was expecting to find one marked *purloined files*. It made it a quick task to thumb through the individual folders. Nothing.

He then went through the desk drawers and closets before examining more unusual spots like under the mattress and in the freezer. If Pia had hidden the files, they certainly weren't in the house, or at least not in any place that was easy to find. He might as well go back to the office and see if Jack had heard from Larry.

As Bernie left, he pushed in the bottom lock, but didn't worry about the dead bolt. Let her think she had forgotten to lock it.

Walking out the front gate, he caught the reflection of something from the front room of the house across the street. Damn it! Who'd been watching? He made a quick decision to go over to the neighbors and calm down any possible misunderstandings. The last thing he needed was someone calling the cops on him.

Mrs. Arlington watched the man leave Pia's, cross the street, and walk up the short path to her front door. Oh dear. What was she going to do? He didn't look dangerous, but she had seen him go into Pia's house and she knew her neighbor hadn't been home for a few days. When he rang her doorbell she grabbed the nearest weapon she could find, which happened to be her bowling trophy that rested on the mantle next to the paint can containing Mr. A. Not that she had been bowling in many years, but Mrs. A could still wield a mean throw.

"Hello," said Bernie when she answered the door, noting the large, solid trophy held in her right hand and the binoculars hung around her neck. "I was wondering if you could be of some help. Your neighbor Pia works for me and she hasn't shown up for a few days. I was just checking to see if she's all right."

Mrs. A looked at the well attired gentleman that stood in front of her. He certainly looked harmless and had a real bit of class about him. Still, you could never be too careful.

"You seemed to be waiting at her door for quite some time," said Mrs. A, thinking it better not to mention that she knew he had been inside the house.

"Pia left a key to her house at the office in case something like this ever happened," Bernie explained, surprised at how quickly he was able to formulate lies. "I was checking to see if maybe she left a note. We've been worried about her lately. I'm concerned that she might have done something to herself."

"Done something? I don't think so. I can't say I even really know her, but she never struck me as someone who might be suicidal."

"And aren't they the type that always slip through our fingers?" Bernie gave his best impression of deep concern. "You wouldn't have happened to have seen her or noticed anything out of the ordinary lately, would you?"

He could see that Mrs. A was deciding whether or not to trust him. He needed a different tactic or he might lose the chance for valuable information. Bernie pointed to the trophy. "Is that yours? What sport do you play?"

Mrs. A had all but forgotten about the heavy piece of metal she was holding. She brought it up so Bernie could see. "Oh this? Just a bit of memorabilia from my younger days as a bowler."

"That's quite some trophy." He leaned over to read the inscription. "First place in the Bowler's League. Well, that certainly is quite an accomplishment!"

"Those were the days," said Mrs. A, remembering back to when she could thrash any bowler within one hundred miles of the Monterey Peninsula. "But now it seems I've turned into an old lady."

"What?" asked Bernie. "You could have fooled me. I bet you can still bowl quite a few strikes." Mrs. A blushed.

"You know, I don't like to get involved, but if my neighbor is in danger, maybe I could help you out. There have been more than a few strange things happening over there lately."

"Really?" said Bernie, for once thankful for a nosey neighbor.

"Would you like to come in? I was just about to put on a fresh pot of coffee."

"That would be delightful," said Bernie, following Mrs. A into her living room.

Once the coffee was brewed and served, and the conversation about bowling tournaments had run its course, Bernie felt it was safe to get back to topic at hand.

"So you said there were some odd things going on at Pia's" he commented.

"Now I don't want you to think that I spend my time spying on neighbors, but ever since I lost Mr. A," here she pointed to the paint can on the mantle, "I've had to be extra vigilant." Bernie glanced at the rusted container and hoped he hadn't run into a real kook.

"I understand," he said sympathetically.

"It started several days ago, very early in the morning. I saw Pia walk out into her front yard and pick up a gun off the ground."

"A gun, you say?"

"Yes. And it was one of those fancy deals with a silencer." She thought Bernie might be having a hard time believing this. "Oh, I know my guns and I know what a silencer looks like, especially with binoculars."

So Pia had found the gun outside, thought Bernie. This was an interesting twist.

"And then the next day," continued Mrs. A, "I saw some big lug sneak through her front gate. Seemed to me he was searching around the same area where the gun was found. Then he tried to look in through the window, but I guess he spotted that surfer who's been hanging out there, and he took off."

Bernie's brain quickly put things together. Could Larry really have been that inept to have dropped his gun in Pia's front yard? And was that the one he himself had seen on the kitchen counter? Jack was going to blow a gasket if this were true.

"Can I pour you another cup of coffee?" Mrs. A asked, noticing that Bernie had become a little distracted.

"Thank you, but one cup is enough for me," he answered. "And no one else has come by?"

"Not until you showed up. But I'll keep an eye out. If you leave me your phone number, I can call you if I see any activity over there." It was so nice to have a gentleman caller in her living room. The last time she'd had a pleasant conversation over coffee had been when Mr. A was still alive. "Or you could just come by and check whenever you wanted and I'll have coffee ready in no time."

"That's very kind of you," Bernie said, pulling a pen out of his pocket. "Do you have something I can write my number on?" This was perfect; his own security woman keeping an eye out. He wrote down his number, thanked Mrs. A, and headed back for the office.

20

Pia looked at her image in the mirror. She liked what she saw, even if she barely recognized herself. Arturo had given her shimmering, peacock blue eye shadow, thick black eyeliner, and bright red lips. She had called a stop to the false eyelashes knowing they'd drive her crazy. He'd ratted her hair into some sort of modern beehive and shellacked it with half a can of noxious hairspray. She always had liked playing dress-up as a little girl, and this was far better than anything she could have dreamed up.

Anastasia had dressed Pia in blue leggings, nearly the same color as her eye makeup, topped with a purple and blue paisley tunic that swished around when she walked.

"And now for the purple scarf around your neck to hide the Adam's apple," Anastasia told her.

"But I don't have an Adam's apple," Pia insisted.

"Exactly," replied Anastasia.

When the makeover was finally completed, Pia stared at the image in the three-way mirror. Darned if she didn't look like a drag queen.

"So what am I supposed to do now?" she asked.

"Baby," said Arturo, tucking in a loose strand of hair, "now you go out in public and get used to your new image."

"I have no problem flaunting my new look, but how is this going to keep me anonymous? Everyone will be starting at me."

"Maybe they'll notice *you*," said Anastasia, "but no one will recognize Pia."

Anastasia stood back and studied the total package. "We'll have to give you shoes, and as much as I'd prefer something with a heel, I hear you might have the necessity to make a quick dash."

Pia was very grateful that she would not have to argue about shoes with Anastasia. While she did pride herself on her keen fashion sense, she truly hated high-heels. In her old job she would wear them only between the car and the office and at meetings with clients. At Houston and Melrose, she wore sensible shoes every day and was never questioned about it.

"Why don't you and Arturo go to the front of the store and get a cold drink while I pick out some footwear and we wait for the boys."

Arturo had just opened two bottles of soda water when the phone rang and they heard Anastasia pick up the extension in the back. Still talking on the phone and carrying a pair of flat, silver sandals, she walked over to Pia.

"It's Brad. Something about not being able to drive." She handed the phone to Pia.

"Hello," Pia said, then listened to Brad. "Hold on a sec." She turned to the others. "Apparently, they left the car at the surf shop, walked to some restaurant, and now aren't legal to drive."

Anastasia motioned for the phone. "Put Skip on... Where are you? ...OK, I'll drop her off and then you can walk back to your car." She placed the phone on her desk and bent down to pick up her bag.

"Arturo, I'll be back in twenty minutes." She turned to Pia. "It's show time! Let's see what the boys think about the new you!"

"I'm ready," she said, eager to spring the new look on Brad and Skip. "Hey wait a minute. I'm not leaving until tomorrow. As much as I like the whole theater aspect of this, I can't possibly sleep in all this makeup."

"You're right," said Arturo, "I forgot that you're not leaving until tomorrow. What do you think, Anastasia? The hair has to stay. I'll give you a hair net, but we'll have to re-do the makeup tomorrow."

"Problem solved," said Anastasia. "Just come in an hour before the bus leaves and we'll fix you up."

Ten minutes later, Anastasia pulled up in front of the café. The guys had taken over a table on the front patio, now covered in empty beer bottles and dirty plates.

"What do you think?" Pia asked Anastasia, pulling down the mirror on the sun visor. "Do you think those drunken surfers will recognize me?"

"If they were women, yes. But men...maybe, but not at first glance."

"There's only one way to find out," Pia said, opening the car door. "Thanks for all the help. I'll see you tomorrow."

Anastasia honked her horn and waved to the guys. "Go get 'um!" she said, and drove off.

"That's Pia?" asked Beamer, staring at lady walking over to them. "Damn, Brad—you didn't tell us you'd turned into a poofter."

Brad was a little too shocked at Pia's new look to say anything until she'd reached the table and sat down.

"Girl-dude," Brad said, "you could righteously pass for a dude, trying to be a girl."

"My friend certainly does good work," said Skip. "I might even fall for Pia being a girl."

"You mean she's really not a girl?" asked Topper. "I thought you said she was."

"Brad, darling," Pia said, trying to imitate a guy dressed like a girl, "Why don't you introduce me to your friends?"

Beamer leaned over and whispered into Brad's ear. "This how they dress up in Monterey? She's not a girlfriend, right?"

"Pia, this is Topper and Beamer. Old friends." He turned to the guys. "Maybe one day I can give you the story behind this, but for today, don't ask. And no, Beamer, she's not my girlfriend and this isn't how they dress up north. Or at least not the ladies I know."

"Cool," said Beamer. "Can't wait to hear the tale behind this one."

The guys continued to stare at Pia.

"How about if one of you gentleman get me a beer?" she asked. Might as well play this for all it was worth. Beamer waved to the waitress to bring another round.

"So Skip," Pia started, "did you find out if there's an APB out on me down here?"

"Damn, Brad," said Topper, "no wonder you're going in for the disguise! What's she wanted for?"

"I'm not wanted for anything down here. Or at least I hope I'm not," Pia cut in. She turned back to Skip. "What did you find out?"

"Oops," said Brad, looking over to Skip, "I think we got too involved with catching up and he forgot to call."

"I'll do it now," Skip said, standing up and walking to a more secluded area of the patio.

The waitress arrived and set down another round of beers. Pia grabbed a bottle and took a lady-like sip. She probably should ask for a glass but decided that it wasn't necessary. She might even look more like a guy pretending to be a gal if she drank straight from the bottle.

No one spoke, not quite knowing how to continue the conversation now that a chick was at the table. And she wasn't exactly the type the boys had been hoping to attract. Beamer thought that Pia might even be really good-looking without all the weird clothes and makeup, but he and the boys had had their hearts set on nubile young bikini-clad gals. Finally, Skip returned.

"Bad news, friends," Skip announced, taking a seat at the table. "Pia's info is with all the police agencies in the area, which means it's all over California." He took a look at Pia. "But I think you'll be OK until we get you out of town tomorrow. They're looking for a well-dressed, middle-aged, professional woman. Still, I think it's' better if we get back to the house."

They finished their beers, settled the tab, and the gang headed back over to the surf shop.

"Want to come in and see our place?" Beamer asked Pia.

"Thanks Beamer, but I think it's better if I'm off the streets."

With Pia in the driver's seat of Skip's surf-mobile, they left Pacific Beach and headed back to the house on Sunset Cliffs.

21

They'd been back at Skips for several hours when the novelty of the playing dress-up had long since passed. Pia needed to get out of the polyester clothes and wash off the thick layer of makeup. She was tired of sitting in the living room and up in her bedroom and had finally gone out to patio.

"Tell me again why you think I still need to stay in drag?" Pia asked the guys. "It's not exactly comfortable and I'm cooking inside all this synthetic fabric and heavy makeup."

"Since we know that the San Diego police have you on their naughty list," Skip said, "I think it's better if you stay this way. The fuzz cruise the cliffs all the time and we can't take the chance that one of them will spot you."

"Skip," Pia tried to reason, "I'm sitting in the back patio of your house. How's anyone going to see me from the street?" She had been doing her best to adhere to her host's requests, but was rapidly approaching her breaking point and in danger of making a few rude remarks.

"Girl-dude, they got police choppers here," said Brad. He looked up to scour the skies. "Might even have a few drones."

"Maybe, Brad, but I haven't seen any flyovers. And I honestly don't think I'm on their top ten list." She abruptly made up her mind and stood up. "That's it. I'm getting out of my party clothes. I'll leave the hair, since I don't even want to try getting this rat's nest down, but the clothes and makeup are coming off."

"Fine, Pia," said Skip. "But then you'll have to stay indoors until tomorrow."

"Not a problem."

Pia walked back inside thinking that the guys were being overly cautious. Did they really think there were cops driving by houses looking for her? Not likely.

Passing by the front door to grab her bag, she decided to walk out and gauge just how much traffic and/or cops really patrolled the area. She sauntered out to the street and it was just as she had thought; a few cars sped by the house but not a patrol car in sight. Had Pia taken a little more time to survey the parked cars across the street before returning to the house, she might have noticed the man crouched behind the black Jeep.

Larry pulled the San Diego Zoo ball cap down over his eyes, further shielding his face from any curious neighbors who might be wondering what some guy was doing checking out the house on the other side of the street. He saw someone walk out of the house and squinted. Who the hell was that? Some matron in too much makeup and a hairdo he hadn't seen since his Gramma June passed ten years ago. Hell. One more fucking complication, not that the broad would pose a problem. But that meant that Pia now had three other people in the house with her.

He'd had such a great day with the gals at the zoo and hated to leave them while he did some reconnaissance on the surfer's house. It would be over tonight, he told himself. And he'd get one more memorable night before returning to Monterey.

Larry stood up and continued his walk along the cliffs for another two blocks, then crossed the street and headed back the way he'd come. At the corner of the cross street before the surfer's house, he turned right. Hoping to get a view of the back of the house, he turned left onto the street that ran behind Skip's, and walked up to the house that backed the surfer's. Now he could only hope that no one was home and he could sneak into their backyard. He casually walked up and rang the doorbell. To anyone passing by, he wouldn't look suspicious. Still, he pulled his cap low on his face in case of any security cameras.

It must have been his lucky day. No one home and no surveillance cameras. Even if any video might catch him from a neighboring house, he wouldn't be breaking and entering so there would be no reason for anyone to check their tapes.

Larry generally was very good at the stealth part of his work. He could usually sneak in and out of a back yard with no one ever being the wiser. However, he had never had to deal with Southern California landscaping that included a whole lot of spiky cactus. Already bleeding from his arm brushing up against one of the assailant plants, Larry figured this probably wouldn't be a good route to use later that evening.

A six foot adobe wall separated the back yard from the surfer's. He could hear a couple of men talking and got a whiff of Mary Jane. Fucking surfers were the same no matter which end of California they came from. Grabbing a wooden Adirondack chair, and placing it next to a large avocado tree for cover, Larry eased himself up and carefully looked over the edge of the wall. No sign of Pia or the other broad in the back yard. He glanced up to the second story hoping that maybe he could see someone in a window. It was going to be hell trying to locate the target in a house this large. Pia's Pacific Grove home had been easy, being only one story and rather small. His only hope was that the guys would get so wasted they passed out and wouldn't hear him when he searched for Pia. He took one final look at the back layout. A path lead around the right side of the house, and he could just make out a side door off of it. That would be his best bet.

Before getting down from the chair, Larry reached up and picked two avocadoes. Fondling them in his hands, his mind wandered to guacamole, then to margaritas, and finally to the frisky Swedish babes. He checked his watch. Still several hours before he could go after the target and nothing to do until then. His leg brushed up against a cactus, but even the stinging pain could not dampen his lusty thoughts.

He was halfway back to the hostel when his phone buzzed in his jeans pocket. *Fuck it.* It had to be Jack wanting another update. He'd already decided that letting Jack's calls go straight to voicemail would be the wisest move until he had taken care of business.

A block away from the hostel, Larry sat down on a bus bench to listen to what Jack had to say. It wasn't exactly coherent, what with all the swearing and yelling, but Larry got the gist of it. Somehow they had found out that he'd lost his gun at Pia's. Shit. There was nothing he could do about it now. He'd figure out a plausible lie when all this was done, if Jack would even care by then. For now, he had a dinner and nookie date with a couple of hot tamales.

~~~

"Girl-dude, get away from the front window," Brad called out.

Pia turned around to face him on the sofa but didn't move. It was nearly ten o'clock and the sun was long gone. She'd washed off the make-up and replaced the drag outfit for pale rose yoga pants and a racer-back tank top hours ago.

"Relax, Brad, I'm just trying to see if there's enough moonlight outside for me to see the ocean."

"And if there is, are you planning on walking down to the beach?" She ignored him and turned back to the front window. "Skip, maybe you can talk some sense into her."

Skip pushed the pause on the DVD remote. "Brother, I think she'll be OK for now. No one can see into the living room from the street."

"Fine. Don't blame me if the fuzz come a-knocking." Brad picked up his beer and signaled Skip to start the movie again.

Pia walked back over and plopped down on the other end of the couch. She'd just closed her eyes when Skip's phone rang.

"People call you this late?" she asked as Skip got up to grab the phone.

"It's not late," Skip said, picking up the phone. "Yeah," he said into the receiver, "come on by, we're home. Anastasia can give you the address."

"Who's coming over?" Brad asked.

"Arturo. He's bringing a hairnet for Pia. Said he'd forgotten to give it to her earlier today." He turned to her. "Is that really necessary?" He shook his head. "The crazy things women have to do for beauty...."

"Skip, the last person I knew who slept in a hairnet was my Great Aunt Fannie," Pia answered. "I didn't even know they still sold the things." She stretched and yawned. "Darn, I was just about to call it a night."

"Arturo will be here in about twenty minutes," said Skip, "then you can run off to bed."

~~~

Larry, kicking it into specialist gear, cleared his mind of all things sexual while he made his way up Sunset Cliffs Boulevard. It was a perfect night for a job; warm, clear skies, and no moon. He'd picked up a Hawaiian shirt at a used clothing store that not only would help him blend in, but also covered the small bulge in his back pocket where he'd stashed the tiny Derringer. Just enough light from streetlamps and houses ensured he had no problem finding Pia's hideout, and there were still plenty of shadows for cover.

A block from the surfer's house, Larry could see light shining through the living room window. Damn, he hadn't expected to find people still awake. He hadn't given it enough thought, and just assumed Pia would knock off at her usual Pacific Grove time, and that the surfers would be too stoned to stay up late. What the hell, it was a nice warm night and it would be no big deal to wait them out. Looking for a darkened area to hide in, Larry came to an abrupt halt. Holy fuck! He'd recognize that beat-up, black VW bus anywhere. What the hell was the gun supplier doing parked in the surfer's driveway?

His first thought was to call Jack but then remembered that his boss was really pissed off at him. And anyway, he didn't even know the name of the guy who'd furnished the weapon. Maybe he was jumping to conclusions. Maybe this wasn't the gun dealer's ride. He needed a closer look.

After creeping up the darkened side of the driveway, Larry scooted under the front window, over to the right, and then stood up. He knew that he couldn't be seen on the unlit front lawn and was thankful the curtains had not been drawn. He chanced a quick glance inside. It had only been a fraction of a second, but what Larry had seen gave him pause. The back of some quiff-looking dude standing behind the old lady with the grandma hairdo. He didn't see Pia or the other men. He'd have to risk another look through the front windows before deciding what to do next.

What the fuck? thought Larry, standing at the window a little longer than he should have.

175

From inside, Arturo blinked but didn't turn towards what had caught his eye.

"Someone's out there," he told Pia in a calm whisper, not moving from his hairnet ministrations. "Act like nothing's wrong."

Seeing as how Pia hadn't seen or heard anything, it was easy enough to go along with the request.

"I didn't hear anything," she whispered back. "Are you sure?"

"Baby, I know what I saw." Arturo fiddled with the last section of the hairnet. "Some guy, right up along the side of the front window."

"So what should we do?" she asked.

"You don't do anything but slowly walk back to the kitchen. I'll be right behind you." Arturo placed his hand on Pia's back and steered her straight ahead.

"God damn it," Larry swore under his breath. If it wasn't the little fucker who had sold him the little gun! And now that the broad had removed all the clown makeup, Larry clearly recognized Pia. But what the fuck had she been doing dressed like his gramma earlier in the day? More importantly, what was the little shit doing at the house?

This was all going south way too quickly for his taste. He obviously couldn't get the job done right now with at least two people wide awake, one of them being a gun dealer. He'd have to give it at least an hour and hope the little guy would leave. As long as he was already here, he'd do a little more surveillance before leaving. Might as well check out the side door and see if it had easy accessibility.

Inching down the pathway that he had spotted from the neighbor's house earlier in the day, Larry had just about reached the side door when he felt a fist slam into his side, narrowly missing the spot that would have had him doubled over and gasping for breath.

He swung a left hook and got a piece of whoever it was, but it didn't seem to do much harm. It was difficult to see in the narrow, darkened pathway but Larry knew it was the little gun dealer. He might have stopped to ask what he was doing there, had the man not literally leaped into a flying kick, his foot landing on Larry's right shoulder. In better light, he had no doubt it would have struck him in square in the face. Deciding if he should pull out his knife, and then remembering it was still up in Monterey getting sharpened, Larry quickly considered his options.

"What's going on?" shouted a man, running from the back of the house towards the fight.

Time for Larry to go. He quickly fired off another left jab, turned, and sprinted back towards the front of the house and out onto the street, where he kept running.

Skip reached Arturo and yelled out over his shoulder, "*Intruder.* Turn on the outside lights!"

"Where's the switch?" Pia hollered back.

"By the side door."

By the time she'd found it and run outside with Brad, Skip and Arturo were already on the street looking left and right for the interloper.

"Girl-dude, was that someone after you?" Brad asked Pia while the two walked out to join the others.

"How should I know?"

Skip and Arturo, seeing no sign of the man, joined the others. "He's gone," said Skip. "Let's get back inside."

The first thing Arturo did was to turn on the front porch light and draw the drapes.

"You think it was someone after Pia?" Skip asked the others.

"Unless you're on someone's to-do list," replied Arturo, "I'd bet on it."

"Damn, girl-dude," said Brad, "how did they find us?"

"I have no idea," she answered. "No one knew I was headed down here, right? How could someone have found me so quickly?"

"Can't say we didn't warn you about staying in disguise," Brad offered. "I told you about the cops and their drones."

"There were no drones, Brad. Anyway, that wasn't a cop. Cops don't sneak around and attack people."

"Yes they do," Brad reasoned. "Or at least I know of several cases."

"It wasn't a cop," said Arturo, rubbing his fist. "It was some big guy who knew how to take care of himself."

"Apparently, so do you," said Skip. "You're a bit of a surprise."

"Ex-Marine," Pia explained. The surfers nodded their heads in understanding. "Arturo, did you get a look at him? Can you give us a description?"

"Sorry, but it was too dark and then he got away." He took in the concern on the faces around him. "I'm pretty sure you'll be OK for the rest of the night, but I could stay here if you wanted."

"We got it, Arturo," said Skip. Brad and me will take shifts."

"I can also take a shift," said Pia.

"No, you need to stay out of sight," ordered Arturo. "Stay in your room with the curtains closed. Maybe leave the light off." He turned to Skip. "What time does the bus leave tomorrow?"

"Anastasia told us to meet her at the store at eleven in the morning. The bus leaves at noon," answered Skip. "Pia, we might have to sneak you out in the trunk of my sports car tomorrow."

"That's not going to happen, Skip," Pia assured him. "I don't do car trunks. Especially in the fancy dudes Anastasia lent me."

The men looked at each other, none wanting to make the next comment. Pia, seeing that no one was going to challenge her, got up from the chair.

"Great. That's settled. I'm off to bed and I'll see you in the morning."

Walking up the stairs to her room, Pia had already started to work on a strategy to keep safe for the night. She just wasn't convinced that Brad and Skip were up to stopping a hired gun aiming for her, not that any of it made any sense. Who could it be? There was that Larry guy up in Pacific

Grove, the reason she fled to San Diego in the first place, but what could he have to do with anyone down here?

Once in her room, which doubled as Skip's office, Pia shut the door and grabbed a pen and paper off the small desk. After drawing a timeline and carefully recording all her movements from her departure in Pacific Grove until the incident with the intruder, she still couldn't work out how she could have been tailed to Skip's house. Had Jack planted a bug and been able to follow her? Now she was really getting crazy.

She got up and, disobeying orders, peeked through the curtains down onto the driveway. Arturo's VW was already gone and no one appeared to be out on the street. There must be something she could do other than sit around and wait. Her eye caught sight of the telephone on the desk. Who could she call? Pia checked the clock. Bob would still be at work. He may not have any answers, but at least she might feel better if they spoke.

"Bob," she said when he answered, "it's Pia."

"Pia?" said Bob, accompanied by the background sounds of conversations and soft music. "What are you doing calling me? Where are you?"

"I'm in San Diego at Brad's friend's house."

"You're not using your phone, are you?"

"No, I'm using the house phone. Still, I should make this quick." She paused for a moment not quite sure what she was going to say to her friend. "Bob, we think they know where I'm staying. Some guy was lurking around outside but we scared him off. I just can't figure out how anyone could have tracked me here. Can you find out anything on your end?"

"That doesn't sound good Pia, but I'll see what I can find out. Give me your phone number there, and I'll get back to you. Hey, I thought you were headed south of the border."

"That's the plan for tomorrow, if I can actually make it to the bus that will take me across."

"Hang in there."

"Thanks Bob."

~~~

Larry, still breathing a little hard, sat down on a bench on the pier. After taking off from the surfer's pad, he'd jogged a zigzag pattern through the neighborhood until he felt it safe enough to get back on Sunset Cliffs Boulevard and make his way into town. He might have been able to walk the last few blocks, but the endorphins had kicked in and he'd just kept on running.

He knew he'd blown it. No way in hell he'd be able to take out the broad now that everyone in the house had been alerted to his attempts. And fuck! What was up with the gun dealer? All Larry knew for sure was that the man knew how to fight. As much as he hated the idea, he knew he'd have to call Jack. At least he could place the blame on Jack's friend, saying that the gun dealer sure looked like a good friend of Pia's.

He decided it would be better to not mention the weird hair and makeup that Pia was wearing. Or maybe that was how she always dressed. It certainly didn't look like the picture Jack had given him of Pia dressed in some high-dollar outfit. But seeing how nothing was going according to plan, he wasn't about to waste time trying to figure this one out. It was probably just the way old gals dressed in Ocean Beach.

Twenty minutes later, with his heart rate back to normal, and with a story that should satisfy Jack regarding the lost Berretta, Larry punched in his boss' number.

"Larry," Jack boomed, "where the fuck you been? And what's this about you losing your gun at Pia's? Never-the-fuck mind, just tell me you got the job done."

"Jack, we got a problem," Larry replied in a calm voice, hoping it would help to cool Jack down a little.

"Damn it! I knew this would happen. You screwed up, right? You calling me from jail?"

Maybe Jack would work himself into a heart attack and Larry could just forget the whole job. "Calm down, Jack. I'm not in jail, and I'm not about to go there. Tell me, how well do you know this guy who got me the gun?"

"I told you. I don't. He's a colleague of an old friend. And what the hell does that have to do with anything?"

"I'll tell you what. I was just at the house to do the job and who do I see hanging out with the target but the guy who gave me the weapon."

"What?" Jack screamed into the phone. *"He's a friend of Pia's?"*

"How would I know? You're the one who set this up."

"Christ! Can't anyone do anything right?" Larry didn't respond. He could almost hear Jack's blood pressure spiking over the phone line. "OK, OK. I'll give my buddy a call. Hopefully I'll wake his sorry ass up. I knew I shouldn't have trusted him." With the noise of few cars driving by, Larry hadn't been paying attention to the background chatter on the other end of the phone. Now he noticed it.

"Why's there so much noise, Jack? Where are you?"

"Just down at Saul's having a nightcap. I'm gonna get one more cocktail before I call my friend."

"Just get back to me as soon as you can."

"Yeah, I know, you want to get the hell out of there and get back home. Look, I'll make this worth your while. Just hang in there."

"That's right Jack. You told me this would be a quick job." Let Jack think he was itching to get home. Larry's mind was already contemplating what he could do with the girls in the extra time he now had.

22

"Pia?" Skip called through the door the following morning, "You up?"

"Huh?...Sure...What time is it?" Pia rolled out of bed and Skip opened the door.

"Your friend Bob just called. He said it's important and to call him right away."

Pia glanced at the clock on the desk. It was just past 6:00. "Thanks," she said, climbing out of bed. "Sorry to get you up so early."

"You didn't. I was just out on my way to catch some waves with Brad."

"Did you say that was Bob?" Brad called out from down the hall. He reached the door and looked in. "Girl-dude, this must be important. Bob's never up this early." He turned to Skip. "I think I should wait to hear what Bob has to say. You go ahead. I'll catch up."

"I'll stay around until we see what's up," Skip said. "You might need my help."

"I'm OK," Pia told the guys. "Both of you can go." She picked up the phone from the desk and punched in Bob's number. The surfers didn't move.

"Bob, it's Pia," she said into the phone. "Uh huh...you're kidding...I understand...I'll figure it out...OK, thanks Bob."

Pia set the phone down and turned to the guys, still standing in the doorway. "I'm dead meat. It seems that was Larry outside Skip's house last night."

"*What?*" asked Brad. "How the hell does Bob know that? And how could Larry have found you?"

"Who's Larry?" asked Skip.

"Dude, don't you remember?" said Brad. "Larry the Lawnmower. The hitman from Monterey."

"Right," replied Skip, "I'd forgotten the name." He turned to Pia. "So what did Bob tell you?"

"Apparently, Jack was sitting at the bar late last night and Bob overheard his phone conversation with Larry." She looked at Skip. "People assume Bob's hearing's gone. No such thing. He picks up on a lot of mostly useless information, but not this time." Pia rubbed her eyes. "Let me just throw some water on my face and I'll explain it all. Skip, do you still have some coffee left?"

"I'll go grab you a cup," he replied, already on his way down the hall.

Five minutes later, standing in the kitchen sipping coffee, Pia told the men how Bob had heard Jack asking Larry if he'd finished the job. Next, Jack called some other guy named Alan and yelled at him about his man who was supposed to get a gun to Larry, and how that same man later turned up at Skip's.

"Arturo?" Skip and Brad said simultaneously.

"That's what I don't get either," Pia responded. "Maybe we should call Arturo and find out what's going on."

"Arturo and Larry the Lawnmower are working together?" asked Brad. "Damn Skip, looks like you righteously screwed up."

"Hang on there, brother. Arturo works for Anastasia. He's one hundred percent reliable. There must be some mistake."

"Why not check with Anastasia?" Pia suggested. "We're supposed to be there at eleven o'clock, but I think we need to figure this out before then."

"No," said Skip. "This doesn't involve her. Pia, do you have Arturo's number?"

She walked to the living room where she had set down his card the night before and brought it back to the kitchen. "I can call him, but what am I going to say?"

"Let me handle this," Skip said, picking up the phone. He punched in the number and waited.

"Hope we aren't calling too early," said Pia, just as Ship started to talk.

"Arturo? Skip here. Can you come over? We need your help with Pia's hair. It's a mess….great, see you soon."

Pia put up a hand to pat the hairnet that she'd left in place so that she wouldn't be able to see exactly how messed up her hair was. "Is it really that bad?" she asked.

"How should I know?" said Skip. "I thought that was a better line than *do you sell firearms.* Anyway, Arturo will be here her shortly."

"OK," said Pia. "I'll just take a quick shower."

~~~

187

Arturo walked into Skip's house with a makeup box and a large canvas bag filled with hair styling paraphernalia. After setting down his belongings, he immediately walked over to Pia, shaking his head at the state of her *do*.

"I thought I told you to sleep on your back with a neck pillow. This is a mess. And why is it wet?" he asked Pia while removing the hairnet.

"Honestly Arturo, I tried. I must have turned on my side sometime during the night." She hadn't actually tried to do anything other than sleep, but there was no need to further upset a man who might be a gun dealer.

"Well it's a good thing you called. This is going to take more than a few minutes to fix." Arturo pulled out a comb and a brush from his bag.

"Before we start," said Pia, "there's something I need to ask you…..I'm not really sure how to put this…."

"Dude," Brad cut in, not wanting to waste anymore time, "did you sell a gun to Larry?"

Arturo's hands froze above Pia's head. "Who's Larry?"

"The guy who attacked you last night," said Pia.

"I already told you I didn't see who it was," Arturo replied. He returned to working on Pia's hair. "Anyway, I don't know any Larry's."

"Maybe," said Pia. "But do you sell guns?"

This time Arturo set down his styling equipment and took a few steps back. "What's going on? I thought you called me over to get Pia ready for the trip."

"Well, we did," Pia answered. "But we also found out that the guy who was lurking around the house last night was a hitman from Monterey. AKA Larry the Lawnmower, and that you may have furnished him with a gun."

"And when was I supposed to have done that?" asked Arturo.

"In the last day or two," said Brad.

Arturo said nothing. The only thing that moved were his eyes, shifting from one of his accusers to the next.

"Look Brother," said Skip, "I know you. You work for a good friend. It's probably all a mix-up but we need to find out what's going on. So just come clean. Did you sell Larry a gun?"

"I told you, I don't even know anyone named Larry," Arturo asserted.

"But did you sell a gun to a man within the past few days?" Skip again asked.

Arturo paused a moment debating just how much he should reveal about his alternate line of work. If this group hadn't been good friends of Anastasia's, he would have been out the front door the minute firearms had been mentioned. But if the big guy from the night before really was the one he'd delivered the gun to, he needed to find out. He grabbed a stool at the breakfast bar and slumped into it.

"I *knew* this would eventually catch up with me." The exasperation in his voice was quite clear. "But you have to believe me, I have no idea who this Larry is." He looked over to Skip. "Think I could get a cup of coffee?"

Skip poured a cup and handed it to Arturo. The friends calmly waited for him to take a few gulps before he continued.

"You know, I didn't even really sell it to him." Arturo waited for a comment from the others, but there was none. "OK. So a guy I know sometimes asks me to get a hold of weapons. I don't do it often, but how much money do you think I can make working for Anastasia? Anyway, this contact asked me to get a weapon to a guy who was new in town. Said he would settle with me later. And that's all I know."

"So you don't know Larry's name," said Brad, "but what about the name of the man who called you?"

"I don't like to reveal that sort of information," Arturo answered.

"Even though it turned out that you had to defend yourself against someone you sold a gun to?" asked Pia. "It seems to me like you might not owe this contact too much loyalty."

"Maybe. But giving up names isn't always advisable," Arturo reasoned.

"Look Arturo," said Skip, "this will just be between us."

Arturo looked at the people grouped around him and considered his options. There didn't seem to be any. "OK...but you didn't hear this from me." The others nodded their head in agreement. "The guy who set it up is named Alan."

"Holy crap!" yelled Brad. "That's the name Bob heard Jack say up in Monterey!"

"We should have guessed Jack had connections down here," said Pia. She noticed Arturo's confusion and turned to him. "Jack's my boss up in Monterey. He hired Larry to take me out." Arturo still appeared perplexed.

"Hang on a minute, everyone," Skip said. "Let's get all our information together before we jump to any conclusions. Arturo, can you explain how this gun deal went down?"

"Just the usual. Alan gave me the number of the buyer, who I now assume is this Larry, and I set up a meet down at The Wild Side."

"Hold on," said Pia. "You mean you talked to Larry on the phone?"

"No. I never talk to clients on the phone. I sent him a text message."

"But you do have Larry's phone number?" Pia asked. Arturo nodded his head. "That could be useful." Pia was already plotting out how to use this new information. "By the way, Arturo, what's The Wild Side?"

"Stripper club," Skip supplied. He nodded towards Arturo. "Go on, brother."

"I go into the club and wait a few minutes until I see a guy with two young chicks get up from his seat and walk over to me. We exchanged code words, which is how we do it in the business, and then went out to the parking lot to do the deal. And then I left. That's all there was to it."

"What kind of gun did you give him?" asked Brad. He reminded himself to ask about the whole code word thing at another time. "He lost his Beretta at Pia's house when he was there to take her out."

"He got the only concealable weapon I had. My granny's little Derringer." Arturo felt no need to tell them that Larry had turned down the AK-47. "I wouldn't worry about him too much Pia, you can't do much damage with a Derringer unless you're right up against the person."

This didn't do much to calm Pia's concerns about being shot. Even if Larry couldn't kill her with a small gun, he could still do a lot of damage. At least they now had confirmation that Larry was in town and armed. It was time to move on that information.

"All right," she said, "let's get a plan together. I need some paper and a pen." Skip grabbed the items, handed them to Pia, and they all watched quietly while she jotted down notes. A few minutes later, she set the pad down on the counter.

"Here's my idea," said Pia, pointing to her notes, "we've got about four hours before the tour bus leaves. Since Arturo is here, I don't have to get to Anastasia's much before then. Skip, can you let her know that Arturo is fixing me up here?" He nodded. She looked back at her notes. "Any suggestions on what we do about Larry?"

"Do you think he knows we're on to him?" asked Brad. "Maybe he doesn't know that we know he was the one outside the house last night. And hell, maybe he doesn't even know that we know that it's him that's after Pia."

"Maybe," said Pia, "but he still has a gun and a contract out on me."

Just then, Arturo's phone rang. He took it out of his pocket and looked at the caller ID. "Isn't this a coincidence? It's Alan."

"A gangster who doesn't have a blocked number?" asked Pia, while Arturo's phone continued to ring.

"I don't think he knows how to do that," replied Arturo. "I'm letting this go to voice mail." They all waited until the message alert beeped, and then Arturo put it on speaker phone.

"Get in touch with me," was all the message that Alan had left.

"I think the best thing for me to do is not call him back," Arturo said. "All he's got on me is a phone number. He doesn't know anything about my life except that I can get weapons."

"So he can't trace you to Anastasia?" asked Skip.

"Nope."

"OK," said Skip, "Arturo will get to work on Pia's hair and makeup while we think of a way to assure that she gets to the tour bus and out of the country on time."

"That's fine with me," said Arturo, picking up his hair styling equipment. "But that means you guys will have to keep a look-out for Larry."

Pia looked at Brad, who looked at Skip, who looked back at Pia.

"Uhh..." said Pia, "we have a problem with that...we don't know what Larry looks like."

"I'm not too up to date on the whole internet thing," said Arturo, "but can't you get on it and find a picture of the man?" He continued to comb out Pia's hair.

"Dude," said Brad, "I don't think we can do a search for Monterey hitmen."

"But we *can* look up his lawn service company," said Skip.

"Skip, my man!" said Brad. "The business mind works wonders yet again! Lead me to the computer." The men walked upstairs to Skip's office.

A few minutes later Skip called out form the top of the stairs. "Arturo, can you come up here a sec?"

When Arturo got to the office, Skip pointed to Larry the Lawnmower's webpage, complete with a picture of the smiling proprietor. "Is this the guy?"

Arturo bent down to take a careful look at the photo. "That's him all right. Imagine that! A contract killer posting his details on the internet." Arturo studied the webpage a little longer. "Maybe I should get something like that. What do you think, Skip?"

"Advertise that you're a gun dealer?" Skip asked in disbelief.

"No, Skip, I'm thinking of a website for *Arturo's Makeovers*. If I could get enough work, I could give up the gun trade."

"You mean you don't even have a blog?" asked his friend. "Brother, you need to get with the twenty-first century. When this current situation is all over, I'll get you set up."

Skip quickly cut and pasted Larry's picture to his computer, sent it to his phone, then on to Brad's and Pia's. Now that they knew what Larry looked like, it would be a lot easier to spot him.

~~~

Alan sat in the living room of his La Jolla home, thankful the wife had gone out to lunch with her girlfriends and not heard the crash of one of her precious Waterford glasses that he'd thrown down on the tiled kitchen floor. He'd clean it up later. Right now he needed to figure out what to do about the situation with his gun supplier. He'd been right when he'd told Jack that they were too old for the game. He'd never had a screw-up like this in his life. A weapons supplier who knew the intended target? And why hadn't that little punk Arturo answered his call? Was he going to have to put a contract out on him? That's what he would have done in the past, but as this had shown him, he was too many years out of the loop to rely on second-hand contacts.

Not knowing what else to do, Alan walked back into the kitchen, swept up the shards of expensive glass, dumped them into a paper bag, and then into the recycling bin in the driveway. The brief respite from the pressing situation at hand had worked to clear his mind. Hell, he reminded himself, he was still the same man that had come from the backwaters of Chula Vista and ended up with a nice chunk of real estate in La Jolla. No little punk was going to mess with him.

Once back inside, he walked into his office and picked up the phone. It was time to call an old friend and ask for favor.

"Sid, Alan here, how 'bout I come over for a visit?"

~~~

"Skip," Brad said, watching Arturo put the finishing touches on Pia's hair, "since we aren't hitting the waves today, and since you told me no smoke or drink until Pia gets out of town, I got a hankering for something sweet. What do you have?"

"You know I don't keep sugar in the house, brother. It's not good for you." Skip looked at his house guests. No one looked very happy and maybe he should go get everyone a treat. "There's a great Danish bakery down on Newport Avenue. How about if I go out and get some pastries?"

"Dude! Awesome plan!" Brad jumped up out of his chair. "Let's go."

"I want you to stay here with Pia and Arturo," said Skip. "It's better to have the coverage. I'll be back in no time."

~~~

Skip parked his van a block from the bakery and was just about to get out when he saw a man walking towards him that looked a whole lot like the one he had just seen on the computer. Sitting in his car, grateful for the dirty windows that made it difficult to see in, he waited until the man was close enough to start snapping pictures with his phone. Once he'd walked by the van, Skip got out and began to follow him. He watched while he rounded the corner and then headed into the hostel. He pulled out his phone and called the house.

"Brad, it's Skip. I think I just spotted Larry. I'm sending you a picture now. Ask Arturo if it's him."

Brad pulled out his phone, waited until the picture uploaded, and showed it to Arturo.

"That's a confirm on the identity, my man," he told Skip. "Where did you say you saw him?"

"I'll get back to you on that."

"Don't forget the éclairs, Skip. We'll need the extra energy if we have to take down a hitman."

Skip walked back towards the bakery thinking about his next move. Larry staying at the hostel was a bit of unexpected luck. His old friend Pedro owned the place but Skip couldn't simply walk in and take the chance that Larry knew what he looked like. Instead, he called him on the phone.

"Brother, it's Skip. Where are you at right now? …Ensenada? Shit… any chance you'll be back in town today? ….It's cool. Just give me a call when you get back."

With his friend Pedro down in Baja for the day, there wasn't much Skip could do. This was too sensitive a subject to deal with across borders. At least he knew where Larry was staying. He walked back to the bakery, bought a box of pastries, and headed home.

23

Larry sat in the back patio of the hostel sipping his double-shot latte. Damn good thing none of the boys back home could see him with this quiche-eaters brew. He'd never be able to explain that it beat the hell out of the McDonald's coffee he usually drank. He smiled thinking about the past few days and all that had gone on how and it had opened his mind to new possibilities.

Saying goodbye to Karen and Karla earlier that morning wasn't all that bad. As sorry as he was to see them go, it was probably for the best. He was getting way too distracted. And with Jack all over his ass he really needed to get the job done and get back to his life in Monterey.

Up until this trip, Larry never thought he was missing out on anything. He liked his life just fine. Hell, he had a good legitimate job and a lucrative side operation. He had a nice little wife who'd kept herself trim and fit and really didn't bug him about much, unlike some of the other guys who he'd grown up with. They were always telling him how lucky he was to have settled down with a good woman. So what was he doing fucking around with the hot babes from Sweden and drinking foo-foo coffee drinks? A slight smile crossed his face when his mind drifted to what he had been doing with the gals just a few hours before. He felt a little ashamed that only the slightest tinge of guilt had crept into his mind.

Still, maybe he should call his wife to check in. After all, she had no idea that he was even out of town. What if he didn't make it back before she returned from Vegas? But he really didn't want to hear her voice. If he could just pretend for a little longer that he wasn't married, he could really enjoy the next day or two. Larry pulled out his phone, scrolled through the contacts list, and punched in his cousin Len's number. Len's wife was one of the other ladies on the Vegas trip.

"Len," he said into the phone, story already lined up, "Larry here."

"Lar, what's up? Enjoying the time being a bachelor again?" Larry was tempted to tell him just how much he was enjoying it, but this was one fantastic adventure he'd carry with him to the grave.

"I'm actually down in....uh...Santa Barbara...got here yesterday. I got a call for some work and I been thinking about expanding. It was great just taking off without telling the old lady, but it turns out I'm going to need to stay here a few more days if I want the contract."

"Sweet—a second Larry the Lawnmower outlet!"

"That's the plan. Anyway, I got a favor to ask. Could you go by the house and make sure everything's OK?"

"No problem. I'll check on it 'till you get back."

"I'm sure the girls will be back before I am."

"Maybe not. Didn't you hear the news? One of them hit a ten-thousand dollar keno and they're now all heading to some hooty-tooty spa out in the desert for a few days. The wife didn't even bother to call—she texted me. No problem here, I'm likeing the none-stop sports and porn on TV. Kinda tired of frozen pizza, but it beats the hell out of cooking."

Larry had never been a particularly spiritual man, but it sure seemed that someone was on his side this time.

"Well, then I guess I don't have to worry. Thanks Len."

Just for good measure, Larry then sent a text to his wife to say he was in Santa Barbara for a job, and that he'd heard about the spa trip. He signed it with a bunch of X's and O's. He picked up his latte and wondered if he should also go buy a pack of smokes to celebrate.

~~~

"Are you sure I shouldn't go on the bus with Pia?" Brad asked, now that Pia was in full regalia, sitting in the living room.

"I already told you Brad," said Pia, "you've helped me enough. If anyone gets arrested it's going to be me and no one else."

"And you wouldn't fit in," said Skip. "Anyway, I need you to stake out the hostel. Too many people in town know me so I can't take the chance that a friend might wander by and mess up any surveillance. You, on the other town, are new in town."

"Yeah, but Larry probably knows what I look like if he's been casing both your pad and Pia's up in Pacific Grove. Don't you think him spotting me is more of a risk?"

"I could help you out with that," Arturo volunteered, eyeing Brad.

"Whoa partner," said Brad, "you are *not* doing me up like Pia."

"I was thinking of doing you up like Skip."

"Huh?"

"Skip," said Arturo, "do you have one of your white linen suits on hand?" Skip nodded. "Good. You bring it out and I'll fix Brad's hair."

Fifteen minutes later, Brad emerged from upstairs in his new outfit. The linen pants were a few sizes too big, but it gave him an edgy look. Arturo had slicked back his locks into a well-groomed pony-tail. The transformation was so striking that it left Pia and Brad speechless.

"Dudes," Brad said, a huge grin on his face, "I'm styling!"

"Wow Brad," said Pia, "I had no idea you could look so good! If I didn't know you so well, I probably wouldn't have recognized you."

"Now *that's* the look I want when I open up a shop in Carmel," said Skip, while Brad paraded in front of them, à la fashion model. "No way would you be taken for guy who lives in his mother's garage."

"Let's go over the plan one more time before I leave," Pia said to the men, getting the group back on track. "Skip, you'll drive me over to Anastasia's in Pacific Breach, right?"

"Yeah," said Skip. "We'll drop Brad off near the hostel and then head over to PB." He looked at Arturo. "Do you need anything else from us?"

"We're done here," said Arturo. "I'll be at Anastasia's in a while to drop off my tools, and then I have things to take care of...like figuring out how to handle the Alan situation. He doesn't know how to track me, but I might just stay low for a while."

"All right, brother, sounds good to me," said Skip. "Once I drop Pia off, I'll check in with you Brad to see if you've spotted Larry. Anything else happens, give me a call."

"Cool," said Brad, looking forward to his stint as an undercover agent. "You say they have a nice little café in the front? Guess I'll just have to check out the female guests."

"Let's do it then," said Pia, grabbing her carryon bag and heading for the door.

~~~

On the drive over to see Sid at the retirement home, Alan again went through the actions of the previous days. He still could not come up with a plausible explanation of how Arturo had known the target. Granted, he had only met the little guy once, and that was only to drop off a payment, but his buddy Sparky had sworn up and down that Arturo was trustworthy. Sparky's ass was on the line as soon as he took care of Arturo.

It had been a couple of years since Alan had last seen Sid. The occasion had been a big to-do given by his kids just before Sid had moved to Pleasant Days Retirement Home out in Lemon Grove.

Back in the day, Sid had been his wing-man in a lot of business dealings. He could always count on Sid to keep his mouth shut and his eyes wide open. That transaction that went sour out in the El Cajon desert was one of his fondest memories. Had Sid not stepped up and clocked the big asshole who was about to run off with all their profits, Alan probably wouldn't be living the high-life in La Jolla.

The two had met up in their early twenties. At the time, Alan had just started a small loan business, and Sid was boxing in illegal fights out at an abandoned warehouse down near the border. Alan, being a boxing aficionado, had already seen Sid in a few fights when their paths crossed at a local bar after a bout one evening. He'd hired Sid to back him up when he'd gone to collect on an unpaid loan, and the men had immediately hit it off it off. Sid was getting real tired of being pummeled three times a week just about the time Alan started to branch out and make some serious dough. Sid left the ring, joined up with Alan, and never gave another thought to prize fighting.

Unfortunately, all those blows to the head had not been very good for Sid. His memory wavered now and then, and the years sometimes became confused. Still, who could Alan turn to at a time like this? He didn't expect Sid to actually take care of the situation, but he would know how to handle it. Or at least Alan hoped so.

Alan pulled into the parking lot of the retirement home and got out. It wasn't a large place. Maybe fifty people lived there. The front garden was well looked after and the mature palm trees offered shade and atmosphere. He stood still for a moment counting his blessings that he had not only been so successful, but that he had a wife who had stood by him all these years. Had things turned out differently, he might be stuck out in Lemon Grove with a bunch of old farts; or maybe even somewhere worse. He made a mental note to stop by the mall on the way home and buy a replacement for the Waterford glass he'd thrown on the kitchen floor.

The woman at the front desk had him sign in before she told him where he could find Sid, which was out back in the smoker's corner. Alan wandered past rooms, most with their doors open, and got even more depressed. How the hell did Sid end up in a little room with a kitchenette? What a way to spend the last years of his life.

Opening the glass doors out to the courtyard where smoking was permitted, Alan didn't have to search for Sid. The scent from his tell-tale pipe tobacco permeated the surroundings. He sat in a recliner next to a lady dressed head to toe in hot pink.

"Alan!" Sid called out, getting up to greet his friend. "How the hell you been?" he asked, crushing him in a giant bear hug. "Come over and take a seat with me and my lady. This is Tallulah. She used to be on the stage and screen!"

"Nice to meet you," Alan said, noting that Tallulah did indeed have the bone structure that must have made her quite a beauty in her youth. "So Sid finally got himself that movie starlet he always dreamed about."

"I sure did! She's got quite a story. Alan, you remember all those clubs the sailors used to go to? Maybe some are still around. You know, the ones with the dancing gals? Back when they really knew how to dance? Tallulah was one of the top strippers in the business." He turned to his gal, "Isn't that right, babe?"

"Oh Sid, your friend doesn't want to hear about me."

Actually, Alan did want to hear the details. He'd met his fair share of nightclub beauties in his younger days but had always figured they'd turn out to me more trouble than it was worth to actually marry one of them. Looking at Tallulah, he wondered if he'd been wrong. She was probably the same age as his wife, but that's where the similarities ended.

"Go on, Tallulah, tell him your life story," said Sid. "And don't stop at the dancing part."

"If you really want to hear...." she started. Alan nodded. "Well all right, then. After a few years doing the circuit between here and Vegas, I got offered a job in the adult movie business." Alan's eyes got very wide. "It was quite risqué back then, but today it might be called soft porn. It was before the business had the budget that it has now." Tallulah sighed. "I know I could have been a mega star in today's market."

"She's not kidding," Sid put in, "just take a look at those knockers! They're the real deal!"

Alan was trying very hard not to look at the low-cut, tight-fitting top that Tallulah wore. She certainly had the best set of tits he'd ever seen on a lady her age.

Alan quickly looked away and cleared his throat. "That's some story, Tallulah. I don't mean to be ill-mannered, but I've got a business matter I need to discuss with Sid. Will you excuse us?"

Tallulah stood up, bent over to kiss Sid on the head, her giant boobs engulfing his face. She straightened up and turned to Alan. "I have to meet the girls for a game of mahjong anyway, so I'll catch up with you later."

If his wife's friends looked like Sid's girl, Alan would take up mahjong on a regular basis.

After Tallulah had gone inside Alan explained the situation.

"An old associate called me from up in Monterey. Said he had a man down here who needed a weapon. So I set him up with a supplier—guy named Arturo. Next thing I know, my associate is on the phone yelling about Arturo being a friend of the intended target."

Sid remained quiet for a minute and Alan thought maybe he hadn't understood.

"I say you let me take this Arturo punk out," Sid finally said. He shadow boxed the air in front of him. "Maybe I don't got the speed anymore, but I sure got the power." He threw a right jab and nearly took off Alan's nose. Maybe Sid's eyesight was also failing.

"I don't know, Sid. I promised myself I was done with the life. Don't you think we could just scare the guy?"

"You mean like take off a finger or two? Sure, I'm up for that."

This had all seemed like such a good idea when Alan was back in La Jolla. Now he wasn't so sure. What if they got caught? Spending the remainder of his years in lock-up would be even worse than at the retirement home.

"Sid, I appreciate your loyalty and wiliness to help, but I think we've got to come up with something that doesn't cause bodily harm."

Sid looked forlorn. "You sure?"

"Hey pal, you got a good thing going here. Nice room, good food. Hell, you got yourself a certifiable porn star! You want to chance losing that all?"

"You got a point, Alan. It's a quiet life, but I like it. Guess that's why you were always the brains and I was the muscle."

"OK. So let's come up with a plan that will scare the pants off that little twit. And then we smear his name. He'll never again work for anyone else in the county."

"Just like old times, Alan. You lead the way."

24

Now that Karen and Karla were gone, Larry's mind was freed up to concentrate on finishing the job he'd set out to do. What he needed was transportation. Screw walking back and forth all over Ocean Beach and getting chased on foot by a gun dealer and a couple of stoners. He considered his options, and renting a car was not one of them. His best bet might just be at the gas station he'd dropped by the other day.

"Hey," Larry said, walking into the mechanics bay. The man who'd told him about Marco's restaurant put down his wrench and walked over. "Just wanted to thank you for the restaurant tip you gave me. Couldn't have worked out better."

"Looks like you had your hands full," he said, remembering the hot babes.

"You can say that again!" The men fist bumped. "You should try heading over the hostel sometime. Seems the foreign girls like a working man. By the way, the name's Larry."

"Benny," replied the mechanic. "Think I'll have to give it a try, seeing as how you seemed to have scored quite a catch."

Larry looked around to see that no one was near. "Look Benny, I need a favor. I need some transportation for a day or two. Maybe you have a junker car I could rent? I could pay cash."

For the right price, Benny would have gladly lent him a customer's car. He could always use some un-reportable income. The problem was that the only car at the station was being picked up later that day. He glanced around to see what else he could offer.

"Can you drive a motorcycle Larry?"

Larry grinned. Hell, a big bike would be even better than a car for sneaking around, especially in this heat. "Damn right I can. What size you got? " He was hoping for something along the lines of a big-ass Harley.

"Right this way," Benny said, leading Larry to the back of the mechanics bay. "Will this do?"

Larry stared down at the itty-bitty pale green Vespa and sighed. What the fuck was going on with his life? "Not quite the image I was looking for," he said.

"For a guy who managed to pick up two hot babes at a hostel, I don't think you need to worry about how you look. Anyway, it's all I've got."

"Benny, you're right. It might even be better if I'm not out on a flashy hog." Thinking it might belong to Benny and he'd offended him, he quickly added, "This isn't yours, is it?"

"Nah. Belongs to a guy who lives in town. He's kind of an asshole. Didn't want to leave his scooter at his apartment while he went on vacation to Cabo. I agreed to watch it before I got any money out of him. I have a feeling he's not going to pay me.... Hey, but that doesn't mean I want any trouble from the law."

"Look, Benny," Larry said reaching to pull out his wallet, "here's a hundred bucks. I'll get it back to you tomorrow unless I need it for one more day. Then I give you another hundred."

Benny sized up the man before him. If he'd wanted to steal the scooter, he could have easily done it when Benny was helping a customer. Besides, if for some reason he didn't return it, he'd claim that was what happened. After all, the jerk had left the keys with the Vespa. He reached over and took the bill.

"Key's in the ignition. Helmet's on the seat. I didn't even see you." Benny walked back out to the front of the garage.

Larry wheeled the Vespa outside and was deciding whether or not he really had to use the helmet. It was too damn hot to have his head trapped in the thing, but he didn't need any cops pulling him over asking for license and registration. He put on his shades, swung his leg over the scooter and reluctantly threw on the helmet without bothering to fasten the chin strap.

He turned the engine over, listened to the pitiful putt-putt and shook his head. It would only be for a day; two at the most. He could do this. He revved it once and headed out onto the street, planning to do a test run around town to get the feel of it.

Passing in front of the hostel, Larry suddenly pulled over to curb, jumped off, and took up a position behind a palm tree. What the hell was that damn surfer van doing in front of the hostel? He knew damn well it was the one that had been parked at Pia's hideout, right next to the sports car. About to take off the helmet and sun glasses, he realized it was pretty good cover. Even so, he kept his body hidden.

Pia, clear as day, sat in the passenger seat, all done up in the old lady outfit. The bald-headed surfer was behind the wheel. They were talking, but weren't making a move to get out. Then the side door slide open and Larry saw a well groomed man with a long ponytail step out, wave goodbye, and head into the hostel. He had no time to try and figure it out because the van was now on the move.

Larry hopped back on the Vespa and followed. With any luck, the surfer had been hitting the dope and so wouldn't notice the big guy on the small scooter following from a car back. He just hoped he wasn't headed for the freeway. Larry doubted he'd be able to keep up. He also hoped there were no tricky maneuvers to follow. This was all unfamiliar terrain and he could not afford to lose them.

~~~

A large group of brightly attired ladies, some accompanied by men in resort wear, spilled out of Tranquility Vacations and onto the sidewalk in front. The tour bus operator moved back and forth, stowing luggage beneath the bus.

Pia and Skip walked through the crowd and into the office. Anastasia stood behind her desk checking in passengers and handing out bus passes. She finished with a tiny gal dressed in a bright orange and magenta shorts set and caught Skip's eye.

"Skip, Pia, I've got your travel documents right here," she said. "Pia, let me see your passport so I can record the number." She held out her hand.

This was not something Pia had even considered. What if this fake passport belonged to someone on a no-fly list? Or any other kind of a list, for that matter.

"Do you really need to record it?" she asked.

"Don't worry. They rarely do anything but glace at the list."

"What if they decide to check this time?"

Anastasia opened the passport and wrote down the information. "Then let's hope Carl doesn't have anything on him."

There wasn't much Pia could do. She'd gotten this far and there was no turning back. "All right. Here's to hoping Carl isn't on the FBI's most wanted list." She raised her arm in a mock toast.

"Skip?" asked a man from behind them. Skip turned around. "Skip of *Skipper of the Seas*?" Skip nodded. "Ladies, look who's here? It's the Skipper himself!" The man wrapped his arms around Skip and held him a few seconds before letting go and backing up a few steps.

"Don't you recognize this?" said the man, indicating his outfit of turquoise cotton cargo pants and matching parrot-print shirt. "It's from your *Paradise Blend* collection. I have two more in different colors."

"Of course I do," said Skip, reaching out to shake the man's hand, "it's still one of our best sellers."

By now, a small crowd had gathered around Skip and Pia, at least half of whom were donning Skip's outfits.

"Anastasia," called out a woman in a Skipper of the Seas fitted caftan in earth tones shot through with gold, "you never told us you knew Skip. Why haven't you sponsored a fashion show? Or let us know you even knew him?"

"People," she answered, "the bus is leaving in three minutes. We'll discuss a fashion show when you get back. Now please, go get onboard."

"Anastasia," Pia said before turning to leave, "I really like several of Skip's lady's ensembles. Why couldn't I wear one of those?"

"And then look like a girl?"

"Right," said Pia.

~~~

From a block down the street, seated in a covered bus stop, Larry watched the tour group file onto the bus. Shit. How was he supposed to follow a whole bus? And where were all those flashy dressers off to? Things sure were a hell of a lot different down here. You certainly didn't see folks like that up in Monterey. Maybe they were going to Las Vegas. They always dressed weird out in the desert. But he'd be damned if he'd ride a motor scooter all the way to Vegas.

Once the bus had taken off, and the surfer had left, Larry sauntered up to Tranquility Vacations and went through the open door. He nearly fell over when he saw the spectacular gal behind the desk. Yeah, she was older than the Swedish girls, but just think of what she might know how to do! Before he had a chance to get too sidetracked, the woman spoke up.

"Can I help you?" she said, getting up from behind her desk. Holy shit! She was even better standing up.

"Yeah," said Larry, back to maintaining a professional air, "I was thinking of taking a little vacation and thought I might get some information. Just saw that tour bus leaving. Off to Las Vegas?"

"Oh no, they're going down to Puerto Vallarta and then on a cruise."

"All the way to Puerto Vallarta on a bus? Isn't that a long ride?"

"The bus trip is only to Tijuana. Flights are much cheaper once you cross the border."

"You don't say."

"We've got another trip going next week, if you're interested," Anastasia suggested.

"I was kinda hoping to take off before then. You know, a spur of the moment idea. Any way I could hook up with the group in Mexico?"

"I might be able to book you on the cruise, but I'd suggest you fly down to Mexico out of San Diego. And you'd have to purchase the cruise ticket from the Puerto Vallarta office. Do you want me to check on flights?"

Larry had no fucking intention of crossing the border. But if that's where Pia had slipped off to, he'd let Jack know and then head back home. No way was he going to take down the broad in Mexico. That's all he needed; to spend the next several years in one of those Mexican jails. But he might as well get flight information. Maybe Jack could send one of his San Diego friends down.

"Sure. Why not?" said Larry.

Anastasia typed away, printed out flight times, and handed the list to Larry. "You could get there tonight in time to meet up with the group for cocktails. Or even early tomorrow morning. The tour is spending the night in Puerto Vallarta before heading out on the cruise. The hotel and address are printed at the bottom."

Larry took the information, thanked Anastasia, and left.

As soon as Larry had walked outside, Arturo stuck his head out of the back room. "Is he gone?" he asked, still keeping his body out of view. "Check the street."

Anastasia looked out the window, saw no sign of Larry, and turned back to Arturo. "What's going on? Did you know him?"

"Where's Skip?" Arturo asked, ignoring her question and walking to the front of the store. "Did he head back to OB?"

"As far as I know," Anastasia answered, still confused. Arturo was now at the window making sure Larry was nowhere in sight. "Arturo. What is it?"

Arturo turned to face his friend. "I did promise Skip I wouldn't say anything, but it looks like it's too late now." He moved away from the window, but kept the street in his line of vision. "That was Larry. He's a hitman from up in Monterey and he's gunning for Pia."

"What?" said Anastasia, taking a seat behind her desk. "Have a seat Arturo and tell me what's going on."

Arturo grabbed the chair in front of the desk and angled it towards the window before sitting down. "I don't really know all the details, but Larry's the reason Pia had to get across the border."

"Silly me." said Anastasia. "I only assumed the whole disguise business was because of a husband or boyfriend she was trying to lose." She closed her eyes in thought. "I must say that Pia certainly didn't strike me as someone who'd have a gangster after her."

"Me neither," Arturo agreed. "I have no idea why this Larry is trying to take her out, but he's serious about it. Now that he knows where Pia is, we've got to act fast."

"You get Skip on the phone," said Anastasia, "and I'll get in touch with one of my tour guides on the bus to give him a heads up." She continued before Arturo could object. "Don't worry. I'll only say to keep an eye on Pia."

Arturo took out his phone and called Skip.

"Skip, it's Arturo. Where are you?"

"Driving back to OB. What's up? Anything wrong?"

"A whole lot is wrong. I'm here at Anastasia's. I was in the back room a few minutes ago when some guy wandered in wanting to know about Pia's tour that had just left. I peeked out and guess who it was? ...Larry."

"*What*? Larry? How did he know where to find Pia?"

"I have no idea. But since Anastasia didn't know who he was, and I had to stay hidden, she told him where he could find Pia in Puerto Vallarta."

"Brother, we're really up a creek." Skip had pulled over to the side of the road as soon as he'd heard Larry's name. "Look, Brad's stationed at the hostel waiting for Larry, but I better go pick him up. We'll head back to my pad and reassess the situation. I don't like this at all. Mexico is out of our control."

"Yeah, I know. Hey, I don't know what I can do, but call me anytime."

"Thanks, brother." Skip disconnected and immediately called Brad.

"Dude, what's up?" said Brad. "Hey, you know any Italian? Got a couple of lovely ladies from Rome at the table with me. I told them I have a friend, so why don't you—"

"Brad, stop talking for a minute," Skip cut in. "We've got serious trouble. I'll be there in five minutes. Be ready."

"What about the babes......couldn't I hang out another thirty minutes?"

"No." Skip hung up and sped off towards the hostel.

"Bummer," Brad said to no one in particular.

25

Larry had driven down the street until he'd found a burger joint. All that outdoor time on the scooter had done nothing to cool off from the heat. He needed air conditioning and fortification before he called Jack and broke the bad news to him. He took his time eating a double cheeseburger and a large order of onion rings. Then he called Jack.

"Larry, you get the job done?" Jack asked as soon as he'd picked up.

"We got complications." Larry took a sip of his coke.

"What did you do now? Lose another gun? Get clobbered by a surfer?"

"Jack, I didn't do anything. It's Pia that did." He took in a deep breath before continuing, knowing Jack would blow his top with the news. "She's on a bus on her way to Tijuana and then onto a plane headed for Puerto Vallarta."

"I don't even want to know how you let her slip through your fingers." Jack paused for a moment and Larry felt it was better not to say anything. "Listen, there's only one choice, get down to Puerto Vallarta pronto. You speak Mexican, right?"

"Are you kidding? Go to Mexico?" Larry all but shouted into the phone. He should have known Jack would come up with an idea like this. "I'm not going down there Jack. It's too damn risky. Why don't you get those friends of yours to do it? Anyway, if the broad's south of the border, what harm can she do?"

"What can she do? What's wrong with you Larry? Too much sun? She can still screw up our whole organization. You don't think they have phones or the internet down there? I'm not asking you again. You do this or you're finished! Not just with your side jobs, but the whole Larry the Lawnmower business. You understand?"

Larry did indeed understand. With just a few phone calls to the right people, Larry could be out on the streets. Or in jail. Or dead.

"So if I go, how the hell am I supposed to take her out?"

"It's Mexico, Larry. Figure it out." Jack hung up. Larry sighed, got back on the Vespa and drove back to Ocean Beach.

~~~

"Darling," said the lady seated at the window next to Pia, "why are you dressed like that?"

Pia knew she was a little over-the-top for Ocean Beach, but compared to the people on the tour bus, she was one of the more sedately dressed passengers. The woman asking the question wore a black, sleeveless top, made of some sort of shimmery fabric, paired with form-hugging zebra-striped pants. Silver bangles hung around both wrists, matching her hoop earrings. Black eyeliner encircled her dark eyes.

"Is there something wrong with my clothing?" Pia asked.

"It's not the outfit.....it's just that I never expected a real girl to dress like that. You're pretty enough without all the makeup. In fact, I'd be willing to bet you look much more attractive sans the getup."

"You mean you can tell I'm not a guy?" she asked.

Her seat partner let out a throaty laugh. "Obviously." She noticed Pia's sudden look of concern. "Don't worry, my dear, you're secret's safe with me. By the way, my name's Matilda."

"I'm Pia. Thanks for not telling anyone, but if you could spot a phony, what's to stop the others? Or the customs agents at the border?"

"Oh, all the other ladies on this bus could make you from a block away—but that's because we know what we're looking at. I can guarantee that no one at the border, on either side, will give you a second look. To them, we're simply a bus full of loonies. They don't like to look too closely or their co-workers tease them about being interested."

"So you've done this trip before? Do they really not check ID that closely?"

Matilda sat back in her seat and really gave Pia a good look. "What, exactly, are you hiding from?"

"It's rather complicated," she said. "Let's just say that the ID I'm carrying doesn't really look like me." She hoped that would be enough information for Matilda.

"Is that all you're worried about? Your passport picture? Honey, *none* of us resemble our photos when we're dressed for travel. Anyway, I've been on a few tours to Mexico and they tend to wave us through. I've never heard of any problems."

It was a point Pia hadn't really thought about. Sure, she was dressed in drag, but so were more than half of the tour. Realizing that suddenly made it seem a lot easier. She hoped that once she got through the border and onto the plane, she might be able to relax. The thought of being detained by either the US or Mexican authorities was not something she needed to add to her resume. For now, she would just have to grit her teeth and hope for the best.

"Oh look," said Matilda, pointing out of the window, "we're almost at the border crossing. It shouldn't be long now and then it's only a quick ride to the Tijuana airport."

Soon the bus had come to a stop in the line waiting to go through border security. Pia leaned back and closed her eyes. If she couldn't see agents staring at her, maybe they couldn't see her. It must have worked because the bus was soon on the Mexican side of the border, driving towards the airport.

"Excuse me, Pia?" She opened her eyes to see the tour guide, Alejandro, standing over her in the aisle. She nodded but said nothing.

"I just got a text message from Anastasia. She wants you to call Skip." He handed her his phone and walked back to his seat.

"Oh dear," said Matilda, "I hope everything's OK."

"So do I," said Pia, punching in Skip's number.

"Skip, it's Pia," she said when he answered. "What's the problem?"

"Now don't get upset...but I have some bad news. Larry knows where you are and where you'll be staying in Puerto Vallarta."

Pia sat up straight in her seat and leaned forward, cupping her hand around the phone. "*What!*" she said in a loud whisper, her heart racing. "How is that possible?"

"I can't go into the details now. Brad's going to meet you at the hotel in Puerto Vallarta, but he probably won't be able to get there until tomorrow. You'll need to be on the lookout for Larry. We don't know if he'll actually come down there, but you have to remain vigilant."

Pia looked out the window and saw that they were pulling up to the sidewalk in front of the airport, giving her no time to mull over the latest developments.

"Skip, we're just getting to the airport. I have to go. I'll call when I get down there."

"Don't worry Pia, we'll figure this out," Skip said.

Pia hung up just as the bus came to a stop and briefly thought about what she would do next. Go into a panic or get off the bus? The latter seemed the only reasonable action, so she stood up and jostled her way through the happy group of travelers, hoping some of their joy might rub off on her. After all, she was on her way to the beautiful beach town of Puerto Vallarta, and what wasn't to like about that? She handed Alejandro's phone back, retrieved her luggage, and followed the cheerful group into the terminal with a somewhat renewed bounce in her step.

A short time later she was strapped into her seat soaring down the coast of Mexico.

~~~

Several hours later, it was Larry who was heading for Puerto Vallarta on a flight out of San Diego. He'd barely had time to rush into Kmart and buy some clothes, toiletries, and a small backpack to carry it all in. Then he'd rushed back to OB, checked out of the hostel, returned the Vespa, and grabbed a taxi to the airport. He got a seat on the next available flight and fell asleep as soon as he's cinched his seatbelt and leaned his head back.

~~~

Meanwhile, back in Ocean Beach, Brad and Skip sat in the patio of the house on Sunset Cliffs and worked out what they were going to do.

"I still think I should have taken the afternoon flight down to Mexico," Brad said. "I sure hope Pia will be OK until I get there tomorrow."

"She's a capable lady," replied Skip, "I wouldn't worry about her. Anyway, we need the time to come up with a strategy."

"I'm all ears, Skip. What did you have in mind?"

"Not much, really. I'm still waiting on a call-back from my Puerto Vallarta distributor. But we know where Pia will be for the night and she'll still be with the tour group so I'm sure she'll be fine. Then tomorrow morning you'll fly down and meet her. Does that work for you?"

"Sounds easy enough, but what about Larry? The dude could be lying in wait."

"That brother, you'll have to play by ear," said Skip. "If you don't see any sign of him, and if I can't get things worked out with my contacts down there, you and Pia should stay at the hotel for a night or two."

"What kind of place is this hotel?" Brad asked. "Is it close to the beach? Can I bring a surfboard?" If he was going to Mexico, he should be allowed to get in at least a few hours on the waves.

"Anastasia tells me it's a block back from the beach but you're not going surfing, Brad." His friend looked a little sad. "Hey, once this is all over, I'll set you up with some friends who own a surf shop in Mazatlan. Surfing's a whole lot better there. For now, let's go through my clothes and get you packed."

26

Pia was extremely happy to be off the plane and into the hotel. Thank goodness for small miracles like breezing through officials on both sides of the border. Matilda had been right about the lack of scrutiny on the part of customs agents. On the American side, the authorities appeared to be happy to get rid of the group. In Mexico, no one even looked her in the eye. She wasn't sure that this would have been the case had she been dressed in drag and travelling alone, but in a group it seemed to work.

The scenery on the ride in from the airport barely registered in Pia's exhausted head. The group's bus cruised through the outskirts of the city, on past giant resorts, and then into the older parts of the city. They passed by the Bay of Banderas, over cobblestoned streets, and squeezed into a narrow alleyway situated in Old Town Puerto Vallarta. From there, they walked around the corner to the hotel.

After checking in, Pia dumped her bags on the bed, ripped off her clothes, and jumped into the shower. Only after she got out did she realize that it might have been better to try and brush out her lacquered hairdo before throwing in the shampoo. Wrapped in a towel, she sat down on the bed and began to gently untangle the mess.

It was such a relief to be rid of the synthetic clothing and heavy makeup, and if she never put on clothes again it would be fine with her. Certainly the weather in Puerto

Vallarta didn't call for much in the way of clothing. Public nudity not really being an option, she slipped into a full-length, Indian skirt, and topped it with a cropped t-shirt.

Pia sat at the small desk and pulled out an international calling card. On Matilda's advice, she'd bought one at the front desk before going up to her room. She wasn't really sure that she even wanted to talk to Brad back in San Diego. She felt completely safe here so why ruin it by hearing what really might be happening with Jack Houston's minions? She picked up the phone and started to punch in numbers three times before finally calling Brad.

"Brad, I'm here," she said when he picked up, remembering not to mention country or hotel. She was sure it wouldn't matter, but keeping Brad calm was important.

"We've been worried about you Pia. Not that anything's happened, but I don't like the idea of you being all alone down there."

"I'm not alone. This hotel is packed with tourists and the travel group is here until tomorrow. It's much safer than in California." Pia wished she could convince Brad to stay in Ocean Beach. "As a matter of fact, I really don't think you need to come down. I can handle this by myself."

"No way girl-dude. I've already bought my ticket. It's nonrefundable. I'll get to the hotel tomorrow in the early afternoon. Hang on...let me get the flight information." He gave Pia the details and then continued with his warnings. "Now make sure you don't leave the hotel until I get there, OK?"

"Sure Brad. That's what I'll do." She hung up, picked up her handbag, threw on her flip-flops and headed out. Spend the day in a hotel room while Puerto Vallarta beckoned? No chance of that. Anyway, if she got shot on the beach, at least it would be a lovely place to die.

The hot sun felt absolutely fantastic, but even with sunglasses Pia found herself squinting. She popped into the nearest souvenir stall, purchased a floppy brimmed hat, and then continued on her way.

From there she strolled down to the beach, walking along the edge of the sand and letting the water brush over her feet. The aroma of shrimp grilling caught her nose and she made a beeline for one of the seafront eateries a few yards away.

With a plateful of shrimp in front of her and a beer in her hand, Pia could almost imagine that she had come to Puerto Vallarta on vacation. She concentrated on the sounds of the waves breaking on the shore, the ocean breeze rustling through her hair, and the brilliant sun warming her body. She might just stay at the restaurant all afternoon.

~~~

Larry arrived in Puerto Vallarta just as the sun was setting. Once through customs, he walked over to the airport taxi booth, handed his hotel information to the lady behind the counter, and paid the fare. A young man escorted him to the taxis lined up outside, ushered him into the one in front, then handed the hotel information to the driver. Had Larry known it was this easy to navigate a foreign country, he might have ventured abroad before now.

The weather was even hotter and muggier than in San Diego, and the taxi was like an oven. Fortunately, as soon as he'd closed the door, the driver cranked up the A/C. Leaning back against the seat, he tried to rid his mind of Jack's warnings by concentrating on the music coming from the radio. He thought he caught a word or two that sounded familiar. Maybe his Spanish wasn't as bad as he thought.

Larry's taxi stopped in front of his hotel, a street lined with cafés, bars, and tourist shops. He stepped out, walked around a few sidewalk tables and strolling tourists, and then into the hotel.

Walking into the lobby of The Golden Pineapple, Larry immediately noticed that something was off. It took him a few seconds to realize that there were no women in the lobby and that men held hands with other men. The guy getting in the elevator had just copped a feel of the man beside him. Shit. No wonder he'd never been to Mexico. He pulled out the slip of paper that the gal at the tour shop had given him to make sure he was in the right place. He was.

Maybe he should look for a different hotel. But what did he know about the area? No, the best thing to do was check in, relax a while, and then go look for Pia.

"Hi there amigo," Larry said to the young man at the reception desk, "I need a room."

"Certainly. How many guests?"

"Just me."

"And how many nights? We're running a special—book three nights and get the fourth for free."

"Just one night for now. Tell me, I'm supposed to meet up with a tour group from San Diego. Do you know where they are?"

"Oh yes, the tour from Tranquility Vacations has already checked in. They'll be meeting on the rooftop lounge at seven o'clock...sundown cocktail hour." He looked up at the lobby clock. "That gives you about an hour, but I'm sure they'll be up there until quite late."

~~~

Pia had stayed on the beach for a couple of hours before returning to the hotel, where she set about reading the airline magazine and all the tourist brochures on the hotel desk. Once she finished those, she got up and paced around, looked out the window, and then flopped back down on the bed. Boredom was not something Pia handled very well. It would be a long time before the morning and sitting in her room until then seemed neither pleasant nor practical. She wasn't really in the mood for the Tranquility Vacations rooftop get-together, but it would use up some time before going to bed. Somewhat reluctantly, she got up, threw on lipstick, clipped her hair up, and headed for the roof.

"My, but you look *so* much better in those clothes!" called out a voice to her right. Pia turned to see Matilda, her seatmate from the bus and plane, sitting on a rattan chair. It appeared that the entire tour group was there, either milling around under the awnings, or sitting out in the sun.

"Darn, you can still tell it's me?" asked Pia, taking a seat next to her. Maybe she wasn't as safe as she thought if she were so easily recognizable whether in disguise or not.

"Darling, we *all* know it's you," Matilda replied. "Don't worry….no one will even mention it. In our circles, it's something that just isn't done. But aren't you worried that someone you don't want to recognize you will?"

Pia shook her head. "I don't think that will be a problem here. Or at least for now I hope it's not." A waiter came by handing out speared chunks of fruit. "I have to tell you, it's such a relief to get out of those clothes and makeup." She noticed that her friend was now in a new outfit more fitting for the tropics, but still laden with makeup. "How is it you manage to keep it up? Especially in this heat?"

"It's a badge of honor," Matilda said. "And now I think it's time to mingle." She stood up and took hold of Pia's arm. "You have to try the cocktails here, they really are the best." She steered them towards the bar. "I know it's terribly cliché, but I'd suggest the margaritas."

~~~

After taking a long shower and dressing in his new black cargo shorts and sleeveless muscle shirt, Larry set out to locate Pia. He was pretty sure she didn't know what he looked like, but didn't want to take any chances. Before heading up to the rooftop lounge, he walked up the street a block and purchased a black visor with Puerto Vallarta emblazoned on the headband in bright rainbow colors. Not his style, but it shaded his face, especially when he put on his mirrored aviator shades.

By the time he got back to the hotel lobby, it was just past seven-thirty. Larry rode the elevator up to the rooftop.

He stood at the entry way for a few moments scanning the crowd. There was no way Larry could tell if this group of crazy-looking ladies and men were the ones from the bus in San Diego. He had to trust what the guy had told him when he'd checked in, and that this was Pia's tour group. His mission was to find her and if she were here, that wouldn't be a problem. He searched around the crowd and was about to give up when he spotted her standing in the corner talking to a small group of those gals. Hell, she wasn't even in the crazy get-up anymore.

The problem now was what to do. First of all, he needed to find out her room number and then come up with a plan....like calling Jack and telling him where he could find her so someone else could take care of the situation.

Several staff members, many of them young men in shorts and sleeveless t-shirts, moved in and out of the party-goers delivering drinks and passing out appetizers. One in particular kept glancing his way and smiling. This had been happening since he'd arrived at the hotel. Lots of guys gave him nods of approval. Not that he would ever do a dude, but he had to admit it was good for his ego.

The next time the waiter glanced his way, Larry gave him and wink and beckoned him over with a nod of his head.

"Yes, sir, what can I do for you?" He stood way too close for Larry's comfort, but it would have to be part of the game if he intended to get Pia.

"There's a gal over there who's not dressed like the others—long skirt, not too much make-up. Ya know who I mean?" Larry nodded in the direction of Pia.

The waiter glanced over. "You mean the straight lady who likes the gay men? I noticed her when she came in." He shrugged his shoulders. "We get them sometimes."

"Maybe you could find out what room she's in," Larry said in a low voice. "I could make it worth your while."

The waiter moved in even closer and ran his hand up Larry's leg. Larry barely flinched. Christ, if his buddies could see him now, standing there like nothing was going on instead of decking the guy, his rep would be gone for good. But Larry kept his cool.

"I was thinking more in the way of fifty bucks US. That sound all right to you?"

The waiter quickly retracted his hand. "I get it. You're into the girls." He took a step back and scrutinized Larry. "So why are you staying at this hotel?"

"I figure it's a great place to meet ladies and I don't see a whole lot of competition around." Larry's quick mind worked even south of the border.

The waiter laughed. "I like the way you think. I can get you the room number in a few minutes." He gauged

Larry's reaction a moment longer. "Are you sure that's all you want?"

"That's it. I'll just wait down in the lobby." He palmed the waiter a fifty. "Thanks amigo."

"My name is Pepe," the waiter replied. "Don't worry, you can count on me."

On the elevator down, Larry ran through what he would say to Jack when he called in with Pia's exact location. He had a sinking feeling that it wasn't going to do much good. If Jack had had contacts down in Mexico, he wouldn't have needed Larry to fly down here in the first place. Yeah, he needed to come up with a few plan B's. Maybe that waiter knew of someone who could take care of it for him. *Christ!* What the hell was he thinking? Hiring a sub-contractor? In Mexico? The elevator came to a halt and Larry stepped out into the lobby and made a beeline for the bar. He needed a drink.

Larry was half way though his Corona when Pepe the waiter sidled up alongside him and laid a folded piece of paper on the bar.

"That was quick," said Larry, glancing at the room number and then slipping it into his pocket. You sure didn't get service like that back in California.

"If there's anything else you need, just ask," said Pepe.

"As a matter of fact, there is." Larry took a swig of his beer. "I was thinking it might be better if I waited to make my move until tomorrow. I mean the gal just got here and I don't want to seem pushy. Any way you can let me know when she comes downstairs tomorrow morning?" He'd already figured Pia would most likely stay in for the night. And he could always make an anonymous call to her room to check if she was there.

"For a price, I can do anything," Pepe smiled.

Larry handed him another fifty and told him his room number. "You call my room as soon as you know anything, got it amigo?"

The fifty had already disappeared into the waiter's pocket. "Got it, señor."

Larry watched the waiter disappear, hoping he hadn't just been scammed out of fifty bucks. Then he turned to the bartender and ordered a shot of tequila. He'd need something stronger than a beer before calling Jack.

He tossed back his shot, backed it with the rest of the beer, and pulled out his phone. And then he just stared at it, not wanting to make the call. Fuck it. What could Jack do other than yell? And when was it that Larry had turned into such a pussy that he was too scared to make a phone call anyway?

He punched in Jack's number and hit the dial button. Next thing he heard was a recording of a women's voice speaking Spanish. Shit. Where had that waiter gone? Larry looked around but only saw the bartender. He watched the man finish serving a drink and then waved him over.

"Amigo, I need some help with Spanish." The bartender nodded, waiting for him to continue. Larry hit redial and put it on speaker. Soon the recorded voice came on.

"Sorry, my friend," said the bartender, "but it says that your phone doesn't work here."

That didn't make sense. He'd seen all sorts of tourists using their phones.

"So how do I call the US?"

"Either buy a Mexican phone or get an international calling card. They sell both in the lobby."

Larry decided he wasn't going to do either of those things for now. If he couldn't call Jack, Jack couldn't call him. It gave him more time to come up with a way to either get Pia or get out of this contract.

"I'll take another shot," he said, slapping a twenty down on the counter. He'd like to have gone out and explored the waterfront, but keeping Pia within range was more important at the moment. He'd hang out in the bar for a while then head up to his room to watch TV.

27

Pia awoke the next morning feeling surprisingly rejuvenated. She'd only spent about an hour at the rooftop party before heading back to her room, flipping on the TV, and almost immediately falling asleep.

She took a shower, threw on a sundress, and headed down for breakfast. There'd been no signs of Larry, but that did nothing to alleviate her fears that he could pop up from behind a palm tree at any minute.

It had taken several cups of coffee and a plate of eggs and tortillas before Pia had decided on what to do. The best thing was to check out of the hotel at noon and wait for Brad in the lobby. Once he got there they could move to another hotel.

Pleased with her new strategy, and just about to get up from the table, Pia suddenly noticed a sleazy-looking man smoking cigarettes and drinking coffee at a side table. *Darn.* Just because she hadn't seen Larry didn't mean that there wasn't someone else looking for her. Jack and Bernie knew where she was, right? They could have gotten in touch with some other criminal type right here in Puerto Vallarta.

Pia shook her head, pushed her chair back, and stood up. She was reading entirely too much into every little thing she saw. It was better to ignore these types of thoughts and try to enjoy the sights and sounds of Mexico. Hopefully, those would not include gun shots.

Before going back up to her room, she walked to the corner bookstore she'd passed the day before and picked up some light reading. She intended to spend the next several hours lounging in the comfortable lobby of the hotel, lost in a book.

~~~

It was just after two in the afternoon when Brad sauntered into The Golden Pineapple. He spotted Pia stretched out on a sofa as soon as he walked in and quickly made his way over.

"Girl-dude," he asked, "what are you doing out in full view for all of Mexico to see? I thought you were supposed to be keeping a low profile."

Pia put down the book she'd been reading and swung her legs off the lounge. "Hi Brad. How was the trip?"

Brad sat down next to her. "Again, why are you hanging out where anyone can see you?"

"Even if Larry were here—and I haven't seen any sign of him—what's he going to do in the middle of a hotel lobby? I'm safer here than most places."

"I think holed up in your room would be a whole lot better choice."

"I'm fine here. Anyway, I've already checked out.

"You checked out? How come?"

"Because if Larry does know where I'm staying, and he does come down to Puerto Vallarta, I don't think this is a good place to be. So I decided to wait until you got here and then we could find another hotel. Maybe somewhere not on the main strip."

"Well, at least we have that part taken care of. Skip got in touch with Fernando, that's his clothing distributor friend, and we're supposed to meet him at his store in about two hours."

Wonderful. Someone else she'd have to worry about.

"Brad you know I don't like the idea of involving anyone else. And anyway, what's Fernando supposed to do?"

"Nothing but find us a place to crash. Skip didn't give him any real details. Just told him you needed a contact and maybe a hideout." Brad's stomach growled. "Sorry about that. I haven't eaten today and no way was I buying that garbage food they sell on the plane. Think maybe we can get us some fish tacos down on the beach?"

"Sounds good to me."

Pia was very happy to get out of the lobby and do just about anything other than talk about her current predicament. Keeping up her carefree persona for Brad's sake was no easy task, but it seemed to be working. Brad was thinking about food instead of a hitman. And she honestly hadn't seen any signs of Larry...not that that counted for much. Back in California she'd never seen him, but apparently he'd had no trouble in finding her. She didn't want to think about it anymore, at least for now. Anyway, it would be much easier to get lost in a crowd on the beach than in a hotel lobby.

The two friends walked a short way up the beach, past a few restaurants, and decided on a place that was more rustic than fancy. Like all the other eateries, it hugged the beach along the shoreline, but this one had worn, umbrella-covered plastic tables and chairs set directly in the sand. They happily plopped down, picked up the menus, and ordered a table full of food and drink.

"This ain't a bad hang-out, Pia," said Brad, finishing off the last of several tacos and a bowl of guacamole and chips. He reached for his beer and gazed out at the beach and water in front of them. "Don't see any reason to rush back to California."

"If I could forget about the past week of my life, I might just agree with you," said Pia. "Unfortunately, it's a little hard for me to truly enjoy all this tropical splendor at the moment." She played with a tortilla chip. "Brad, you shouldn't have come down here."

"What? And miss out on a trip to Mexico? Girl-dude, I wouldn't have passed this up for anything!"

"Even if it means getting thrown in a Mexican jail?"

"Why would that happen? If Larry is stupid enough to come after you with a gun down here, I'd say he's the one the *Federales* will be hunting." Brad picked up his beer and drained the last drop. "Think it's late enough in the day for a shot of that good local tequila?" He looked at Pia, but she was staring out at the water, lost in her thoughts. Maybe he'd wait until they met up with Fernando.

Pia opened her bag and pulled out the tourist map she'd picked up at the hotel and laid it out on the table. "So where is Skip's friend's place of business?"

Brad reached into his pocket and took out a piece of paper with the information. "Skip told me it's right on this Malecon thing." He looked down at Pia's map. "Hey, it's just down the way. We can walk there in no time. Are you ready?"

Pia scooped up the last bit of guacamole, popped it in her mouth, and stood up. "Let's go," she said, grabbing her belongings.

They walked a short ways on the beach before turning onto a concrete path that fronted more restaurants, hotels and condos. It took them on a footbridge over the Rio Cuale, then on past more commercial buildings until they reached the main section of the Malecon.

The Malecon, the broad, pebble-paved pedestrian strip, ran along the water's edge of the Bay of Banderas. Wide enough to accommodate a marching band and long enough to get in a good stroll, it was indeed a lovely place. Gardens of palm trees and plants, sprinkled along the way, added to the tropical beauty. Massive brass sculptures by well-known artists dotted other areas on the route. To their left, the walkway edged along the seawall, dropping down to rocks and sand and the rolling tide.

They'd been walking a while when Brad stopped and turned towards the buildings that ran along the street, across from the Malecon.

"There it is," he said, pointing to a shop over a nightclub. "Just in time, I'd say. It's kinda hot out here and I think we could both use some shade."

"You're sure this is OK?" Pia asked, looking up at the bright blue *Fernando's Surf Den* sign. "We're total strangers, remember. Maybe Fernando was just being polite to Skip. Maybe you should go up and I'll just keep walking and find a hotel."

"It'll be fine. If we get some sort of bad vibe once we're inside, we'll leave." Brad waited for his friend to respond, but Pia said nothing. He gently placed his hand on her back. "Let's go."

The two story building below Fernando's housed a nightclub, with security gates pulled back to expose the entire, open-aired front of the establishment. Several umbrella-topped tables on the entrance patio remained empty. A short staircase ran up the middle, flanked by more outdoor tables. The club was painted black, inside and out, with several massive silver figurines flanking both sides.

Pia and Brad walked to the left of the club, up a narrow staircase, and into Fernando's Surf Den. From below, it had looked like a small shop squished on top of the club. Surprisingly, it was a rather spacious. Surf boards lined one wall, bikinis and swimwear along another. Suntan lotion, beach balls, and towels filled display cases down the middle of the room and in the corners of the shop. A few small tables and chairs sat on an outside balcony with a view towards the Malecon and bay beyond. A makeshift lounge ran along the back wall of the shop, complete with a couple of sofa's and a flat screen TV playing a surfing video.

Brad headed straight for the surfboards and was about to pick one up, when a sales rep approached.

"That's a great board," he said to Brad, "but I have a better one."

"I can see you do," Brad replied, acknowledging a board to his right. "But I guess I should meet your boss first. I'm looking for Fernando."

Before the employee had a chance to respond, a man walked out to greet them.

"You must be Brad and Pia. I'm Fernando."

~~~

Larry sat down on a bench to the left of some weird, alien-looking brass sculptures on the Malecon. Thanks to Pepe the waiter, he'd been able to track Pia and the surfer from the hotel, down to the beach, and then to some surf shop. Great. Now what the fuck was he supposed to do? He'd followed her to Puerto Vallarta, just like Jack had instructed. And he'd found out she wasn't alone, now that her surfer friend had joined up. Boy—that had been a real shock. The guy had cleaned up, dressed up, and if Larry hadn't been staking out Pia, he might not have caught on that it was the surfer. It explained why he hadn't recognized him when he got out of the van at the hostel back in Ocean Beach.

None of this helped his current situation. He'd had a good night's sleep, eaten some damn decent food, and had found the target. But now he was stuck. There was no gun hidden in the waistband of his pants which didn't leave a lot of options. Larry didn't do strangulation. He didn't do knives…except in an emergency. And he didn't do crazy shit

245

like this south of the border. He sat there for a good fifteen minutes until his ass started to go numb on the concrete bench. Fuck Jack. He needed to think.

Larry crossed over the pedestrian walkway and continued his stroll past souvenir shops and restaurants, moving out of the way of scantily clad cruise ship tourists of all ages. His hand brushed the phone in his front pocket, and for a brief moment he thought of getting one of those international calling cards and phoning Jack. Fortunately, before he had a chance to do anything more, his eyes caught sight of a group of young babes giggling at the entrance to a corner store. He stopped.

Tequila and Cuban Cigars. Looked good to Larry. He sauntered over.

"You like to try primo Mexican tequila?" asked a young salesman before Larry had even reached the front door.

"Pal, I'm always up for a shot," Larry said smiling. He then motioned the salesman away from the boisterous young ladies. "Tell me amigo, what's up with the girls?"

"That, my friend, is a bachelorette party." Larry looked impressed. "It's a big thing now—weddings in Puerto Vallarta."

"Must be good for business....and maybe even for a guy like you."

The salesman winked. "Best job in town is right here." He poured Larry a shot and took him by the arm. "Let me introduce you to the señoritas."

Within no time, Larry found himself surrounded by bridesmaids, drinking tequila and smoking a Cuban cigar. He had completely forgotten about getting that international calling card.

28

Jack Houston felt his blood pressure rising by the minute. It'd been over twenty-four hours since Larry had headed down to Mexico and still no word. Once again, he had given him explicit instructions to stay in touch and his orders had been ignored. He'd even tried to call Larry but got a recording announcing the phone was out of range. Maybe he shouldn't have sent him down there, but what other choice did he have? He wasn't about to let Pia blow his whole operation after all his hard work. He'd spent years working with just the right clients until he'd secured a name for himself and finally arrived in the big leagues. Maybe it wasn't Atlantic City, but you couldn't get any better in Monterey, California. No way was he going to lose it all now and end up in San Quentin.

If he'd been a few years younger, well maybe a lot younger, he'd head on down to Puerto Vallarta to make sure things were taken care of. Jack knew he wouldn't be able to do that now. If only he had someone south of the border that could help.

"Bernie," he yelled at his partner walking by the open door, "get in here."

"Yeah Jack? What do you need?"

"What I need is a way to get in touch with Larry and find out what the hell is going on. You got any friends down that way?"

"My wife's aunt retired to Guadalajara about ten years ago, but she's old as the hills now and a little batty. She wouldn't be of any use."

"Christ, is everyone we know that old? I tell you Bern, this getting old ain't for people like you and me. We still got a lot of life left in us. Too bad we're surrounded by jerks."

"What about your friend Alan? He's in La Jolla, right? That's only a few miles from the border. He must have connections down there."

"True, but he sure screwed up with that gun supplier who turned out to know Pia. I don't know if I can trust him."

"Jack, you yourself said that it probably was just an oversight—nothing intentional. The way I see it, we don't have a lot of other options. At least give him a call and see what's up."

Jack looked up at the wall clock. "Tell you what, Bernie, let's go out for some chow and then I'll think about calling Alan."

~~~

It was just as well that Jack had decided not to call his friend in San Diego until after he'd eaten. Alan and Sid were too busy on the hunt for Arturo, which was not going well at all.

"Damn it Sid," Alan said, parked in his car in North Park. "How can it be this hard to find one turn-coat gun supplier?" They'd been driving around for several hours and it had gotten them no closer to finding Arturo than when they had started.

"Gee Alan, I just don't know," replied Sid. "Where is it we are now anyway?"

"North Park, just like I told you." Alan had quit worrying about Sid's confusion about their location. It didn't matter where they were as long as they could track down the little punk and teach him a lesson.

"Why would a gun dealer be in North Park?" Sid asked. "I'd think he might be down closer to the border….maybe Chula Vista or San Ysidro. Any place he could make a quick run for Mexico. Or maybe out in El Centro where he could hide in the desert."

Alan glanced at his friend, happy to see that Sid wasn't all that far gone after all. Seemed he still had a fair amount of reasoning skills.

"Sid, if he were a guy who'd had run-ins with the law before, or if he knew we were after his ass, I'd agree with you. But Arturo is clean. He only does this as a side job and not too often."

"So what's his main job? Couldn't we find him there?"

Alan was at a loss for an answer. He had no idea what Arturo did when he wasn't dealing in arms. Once again, Alan was reminded why he was no longer in the business. Back in the day, he'd never needed to go through a third party to find a contact. He'd have a file on anyone he'd even thought of hiring. He'd only driven out to North Park because a guy who knew a guy, who had an uncle there, had mentioned once seeing Arturo. And now he and Sid were sitting in a parked car with absolutely no idea where to go or what to look for.

"Sid, how 'bout we go back to your place and light up a few stogies and come up with a better plan."

"All right. Sounds good to me."

29

By nine o'clock that evening, only Pia and Brad remained in the Surf Den, the owner having already gone home to his house on the hill above Puerto Vallarta. Pia was grateful that Fernando wanted no details of her predicament. All he needed to know, he'd told her, was that she had to stay off the grid for a few days.

Nevertheless, she did not like the arrangement. It would have been better to find another hotel and keep Skip's friend out of it. But since there was nothing to be done about it until the morning, she'd been content to sit on the balcony and watch the sights while Brad talked surf stuff with Fernando and anyone who came into the shop.

Now, with the shop empty, Pia and Brad lay sprawled out on the sofas against the back wall. There was nothing of interest on TV and Pia had no desire to look at any more surfing magazines.

Pia had wanted to book into a hotel, but Fernando had assured her that staying at the Den was much safer. He'd pointed out that with all the security for the nightclub downstairs, she'd be much safer sleeping in the shop. It had made sense at the time, and had seemed like a good enough arrangement until the sun went down and the music cranked up downstairs in the club.

"Brad," said Pia, after about an hour of the incessant racket, "I don't know how much longer I can take techno beats ringing in my ears and shaking the floor. I don't think there's a two a.m. curfew here. This could go on until dawn."

Brad tossed down the magazine he'd been reading. "I'd have to agree with you on that, my friend. Not quite the mellow beach atmosphere I'd been looking forward to."

He stood up and walked to the front of the shop and out onto the balcony. Below he saw a line of people waiting to get into the club. Across the way, families strolled along the Malecon with the Bay of Banderas in the background and a star filled sky up above. With such a beautiful sight, Brad was itching to get out of their make-shift safe house and enjoy the exotic atmosphere.

"Girl-dude," he called out to Pia, "come and take a look at this."

Pia walked out to join him. "It almost makes you forget the noise below us. I'd love to take a walk along the Malecon."

"Don't know if that would be the best idea. We'd be sitting ducks….but how about we take a little trip down to the club?"

Pia still didn't believe that anyone had tracked her to Puerto Vallarta. And even if Jack and Bernie knew she were there, it wasn't exactly like any of their cohorts knew the lay of the land and where to find her. Looking out at the families and tourists walking along the Malecon, she was sure she would blend right in and look like any other visitor. Arguing with Brad about it would not do any good. Subterfuge seemed a better idea.

"OK Brad, the least I can do is buy you a drink."

Inside the club, just as Pia had imagined, was far worse than being in the shop above it. Her ears ached with every beat of ear-splitting music. There was no point even trying to talk to anyone. She motioned Brad over to the bar, set him up with a shot and a beer, then yelled in his ear that she was headed for the ladies.

Squeezing her way through the crowd of writhing bodies, Pia made it back to the entrance. After a few breaths of fresh air, she crossed over to the Malecon to join the pedestrians for an evening stroll. She knew Brad well enough to know that he would not notice her missing for at least half an hour. And she planned on stretching that to an hour.

Young couples, families with small children, groups of teenagers and tourists, meandered along the Malecon. Some stopped to buy food from street venders and then sit on the benches looking out over the bay. Others gathered around the many brass statues sprinkled along the route taking photos and making silly faces. Pia took it all in, loosing herself in the moment, feeling as if she didn't have a care in the world.

That is until she detected some movement behind her, and something caught her eye. A man who had been sitting in the shadows of one of the small gardens suddenly jumped to his feet and flew to where she was standing a few feet away. Before she had a chance to react, he grabbed her arm.

"*Gottcha!*" Larry yelled, swinging Pia around to face him.

Pia, reflexes kicking in, quickly punched him in the stomach. It didn't really hurt Larry, but the unexpected assault startled him enough that he lost his grip. Pia broke free, spun around to her left, and took off heading back towards Old Town as fast as her flip-flops could carry her.

She crossed back over the street to the row of restaurants and clubs with only a quick glance behind her. Larry remained on the other side entangled in a crowd of young tourists taking group pictures. How in the heck had he found her? It wasn't something she could worry about right now. What she needed to do was get off the street.

Just ahead she noticed a corner restaurant with open windows covering both sides. Full of people, it was still far less crowded than the nightclub and had the added attraction of Mariachi music rather than techno-blast. She promptly headed for the entrance, stopped for a moment to compose herself, then walked up a few steps and into the restaurant.

Quickly surveying the clientele, Pia spotted a group of women in their mid-thirties seated around several tables by the front windows. Pitchers of margaritas and baskets of tortilla chips and guacamole covered their tables. Although younger than she was, they were old enough so that she wouldn't look completely out of place like she did in the club.

Here goes nothing, she thought, and walked over to an empty chair.

"Excuse me for barging in, but would you mind if I joined you for a few minutes?"

They may have had a few cocktails, but these women knew that something was up.

"Are you OK?" asked the woman with bright red hair to her right. The others immediately stopped talking and listened in.

"Some strange guy just grabbed me out on the street and I thought it would be a good idea to get inside and join a group."

Pia hoped she was doing the right thing. Had this been back in Monterey, she would never have sat down with a group of strangers. The rules changed in a foreign country. She couldn't see Larry being much of a real threat down here and the encounter had just proven her point. Had he really wanted to detain her out on the Malecon, he would have had no problem.

"What did he look like?" asked another woman from across the table. Her skimpy tank-top showed off well toned arms. "Local or tourist?"

"He's American, over six feet, solid build, mid-thirties. He was wearing dark shorts, a sleeveless shirt, and a visor."

"I'll just make a quick sweep of the premises," the muscle-armed lady continued.

"Please don't bother," said Pia. "I'm sure he's already lost interest."

"Maybe, maybe not. Or maybe he'll try to grab someone else." Saying nothing more, the woman walked to the front of the restaurant and out onto the steps.

"It really isn't necessary," Pia apologized to the rest of the group. "I'm sorry if I interrupted your meal."

"No problem," said the redhead. "We like to help out where we can. My name's Liz, and the gal who just left is Danni."

"I'm Pia." Liz then went around the table, introducing the other six women.

"I didn't see anyone fitting your description," Danni said, returning to the table. "But it doesn't mean he's not hiding somewhere, just waiting for you to leave. Best you stay with us for a while."

"If you're really sure you don't mind," Pia answered. "I hate to spoil your party and I certainly don't want to cause you any trouble." Looking at the ladies, she had no doubt that that trouble was the one that usually avoided them.

"Hell, it just adds to the exotic atmosphere," said Danni. "What do you think, girls?" She raised her glass in a toast. "Here's to a little more adventure!"

Pia liked this collection of bold women. She'd had a few friends like them in the past, but most had settled down into a more socially acceptable lifestyle. Just like she had. The thought of a life on-the-run began to sound rather intriguing, if this were an example of what she could expect. She was snapped out of her thoughts by the woman next to her.

"So what brings all of you to Puerto Vallarta?" she asked Pia.

"Oh, I just needed a few days away from my job...you know how it is."

"Boy, do I ever! Me and the girls try to get away at least once a year." She might have gone on, but Danni suddenly shot out of her chair, yelled something unintelligible over her shoulder, and the table instantly emptied. Pia ran after the women, now bounding down the steps and out on to the street.

"We got him, Liz," Danni called out, "but we need Pia for a positive ID."

Liz took Pia by the arm and steered her over to where Danni and three of the other women had someone pinned to the sidewalk.

"This him?" Danni called out, turning Larry's head-locked face towards Pia. All Pia could do was nod.

"Listen, a-hole," Danni yelled into Larry's ear, "you need to learn to leave ladies alone." She tightened her grip and Larry started to turn an unnatural color. "We're letting you go with a warning this time, understand?" Larry might have indicated that he did, were he able to move his head. Danni then nodded her head to the other ladies pinning his legs and arms. They all got in a few punches and then let him up.

Larry, eyes wide and coughing, backed up a few steps, then turned and quickly walked away from the restaurant.

"This calls for at least one round on me," Pia announced. Walking back inside the restaurant, she stopped by the bar and ordered two more pitchers of margaritas.

Once everyone had a drink, including Pia, she raised her glass. "Here's to the best bunch of new friends a person could have!"

"And here's to our new friend who added another story to our trip!" Liz added.

"You sure are a tough group of women," said Pia.

"Oh, this is nothing," said Danni. "We all skate together out of Tarzana. We're the top roller derby team in the area. *Jane's Revenge.*"

~~~

Pia hadn't enjoyed herself this much in years. She couldn't remember the last time she'd hung out with a group of women who really knew how to have fun. Their lives back home weren't that much different from other women their age. Married, divorced, single—several kids or none, jobs ranging from teacher to waitress to lawyer. So when had she changed so radically that she no longer knew how to live it up with a pitcher of maggies and some hilarious stories? Pia could have stayed with the group all night, but it was time to go back and find Brad before he did something stupid like call the American embassy and report her missing.

The women wanted to escort Pia back to Fernando's, but she insisted on going alone. With so many people out and about, there was no chance Larry would try another attack. Evidently he knew where she was spending the night, which was not a comforting fact. But that's the way it would be, at least for the night. And as Fernando had pointed out, the security guard for the nightclub would keep persons like Larry at a distance.

She found Brad sitting in front of the club, not at all pleased with her disappearance.

"Girl-dude! Where the hell have you been? I've been freaking out thinking that Larry had nabbed you."

"Let's go in Brad. I'll explain it when we get upstairs."

~~~

Larry sat at a table in the bar at The Golden Pineapple sipping on a tumbler of iced rum and coke. He could still feel where those crazy women had punched him, and rubbed his hand over his neck. He'd known that this whole idea of following Pia to Mexico would be a disaster and it was. From the get-go it had been a train wreck. He reviewed everything that had gone wrong since Jack Houston had first hired him to get rid of Pia. Nothing, absolutely nothing, had gone right. He didn't need this. He had a good life back in Monterey. Had a nice wife, a good lawn maintenance business, good friends, a nice house. Yeah, the extra money from the side jobs was great, but he needed to re-evaluate what he had thought was excitement. This was not excitement. This was humiliation. Once more he pictured himself rotting in some disgusting Mexican prison while Jack lived it up in Monterey.

"So how did it go with the lady?"

Larry turned to see Pepe, the waiter who'd supplied him with Pia's information, standing next to him.

"Not at all well, amigo," he answered. "I'm thinking I need to make a change in my life."

Pepe moved in closer. "So maybe I can help with that?" He placed a hand on Larry's thigh.

Larry only shook his head. "Sorry amigo, it's just not my thing." Pepe removed his hand. "Got me a nice set-up back in California," Larry continued. "Even got a beautiful wife. I don't know why I even came down here."

"Maybe you are here to find answers," Pepe suggested.

"Answers?"

"Sí. Maybe you come here because you think the life is missing something."

Larry shook his head. "Not missing anything."

"But you say you have a beautiful lady at home. And then you are interested in the old lady in the bar. Why?"

"Can't really go into details, amigo. But I think you got a point. Maybe I'm too old for this life." He looked at Pepe. "Ya know, maybe you need to get out of the hotel business and work on one of those talk radio programs. Giving advice. You're pretty good at it."

"You think so? I never thought of that."

"Tell you what, partner," Larry said, signaling the bartender, "let me buy you a drink and I can give you some advice on going into business for yourself. You won't get in trouble for drinking with a customer, will you?"

"It is all part of the job," Pepe said. He took a seat next to Larry. "But maybe this time I will really get something out of this conversation."

262

~~~

That night, Larry slept like a baby. Pia and Brad had had enough cocktails to ensure sleep, if not sweet dreams. Alan was back at his house in La Jolla and Sid back at the retirement home. Jack had indigestion all night.

30

Sitting at the bar in Saul's the next day, Jack tried to forget all the shit that had gone down since Pia had butted into his affairs. His life had had its ups and downs but for the most part, it had been damn good. Yeah, there'd been the hassles that went along with his special clients, but nothing he couldn't handle. It kept him on his toes and added a whole lot of excitement to what could have been a boring profession. Damn; he hated to admit it, but Alan might have a point. Maybe he was getting too old for the business. And where the hell was the man anyway? He'd been trying to reach him for a couple of days but Alan wasn't answering his phone.

He picked up his cocktail and turned his attention back to the ballgame on the TV above the bar, not that Jack even knew the score or the inning. Just as a batter was starting to get into it with the home plate umpire, the ballgame was abruptly replaced by a multi-colored screen announcing *Breaking News.* Probably some more shit about a high-speed chase or a bomb going off in some foreign country. Jack reached for the bowl of pretzels and stopped mid-reach.

The live TV shot showed the commercial end of the Monterey Marina, not too far from where Jack was sitting at that very moment. With the volume on low, it was difficult to hear exactly what was being said. However the words *Drug*

Bust plastered below the newscaster were more than enough clear. Jack felt his heart begin to pound in his chest. The live feed continued, this time zooming in on the boat dock where three men in handcuffs were being escorted away by DEA agents. The man in the middle turned his head directly towards the cameraman, flashing a menacing stare. Holy shit! It was Joe!

Jack nearly started to hyperventilate. He was gonna kill Bernie for letting the man meet him at the office. If Joe hadn't gone there, Pia wouldn't have overheard the conversation that led her to stealing the files. Not only did the nosey broad have the files, she could now provide proof that Joe had been to the office, which would tie the firm to Joe's drug baron father. Jack sat on his barstool for another full minute before throwing some bills on the counter and casually leaving the bar.

Once outside, he walked down the pier and then onto the footpath leading to the parking lot. He checked that no one was around before grabbing a seat on a bench. He punched in the office number.

"Bernie," Jack said quietly when his partner picked up. "Listen to me carefully. You need to destroy the files right now, you understand?"

"Jack, what's up?" Jack's instructions belied his calm voice.

"Just do what I say and then turn on the news."

"You sure about this? You want me to execute the dump and destroy protocol?"

"We've talked about this Bern. We knew it could happen one day and there's no time to spare. Just get on it."

Jack was so calm sounding that Bernie wondered if maybe his friend was getting ready to faint.

"You OK Jack?"

"I'll be fine once you get on with what you're supposed to do. I'll be back there in a few minutes." He hung up before Bernie could ask anything else. Now was not a good time to be making calls. He did a three-sixty just to satisfy himself that no one was around. Then he headed for his car and drove off.

Too bad Jack hadn't been as observant back at Saul's where Bob had just watched enough of the newscast to get the gist of what was going on. A major heroin bust, details to follow. From the way Jack Houston had skedaddled out of the bar, Bob knew it had to be a bust of the infamous Fishing Run operation.

He walked to the phone at the end of the bar and made a quick call to Skip. The news probably wouldn't be covered in San Diego until the evening and someone needed to get in touch with Pia and Brad. No telling how this might affect them.

~~~

"What else do we need to do?" Bernie asked Jack while the two men hastily fed documents into the shredder. He'd already wiped his computer and destroyed the hard drive.

"I probably should get in touch with Larry and call off the hit, but since he's been dragging his ass since I first hired him to take care of Pia, I'm not in too much of a hurry. Let him sweat it out a little longer."

Jack leaned back in his chair and pulled out another cigarette. He'd bought a pack on the way back to the office. Bernie's eyes were burning from all the smoke, but the nicotine certainly seemed to be having a calming effect on his partner. In fact Bernie had never seen the man so relaxed, especially in view of the current situation.

"And what if he gets arrested down there? We don't need that Jack."

"Screw him," Jack replied. "He's fucked up the whole job since day one. Might serve his ass right to get busted down in Mexico."

"Maybe. But I don't think he'd keep his mouth shut, do you? We have enough to worry about on this side of the border."

"Yeah, I guess you're right," Jack said, getting up from his chair. "Problem is I can't get through to the guy. His phone don't work down there."

"Have you tried the hotel? Didn't he leave you with the information?"

Jack didn't like the idea of calling a hotel in Puerto Vallarta. Maybe they weren't as sophisticated as in the US. Maybe hotels down there didn't keep meticulous records of international calls. But why take the chance? Normally it would be something to avoid, however, it didn't look like he had much of a choice.

"OK Bern, I guess we got to take that chance."

Jack reached into the top desk drawer, rummaging around until he found the piece of paper with Larry's hotel in Puerto Vallarta.

"The Golden Pineapple." Jack said looking at the paper and shaking his head. "They come up with the damndest names down there." He picked up the phone and paused. "Bernie, what if they don't speak English? How am I supposed to get a message to Larry?"

"The hotel's name is in English, they deal with tourists all the time, so I wouldn't worry about it. At least give it a try."

Jack huffed, but dialed the hotel's number. He was surprised at just how good the receptionist spoke English, and how quickly he was put through to Larry's room.

"He's not answering Bern, what should I do? ....wait...it's asking me to leave a message. Think I should?" Bernie nodded his head. Jack put his hand over the receiver. "I sure hope you're right."

Jack cleared his voice before talking. "Just want to let you know that I won't be needing your services anymore." He was about to hang up but couldn't stop himself from adding a little more. "And I don't have to tell you not to fuck this up. Call me as soon as you get this."

~~~

"Girl-dude, maybe we got lucky," said Brad. "Maybe it's safe to go back to California."

269

Brad and Pia sat on the balcony of Fernando's Surf Den sipping coffee. They'd just spoken to Skip who'd told them about the drug bust back in Monterey. Brad had been waiting for Pia to say something but she just stared out at the ocean.

"Course, if you'd rather stay here a while, I think I could manage it." Brad had really taken a shine to Puerto Vallarta and was in no real hurry to leave. "No thoughts on the matter?"

Pia finally turned her head to face him. "We're not doing anything just yet. We don't know for sure if the heroin bust had anything to do with Houston and Melrose."

"You heard what Skip said. Bob saw Jack nearly keel over when the news came on the TV. Why else would your boss man react that way?"

Pia picked up her cup of coffee. "Maybe he had heartburn." She sipped some of the brew. "I at least want to wait until the police release some names. Better yet, wait until they pick up Jack and Bernie." She turned her head back to the view out over the water.

Even before they'd gotten the call from Skip, Pia had been mulling over her options. Staying off the grid in Puerto Vallarta had not been on the top of her list. Yes, she had files on her bosses that were awfully incriminating. And taking those files had led to threats on her life and a hitman on her trail. However, she couldn't put up with this type of life for very much longer. Again she reminded herself that she was not in some sort of movie where people simply disappeared off the streets. Did she really think Jack would have her killed, especially since she had evidence against him? Stay on the run or return to Monterey. Those were her only two choices.

"Tell you what, Brad," she said, "we'll give it until tonight and then I'm calling Jack's bluff."

"Bluff? Are you nuts? That gun in your front yard was no bluff!"

"Possibly. But no one used it. And what can Larry do down here? I bet Jack only sent him after me because he doesn't know anyone in Mexico. And what's Larry supposed to do? Buy a gun off the streets of Puerto Vallarta?" Pia shook her head. "No. If Larry had really wanted to harm me, he would have done it last night. I think he's having second thoughts about committing a crime in Mexico."

"So what do you plan to do? Go and ask Larry what he's up to?"

"Actually, that might not be a bad idea."

"No way, my friend. This is where I'm gonna get all tough on you. Talking to Larry is *not* an option. What if some of those *Federales* are on to him? Thought of that? We don't know how things run down here and we can't take the chance."

Brad had a point. Avoiding the police in California was one thing. And even if she did get arrested, at least there she had rights. That would not be the case in Mexico. As much as Pia wanted to take charge of the situation, the only real option was to wait it out a little longer.

~~~

Larry, eating lunch in the rooftop restaurant at the Golden Pineapple, thought about the message Jack had left on the hotel room's phone. The boss didn't need his services anymore. Did that mean Larry was a marked man? Not likely, since Jack Houston only had one enforcer and that was him. He also knew that Jack had no contacts south of the border, otherwise why would Jack have sent him down here? None of it made any sense.

Larry had spent several hours the night before talking with Pepe about life choices and options. It wasn't quite an epiphany, but Larry had evolved. Who would have thought that a simple contract on an aging broad would have led him on an inner discovery of what was important in life? Except for the fling with the gals in San Diego, he was beginning to think that he might be turning into a better person. He could never have imagined that not only would he hang out in a gay hotel, but that he'd have a meaningful conversation with someone like Pepe. And most importantly, he had come to the decision that he was hanging up the Berretta for good; at least for any illegal activities. He'd have to buy a new handgun of course, but that would be only for self-defense. And he had decided to give Jack a call and tell him all of this. Well, maybe not the part of befriending Pepe, but certainly his decision to quit the game.

Larry picked up his phone and the international calling card and punched in Jack's number.

"Larry, where the hell you been?" Jack said. "You get the message?"

"Yeah, boss, I did." Larry had already decided to wait for Jack to say what he had to before going into his rehearsed talk.

"Look, I can't go into details right now, but big things are going down up here. Let's just say that some fisherman down at the wharf got nabbed yesterday.....we're in the middle of tidying things up at the office. So you can just forget about our arrangement and head on back."

Larry could only assume that Jack was referring to a big drug bust. He quickly ran through how this could affect him. If Houston and Melrose were implicated in any of this, he could be screwed. At least for now, he wouldn't have to explain to Jack why he was getting out of the business.

"So I'm good to head home?" Larry asked, just to make sure.

"Yeah. And maybe don't call me for a while. I'll get back in touch if I need you."

Larry hung up, finished his meal, then headed down to the lobby to use the hotel's free computer. He needed to make sure that Jack wasn't setting him up. Once he found confirmation about a large drug seizure in Monterey, he was taking the next flight back to San José. Or maybe he'd have a celebratory margarita back up on the roof before packing his bags.

~~~

Alan and Sid sat at a booth in a Denny's in El Cajon. Another tip had them believing that Arturo lived in the neighborhood.

"Sid," said Alan, resting his fork on his plate, "I think we're on the wrong track. This sounded like a good lead until we got here. What are we supposed to do? Hang out drinking coffee until Arturo walks by? Not much of a chance of that happening."

Alan had been fairly sure that they were on a wild goose chase, but found himself enjoying the hunt, even with less-than-reliable information.

"I think your right, Alan. But it's been fun, hasn't it?"

"It sure has. And I really hate to give up on finding that punk, but what can we do?"

"You tell me, Alan. I'm happy to go along with anything you want."

Alan had been thinking about it and the only sensible thing to do was to call it off. For now. "I figure we lay low and wait for the next time we get wind of Arturo. He can't stay underground forever, you know."

"He's sure to slip up somewhere," Sid added.

Had either of the men known that Arturo was taking a much needed vacation in Palm Springs, and had never been to El Cajon in his life, they wouldn't have cared. It was better to think that they still had the skills to track down a man and bring him to his knees.

Alan looked at his watch. "Guess we'll call it a day for now." Sid looked a little sad at the thought of returning to his life in retirement. "Don't look so glum, Sid. It's not over yet. Just a little breather. Call me if you hear of any new sightings and I'll do the same."

"You can count on me, Alan."

31

Ray sat in his living room absentmindedly toying with his 16 Mile Drive Security badge, hashing through what his mother had just told him on the phone. He'd been watching the news coverage of the drug raid down at the wharf when she'd called asking what he knew he knew about it.

"What would I know about it?" he asked, rather confused. He didn't need to remind her that he still only worked for a lowly home security company. And why would his mother want information about a drug bust anyway?

"Well...." his mother started, "...remember that call I made to you several days ago? Asking about an APB on that accountant named Pia?"

Ray did, and also remembered thinking it was strange. Hell, he hadn't even known his mother knew what an APB was. But that was also the day after his unfortunate encounter with Officer Jackie up at the house where he'd found the Beretta. At the time, Ray was still so ticked off, that he'd all but forgotten about his mother's odd request.

"Yeah....I remember," he told his mom. "But what does that have to do with what went down at the wharf?"

He could hear his mother breathing, but she wasn't saying anything.

"Mom? You OK?"

"I hope so. But I'm worried I may have gotten you in trouble. Or maybe they'll just arrest me."

Ray sat forward in his Barcalounger. "Mom, what are you talking about? Arrest you for what?"

"Knowing a drug king pin."

Maybe his mom had been hitting the gin and tonics a little too often. Like she had when his father had walked out when he was in high school.

"OK," Ray said, "why don't you tell me what's going on?" When his mother didn't say anything, he continued. "How about you start with the call about the APB, OK?"

"All right…but first I should give you a little background. Back when I was working at the Chevy dealer's up in Seaside, I used to get lots of….how should I call them…colorful clients. There's a lot of money that flows through this area and some people knew we'd take cash and not ask too many questions. I was never part of that….I worked in sales only. Anyway, there was a man who used to come in now and then. I must have sold him at least three cars and he also brought in friends for more sales. His name was Jack Houston. He's accountant here in Monterey." At that point, Ray's mother stopped talking.

"OK. So you sold a few cars to an accountant. Like you said, nothing wrong with that."

"But maybe there was. These were cash deals, you know."

"Did you handle the cash, or make any special offers, or falsify records?" Ray asked, beginning to wonder if he really knew his mom as well as he thought he did.

"Of course not!"

"Mom, then you didn't do anything wrong. Anyway, you haven't worked there for a few years....and what's that got to do with the drug bust?"

"It has to do with me calling you about the APB. It was Jack Houston who called me and asked if I could contact you. I thought it was a little odd, but nothing illegal."

Actually, what Ray had done by giving her the details of Pia's APB really wasn't all that legal, but why scare his mom? "It was nothing. So why are you worried?"

"When I was watching the news just now, they showed video of a man being arrested down on the wharf. The newscaster said he was suspected of being a drug baron." His mother paused and Ray thought he heard a slight sob. "Ray, I know that man. His name is Joe. He was one of the men Jack Houston used to bring to the dealership. I sold cars to him, his father, and several others in their family. I sold cars to drug lords!" This time Ray really did hear his mother crying.

"Mom, mom, what are you worried about? You sold a few cars. It doesn't matter who you sold them to. There's no connection."

"Oh no? Then why did Jack Houston, out of the blue, call me and ask me to get in touch with you? It's too much of a coincidence. I don't hear from him for years, then he wants information about some felon the police are looking for, and then his friend gets arrested for importing drugs. I think I could manage a few years in the pokey—I've had a good life.

But thinking that somehow I've gotten my boy involved in all this is more than any mother can bear."

"Mom, you're worrying about nothing. Just forget this Jack Houston ever called you. No one's going to arrest you. Anyway, you can count on me and Cousin Jackie if anything happens. She's way up there in the force these days."

It took a good five minutes to get his mother calmed down, but eventually she agreed to not mention the call from Jack to anyone else, and to maybe stop watching the news for a few days.

And now Ray was faced with a very interesting situation. He thought about how he'd missed his chance for real notoriety when he'd found the Berretta. As much as he'd like to blame Cousin Jackie for that one, he grudgingly admitted that she was only doing her job. But it now seemed that he might just have an opportunity to change his luck. Maybe this really was the big break he'd been waiting for.

Could it be that Jack Houston not only knew the guy picked up in the drug raid, but kept books for him? It made sense to Ray. His mother was right, it was all too coincidental—the ABP on the lady with the Berretta, Jack Houston contacting his mother about it, and then Houston's associate getting nabbed for importing drugs. If this was all true, things might get a little dicey. Bringing down a drug lord's accountant was on a whole different level from finding a weapon. This was big time.

There had to be a connection between all of them and Ray was going to find it. It would mean finding a concrete link between Joe the-drug-dealer and Jack Houston, and then a connection to the lady named Pia.

Ray briefly considered calling his buddy Alvin, but seeing as how he'd cut and run as soon as things got a little sticky up at the house on the hill, he quickly dismissed the thought. This was going to be a solo effort. And no way was he going to call Officer Jackie this time.

Ray got up off the Barcalounger and paced around his small apartment trying to come up with how he was going to get the intelligence he needed. He already knew where Pia lived, and he could easily find out where Jack Houston worked, which was at least a starting point. From there on in, if he wanted to obtain the information he needed, it would all have to be carefully planned out.

He walked into his bedroom and pulled out the large whiteboard and markers he kept under his bed. He carried them back into the living room and hung the board on the hooks in the wall. Then he began to map out the connections he already knew about, and list possible means of getting further information.

It was going to be a long night, but Ray couldn't think of a better way to spend the evening.

32

"I can't take this any longer," Pia told Brad while they sat eating breakfast at a beach café. "We've given it a day, and now I'm making my move."

The two had spent the previous day anxiously awaiting updates from Bob and Skip on the state of the drug raid down on the wharf in Monterey. Between calls to California they'd checked the internet for any other possible information. But there had been no new information from any source—and no mention of Jack or Bernie. At least they hadn't seen or heard from Larry.

"And what move are you planning to make?" Brad asked.

"I'm calling Bernie and offering him a deal." Pia signaled the waiter for more coffee.

"How's Bernie going to be of any help?" Brad asked. He waited until their coffee cups had been filled. "Wasn't it Jack who was doing the threatening and then hiring Larry to take you out? Remember, I met Bernie. Don't think he holds a whole lot of weight at your office. That Jack dude seems to be calling all the shots."

"Not at all. Jack does all the talking, but Bernie's a full partner and makes a lot of the decisions. And I think I can reason with Bernie. Jack….I doubt he'd listen to me."

"Even so, what are you going to tell Bernie?"

"Easy. I'll give him back all the files I stole, but he's got to call off Larry and drop this whole fiasco."

Brad looked at his friend in disbelief. "Are you kidding? After all we've done, you're just gonna hand back everything?"

"Look Brad, they busted the dealers and that's what's important, right?" Brad didn't respond. "What do you expect me to do? I'm certainly not going to hide out for the rest of my life. This seems like the only logical trade-off."

"If you put it that way—the dealers getting busted, I kinda see your point. But don't you want to take down Houston and Melrose? I thought that was the whole point of this."

"The whole point was to stop the heroin from getting into Monterey." Pia sipped her coffee. "Anyway, the money trail should lead the authorities to Jack and Bernie. I think I'll let the professionals take care of that part."

"Do you have to call him right now?" Brad asked, looking out to the water. "I'd like to pick up a gift for my mom. She always did love Mexico."

"We've got some time. Why not enjoy a few more hours and try to forget about it all. Who knows what will be waiting for me once we get back home."

~~~

Larry walked out of the Golden Pineapple to grab a taxi to the airport. He took one final look at the hotel. Maybe he could bring the wife to Puerto Vallarta on a vacation one day. Of course, he wouldn't be staying at this hotel, but there were lots of nice places to choose from. Judging by the tourist brochures he'd glanced at, the area had a lot to offer. He was sorry he didn't get a chance to go to the botanical gardens or on a whale watching trip. Yeah, the little lady would love that.

~~~

Back in Monterey, at the office of Houston and Melrose Accounting, no one was feeling all that happy with life.

"Jack," said Bernie, "you've got to calm down." They were sitting in Jack's office, on their third pot of coffee. They'd been in until late the night before, and back again early in the morning.

"How can I calm down? There could be a knock on the door at any minute from the feds."

"There's nothing here to implicate us, Jack. But if they do drop by, and they see you this anxious, who knows what could happen?"

"You got a point, Bernie. But what do we do? Just sit around and wait?"

"That's exactly what we do. Carry on like it's any other day at work. We don't need to act like something's wrong."

The partners returned to their desks and concentrated on with their daily work. Thoughts of getting arrested had almost been shoved to the back of their minds while they went about totaling spread sheets and compiling expense accounts. And then, just past ten in the morning, Jack and Bernie heard the front doorbell ring.

Up until the day before, they'd never kept the door locked during business hours. But these were risky times; precautionary measures were needed.

"You got an appointment Bern?" Jack called out from his office.

Bernie was at his door in two seconds flat. "No. But let's not jump to conclusions. It could be anyone. You stay here. I'll get the door. It would be too suspicious if we both went."

Bernie unlocked and opened the door to see a medium sized man dressed in a leather jacket, blue jeans, and dark glasses. The man had a long moustache, and the strangest head of hair Bernie had ever seen. The shoe-polish-black mess stuck out on the top, was short on the sides, and brushed down the back of his neck. The whole outfit reminded Bernie of a cheap Halloween costume.

"Can I help you?" Bernie asked the stranger.

"I wants the skinny on setting me up a business account," replied the man.

Bernie squinted his eyes and turned his ear towards him, hoping he'd understood the man's odd speech. He wasn't their typical client, but times might be getting a little tough and any extra business would be welcome.

"A business account you say?" Bernie asked, and got no reply. "We can help you. Do come in."

Bernie stepped aside and the strange fellow entered the premises just as Jack arrived in the reception area.

"Maybe we's can talk in your office," the man said to Jack and Bernie. The partners didn't move.

"OK, let's just come to the point. I hears you know something about this raid down on the wharf," the man said.

Jack and Bernie stared at the guy. What kind of weird accent was that? And what was up with the handle-bar moustache that was peeling off the right side of his face?

"We don't know what you're talking about, pal," said Jack, easing over to the reception desk and feeling around for anything that could be used as a weapon.

"Didn't you mention something about needing our services," Bernie asked, keeping an eye on the door and possible escape route. This man was not acting rationally.

"You understoods me. Just tell me whats you twos know about that drug bust."

"I didn't get your name," said Jack, trying to stall for time. The only thing his hand had found behind the desk was some sort of small stuffed animal that belonged to his niece.

"My name? That's for me to know and for you to figure out."

The accountants looked at each other again, not quite sure where this was leading or what to do.

"Didn't you tell me that you wanted to set up an account?" Bernie asked. "How can we do that if we don't know your name?"

"I'lls makes it real easy. You tell me whats you know about the drug dealer, and I'll be outta here in no time."

"What we know about *what*?" said Jack, clearly starting to get ticked off at this clown who was wasting their time, whether or not he posed a threat.

"Don't tries to fool me, hombre. I knows you all are involved with that drug raid down on the wharf."

Jack had reached his limit. "Listen, punk, I don't know what you think you know, but you're barking up the wrong tree. We run a clean business here. Hell, look at us. We're a couple of old farts about to retire. We really look like drug dealers?"

"Maybe youse just is funning me."

That was it. Jack had had enough. He grabbed the man by the collar and pulled him towards the door. "I'm only gonna say this once, asshole, get the fuck out of my office and don't come back!" He then pushed the man outside, closed the door and locked it.

Jack put his finger to his lips and pointed to his office. Once he and Bernie were inside, Jack looked out the window to make sure the weirdo wasn't hanging around.

"What the fuck was that, Bernie?"

"I've got no idea. But he sure seemed to know something about our connection to Joe and his family."

"Nah," said Jack, sitting down in his chair and reaching for his pack of smokes. "That was no DEA agent. Wasn't even a local cop. Can't say I have any idea who he was."

"I agree. That was no law enforcement official." He thought for a moment. "My guess is that it's someone who knows Joe and his family. Probably trying to blackmail us. Fishing expedition only, I'd say."

"True, Bernie, that sounds reasonable. But even if he's just some low-level punk trying to wrangle a little extra cash out of us, we got to be careful. Maybe we should give Larry a call."

"I thought you were done with Larry. Why would you want to bring him in on something else?"

"You got a better suggestion?"

"Yes, Jack, I do. We wait this one out. That creep is obviously acting alone and doesn't have anything on us. Like I told you earlier, we have to continue like it's any other day and just forget about our connections."

"I sure hope you're right," said Jack, lighting up one more cigarette.

~~~

Back in his car, which he'd parked several blocks away from the Houston and Melrose office, Ray looked at himself in the rearview mirror. Damn! The moustache was half-way off his face and his wig was crooked. Nevertheless, he didn't think that the accountants would ever recognize him again.

Now what was he supposed to do? He'd hoped the direct approach would shake the men up and at least they'd make a slip-up. Maybe mention something useful. But they hadn't said anything of value. And he had nothing else to go on.

Ray drove home, got out of his outfit and sat on the couch. He hated to admit defeat, but what could he do? He was sure Jack Houston and his partner were involved with the drug cartel, and if he didn't let someone know they'd never be caught. He looked at his watch. Time was of the essence. As much as he detested the idea, there was only one choice—he'd have to call Cousin Jackie. Maybe this time she would credit him for his tip.

"Jackie," said Ray when the officer answered her phone, "It's Ray. I've got some important information to give you about that big drug bust that went down yesterday." He waited for a response, but there was none. "You know, the one down at the wharf?"

"Of course I know about it Ray, but why are you calling me?"

"I think I know two guys—accountants—who are tied in with it all."

He could hear his cousin exhale loudly. "Ray, that was a DEA bust. We knew about it, but weren't involved. If you've got information, give them a call."

It sounded like Cousin Jackie didn't quite believe Ray's story.

"Come on Jackie. You must know someone. If you don't do something, these guys will get away."

"Yeah, yeah....fine Ray....Oh, there's a call coming in from the station. Gotta go." Jackie hung up before Ray had a chance to say anything else.

He got up, went to the kitchen, and got himself a beer. For now, there wasn't much he could do. But he'd be damned if he'd forget about it. No, these drug dealer accountants were not going to get away with their involvement in trafficking in his city. Sooner or later, something was sure to tie them to the dealers. Ray was going to keep a close watch on the office of Houston and Melrose and this time, he'd be the one to take them down.

33

"Girl-dude, last chance...are you sure you want to go through with this?"

Pia and Brad sat on a bench at the far end of the Malecon, away from the busier section of the walkway. After breakfast, they'd spent a few hours looking at tourist shops and buying souvenirs for Brad's mom, Skip, and Bob. When they were done, Pia had decided it was time to make that call.

"It's my only option, Brad. As soon as I do this, we're booking a flight back to California." She pulled out her phone and calling card and punched in Bernie's number. "Wish me luck."

"Hello," Bernie said when he answered. He usually looked at the caller ID, but he was preoccupied with more important matters at the moment.

"Bernie, it's Pia." Bernie was half way out of his chair on his way to Jack's office and then thought better of it. He wouldn't be able to understand anything with Jack yelling in the background. Which is what he'd be doing if he knew Pia were on the other end of the line.

"Pia.....where have you been? We've been worried."

"Bernie, you know where I am so let's not play any games. I'll get right to the point. I'm calling because I want to make a deal."

"A deal?" Bernie paused a minute...maybe he should go get Jack. "All right, go ahead."

"Here's the proposition—call off your man, get Jack off my back, and I'll give you back your files and forget about everything I've seen."

"And how will we know if you're telling the truth? Maybe you'll hand that information over to someone else……not that you have anything on us."

"I'm talking to you Bernie, because you're not the loose cannon that Jack is, and because you know my work ethic and know I'm reliable. If I say something, you can trust me."

Bernie really was inclined to believe Pia, but it felt wrong to not first consult Jack. He thought about it for a second and made up his mind. To hell with Jack. He was making an executive decision, just like Jack had when he'd hired Larry.

"OK. I'll call off our man." Bernie saw no need to tell her that Larry's services had already been cancelled. "And I'll talk to Jack. But before I do that, I have to know when we get our files back."

"I can get them to you tomorrow morning. I'll give you a call and we can meet someplace public." She waited for Bernie to reply, but heard nothing. "So Bernie, do we have a deal?"

Once more, Bernie hesitated before speaking. If he messed this up, Jack would be the least of his problems. He had to trust that Pia would do as she said.

"It's a deal, Pia. But I expect to hear from you tomorrow morning." Bernie thought it might be better to add a little incentive, so he continued. "I'm going to tell Jack about this call as soon as I hang up, and if you don't come through, I'm sure Jack will think of something." He didn't like threatening her, but this was too important a matter to leave entirely to trust.

"You'll hear from me," Pia said, and then hung up.

She put her phone back in her bag, hoping she'd made the right decision and wouldn't be walking right back into Larry's arms when she got off the plane in California.

"That part's done," she said to Brad, who was staring out at the water, "now let's go make those plane reservations and pack our bags. By the way, you do know that we'll have to fly into Tijuana and then walk across the border, right?"

"Why can't we fly straight to San José? It's a whole lot easier."

"Remember? I don't have my passport," she reminded him.

"Yes you do." Pia stared at him. "I mean I have it. Bob made me bring it along for just this sort of emergency."

"Then that's settled. Let's go"

Brad looked back out at the bay. "I was hoping to maybe get in a ride or two, but I guess it really doesn't matter. The waves here aren't really worth it...bummer."

"Come on, Brad," said Pia standing up, "the sooner we get out of here the sooner you can get back to the surf in Monterey."

"I guess that's something to look forward to." Brad got up and the two starting walking. "I just hope Larry doesn't try something on our way out of town or that your bosses aren't just setting you up for a takedown in Monterey."

Pia didn't need Brad echoing her sentiments. "No negative thinking for now. We've got this."

34

Pia had never been so grateful to be back in her little house in Pacific Grove. It had been one very long day starting with the call to Bernie, then the flight home, and finally the drive back to Pacific Grove from the San José airport. All the while, she'd kept an eye out for signs of a hitman or any other suspicious looking characters. It was dark by the time Brad dropped her off before heading back to his own apartment in his mother's garage.

Inside her house, Pia opened all the windows to clear out the stuffiness of a house closed up for too many days. Perhaps leaving the windows open was not the best move. Who knew if Larry might be waiting in the bushes to gun her down? But at that point, Pia was simply too exhausted and the house too musty to worry about it.

With the house airing out, and before she did anything else, she retrieved her laptop from inside a pile of clothes in her dryer. She checked that she still had her second copy of the files from the office. Seeing that all was in order, Pia relaxed. They were all she needed as insurance against any future threats from Jack. Not even Brad knew that she intended to keep a backup file on Houston and Melrose.

Closing up before she went to bed, something caught Pia's eye from across the street. Was that her neighbor peeping through the curtains, looking directly into her house? Pia locked the window and pulled the drapes. A nosey neighbor was only a minor nuisance. And anyway, she was too tired to care. She jumped into bed and instantly fell asleep.

~~~

Pia and Brad arrived at Saul's just before ten the next morning. Only a few diehards were in that early, giving Bob a chance to come over and greet his friends.

"Good to have you back in one piece, Pia," said Bob.

"Hey Bob," said Brad, "What about me? I'm also in one piece. I got Pia back safe and sound....think I could get that free beer you offered?"

"Like I said Brad, when it's all over, which it isn't" he turned to Pia. "I've got your papers in the back office. Do you want them now?"

"*What?*" exclaimed Brad. "You left them in the office this whole time? Bob, dude, *anyone* could have gone in there and stolen them."

"Relax Brad. They've only been in the office since this morning. Before that, they were in another location...and I took them out of there before I opened the bar this morning."

"You mean you hid them here? In Saul's? How is that cool?" Brad asked.

"They were safe, that's all I'll tell you," he answered, and set out to get the documents.

Only Bob, who was the oldest employee of the bar and had been there longer than the present owners, knew of the secret safes that had been installed in the original building. He intended to keep it that way.

~~~

"Bernie, it's already ten o'clock and we got no call from Pia." Jack sat in his office chain smoking cigarettes and drinking coffee. "If this doesn't go right, Bernie….."

"What Jack? Are you going to send Larry after me now?"

"I already told you. Larry's off the payroll." As much as Jack would like to have really threatened his partner, he couldn't do it. But he sure didn't like waiting around for Pia to make her move. "Anyway, you got a plan if she doesn't come through with the goods?"

Bernie didn't, and considering Jack's state it wouldn't do him any good to admit it. "We just have to wait it out for now," he said, deciding that this would be a good time to change the subject. "At least we know Joe's not going to be talking."

"That's about the only thing that's gone right with this whole mess," Jack agreed.

The night before, after a long day of destroying files and making sure that Houston and Melrose Accounting had no direct ties to Joe and the others arrested down on the wharf, they'd finally heard from their associates.

It had been just after nine in the evening when a man knocked on the back door holding a sealed letter. He handed it off to Bernie and slipped back into the night before any questions could be asked. Bernie brought the letter back into

Jack's office where the two men had just poured shots of bourbon into their coffee in an attempt to keep their minds focused and their heart rates in check.

There'd been no signature on the typed letter or any other information about who had sent it. No name was needed. Jack and Bernie knew it was from none other than The Captain—head of the cartel and Joe's father. Without mentioning any names, it stated that all parties involved would keep their mouths shut, and that Jack and Bernie were expected to do the same. The Captain was no fool; he knew that if the accountants got nabbed, he could kiss several off-shore accounts goodbye.

Now, their only concern was Pia and they had no choice but to wait for her call. Fortunately, it turned out to be only a few more minutes. The phone rang just as Jack had reached for his cigarettes. He grabbed it before Bernie had a chance to answer.

"I've got your paperwork and files," Pia said. "Meet me in the parking lot of the liquor store on Lighthouse in fifteen minutes. You know where it is, right?"

"This better not be a setup, Pia. And you better be alone. Don't forget we can have you taken care of."

"And how do I know you aren't setting me up?" she replied. "Larry could be waiting for me as soon as I get out of my car."

Damn it! How in the hell had she found out Larry's name? Damn good thing the man was no longer in his employ. What a fuck up he'd turned out to be.

"I don't know who you're talking about....but it will just be me and Bernie. Remember, don't try any funny business."

Pia hung up, put the Houston and Melrose papers in a reusable shopping bag, and stood up.

"OK," said Brad, "I'll be right behind you."

"No you won't Brad. I'm doing this alone."

"Girl-dude, are you crazy? You can't trust these guys."

"No, I probably can't, but this is what I'm doing."

Brad looked around for Bob, hoping the older man could talk some sense into her. Bob was on the other side of the room, picking up glasses. Brad got up to go over to him and that's when Pia made her move. She was out the door and headed for her car before Brad had a chance to do anything.

"Bob," Brad said, helping to load glasses into a bus tub, "Pia's just run out the door to go and meet her bosses unaccompanied. What are we going to do?"

"I think she'll be fine—after all she's meeting them in a parking lot on a busy street. But just to make sure, you should follow her. Maybe stay out of sight."

"I don't have my ride with me Bob. I drove over with Pia."

"Go in the back office. There's a skateboard that someone left in here the other day. You still know how to ride one, right?"

"Sweet!" called out Brad, already halfway to the office, leaving Bob to finish up collecting glasses.

~~~

Jack and Bernie sat in the car in the parking lot not talking to each other until they saw Pia drive up.

"Bern, I don't like this. It's too public. What if Pia tries something?" Jack made no move to get out of the car.

"What's she going to do? Remember, we still have those bogus accounts in her name and she knows it. And honestly Jack, I really do think she just wants out of all this as much as we do." Bernie opened the car door. "Come on, let's get this over."

The men walked over to Pia, now leaning against her car door. All three looked around to see who was in the vicinity.

"Hello Jack, Bernie," Pia said.

"No small talk," said Jack, "just hand us the files."

"Are we clear that you're not going to harass me anymore?"

"As a matter of fact," said Jack, "we hope we never see you again. And just so you know, you're fired. Don't expect any severance pay."

"All I want is my regular paycheck. I assume it will be deposited as normal?"

"Yeah, yeah….now hand over the papers." Jack stuck his hand out and waited.

Just as Pia was taking the files and flash drive out of her bag, a van drove into the parking lot. Even if Pia hadn't gotten a clear look at the driver, the words Larry the Lawnmower plastered on the side told her all she needed to know. She threw the evidence back in her bag and reached for the car door.

"What's going on?" she snapped at the men. "You told me you'd called off Larry!"

Jack and Bernie looked at each other in surprise and then over to the parked van where Larry had just spotted the trio. Jack glared at Larry, making a slicing motion across his neck with his finger. Bernie started to sweat. Larry threw the van into reverse intending to hightail it out of there but just then another car drove in and blocked his exit.

Pia was halfway into her car when Jack leaned forward and tried to snatch the shopping bag holding the stolen files. The two struggled, Jack trying to wrestle it away from her, Pia not letting go. Suddenly, Brad zoomed in on his skateboard, executing a perfect stop right behind Jack.

"Dude, let go of her!" he yelled, reaching out to grab Jack's arm.

"Larry, you're hired again," Jack called out over his shoulder. "Get this punk off of me!"

Larry, seeing that he was no longer penned in, reversed his van out of the parking space and flew back onto Lighthouse. Damn! What were the odds of that happening? He'd have to forget about the expensive bottle of wine he wanted for his wife who was returning that day.

"*Stop this right now!*" Jack, Pia, and Brad froze in their struggle and turned to see Bernie, hands on his hips, looking quite ferocious.

"Cut it out all of you," he continued in a stern voice, "you want the police here? You're causing a scene." Bernie turned to Pia. "Just hand over the files and we'll all be on our way."

"Yeah?" asked Brad. "If that's true, why was Larry here?"

"And why are you here?" replied Bernie.

"I'd also like to know that," said Pia. "I thought I told you I was doing this alone."

"Come on Pia, I knew this was a setup....anyway, Bob told me to run interference. And let's get back to why you called in Larry," he said to the other men.

"We didn't," Jack said, still huffing after the brief struggle. Pia did not look convinced. "Tell them Bern—that was just bad luck."

"It's true," Bernie said, "we had nothing to do with him being here. You saw how he looked when he saw us. He got out of here as fast as he could."

It did seem like Larry had no intention of hanging around to help Jack and Bernie. He'd looked as surprised to see them as Pia had to see him. And they were going to attract a lot of unwanted attention if they kept this up for much longer. Two senior citizens in suits arguing with an older woman and a bum on a skateboard, was sure to draw a crowd.

"Fine," Pia said. "I'm handing this over, but if I even see a glimpse of Larry following me, I'm calling the police." She pulled the papers back out of her bag and noticed that Brad was opening his mouth to talk. "Keep quiet Brad. I want this over and want to get out of here."

From there on in, it was a simple handover. Jack and Bernie got in their car and drove off. Brad picked up his skateboard and jumped in with Pia.

None of them had noticed the car parked across the lot with a man slumped down in the back seat, peering through the back window. After all the parties had left the lot, Ray returned to the front seat. He pulled up the video he had just shot of the entire altercation. It wasn't anything he could use right away, but one day he knew it would prove to be valuable evidence. Until then, he planned on doing some more reconnaissance on all the suspects. And also get the lowdown on Larry the Lawnmower.

35

Three weeks later, Pia and Brad sat at the bar in Saul's, toasting a return to normalcy and their new jobs. Skip's negotiations for his new store in Carmel were almost completed, and eventually Brad would be running the place. Until Brad got up to speed on the complexities of running a store, Skip would be sending his son up to get things rolling. For Brad, the best part was the rent free little apartment over the shop. Who'd ever have believed that Brad would be living in Carmel?

Pia had started working for Skip just that week. She was now head accountant for Skipper of the Seas Clothing, working out of her home and making the occasional trip down to Ocean Beach.

"Hey Bob," Brad called out, "both me and Pia got new jobs…you have any plans? Like maybe retiring?"

Bob polished the bar in front of them. "Retire? Why would I do that?"

"Just asking." Brad picked up his beer and took a gulp.

"By the way Bob," said Pia, "I've been meaning to ask you if you ever heard how the Fishing Run bust came down."

Bob stopped what he was doing, looked around him, and lowered his voice.

"Word on the street is that a DEA agent infiltrated the cartel. No one seems to know who it was and if he's smart, he's already left the area." He paused for a moment. "That doesn't mean Houston and Melrose don't pose a threat to you, Pia. They might have been able to slip the hangman's noose for now, but you never know with these things. You need to keep vigilant."

"Bob, you're worrying about nothing," said Pia. "I just heard that both of them are retiring and closing down the office. They're not going to bother me." And if they ever tried, she'd pull up those files she'd kept and go straight to the authorities.

"Maybe they're retiring, but that doesn't mean that can't sic Larry on you again," Bob added.

"Don't worry, Bob," Brad cut in. "I've been keeping an eye on him."

Pia whipped her head around. "You've been *what?*"

"Hey, it's not like I'm following him…well, not exactly. But I've seen him around town a few times and I make sure he sees me. He won't be messing with Pia again."

"Brad, just let it go…I think Larry is as sick of us as we are of him." Brad did not seem convinced.

"Look," said Pia, "we need to put this all behind us. Worrying about what might happen isn't going to do us any good."

"Girl-dude, you might have a point there." Brad figured it would be better to agree with Pia. He could still keep a close eye on Larry without Pia ever knowing.

"Then it's settled," said Pia. "We're off to a new life in the cruise wear industry. Bob, set us up with another round."

~~~

About the Author

Kate McVaugh grew up in Northern California, but always felt she should be living somewhere else. Preferably, in a hot, tropical climate, exploring the culture and learning the language.

She got her first real taste of that long sought after life as a Peace Corps Volunteer in Brazil in the late 70's. Since then, she has worked as an educator in the US and in several countries around the world.

Long before she seriously put pen to paper, she constantly had stories running through her head. In the most ordinary of places and situations, she would often imagine a different, more intriguing reality.

Her books take place in the foreign lands where she has lived, traveled, and worked.

Proof

Made in the USA
Charleston, SC
09 September 2015